Dinosaur Run

A Jack Tyler Novel: Adventure 1

Dinosaur Run

by

Christopher Jaffrey

Books by Christopher Jaffrey:

Dinosaur Run

Dinosaur Strike

Flight of Horror

This is a work of fiction. The events and places described are imaginary; the characters and settings are fictitious and not intended to represent specific places or persons.

Text copyright 2021 © by Christopher A. Jaffrey. All rights reserved.

To

Max ... for the mandolin;

Dylan ... for the guitar;

And Eli ... for everything.

Prologue

The allosaur was the color of dried mud and reeked of sour, rotting meat.

It crunched over a patch of loose shale, dropping its head from time to time to sniff at the rocks, tracking an unfamiliar scent. A soaring pterosaur screeched as it wheeled overhead, but the allosaur didn't react. Its primitive brain recognized the flying creature as prey, but understood its kind was difficult to catch. If it came across an injured one, *Allosaurus* would attack it. And if it discovered a dead one, it would eat it.

But it would waste no energy hunting it.

The breeze shifted and the allosaur lifted its nose to sift through the variety of scents drifting in the warm air. It detected the smell of nearby brachiosaurs, barosaurs, stegosaurs, and kentrosaurs, all of which it identified as prey. And it picked out several rival predators: ceratosaurs and marshosaurs and—not far away—a male allosaur. Those animals were in addition to numerous small, insignificant scavengers: pesky creatures as common as flies but of no concern to the hunting allosaur.

Allosaurus sniffed again, dismissing the most familiar scents and fixing upon a trace of something different. Something foreign. And unknown. It turned its head, determined the direction of its quarry, and crept carefully toward it.

The dinosaur's open, teeth-lined mouth began to salivate as the animal continued the hunt.

The hunting allosaur was female, nine feet tall at the hips and thirty from the tip of her nose to the end of her muscular tail. Her tough gray skin was heavily scarred from battle. Stealing fresh meat was often easier than stalking, attacking, and killing another large animal. After a kill she was often forced to defend her prize from hungry rivals, just as she often challenged other predators for kills of their own. The resulting battles were invariably fast, fierce, savage, and bloody.

In the allosaur's primitive, prehistoric world, the fight for dominance was every bit as harsh and violent as the fight to survive.

*   *   *

A short distance away, Kayce Decker scrunched in a narrow cleft of rock. She couldn't yet see the allosaur, but she could smell the sickly-sweet stench of sour garbage over the heavy musk of decaying wood and compost that permeated the forest.

A rock clacked and she caught her breath, knowing the dinosaur was creeping closer.

It's got us, she thought flatly.

She looked up and around, gauging the security of the cleft. As a hiding place it wasn't perfect. And a small predator—a young dilophosaur, for instance—could easily squeeze inside.

But this thing's too big to reach us. It'll certainly try, but there's not enough room. Its head won't fit and its arms won't reach. So as long as we hang tight, we'll be okay.

She watched for another second, then turned and held a finger to her lips. Fifteen-year-old Eva nodded silently, her eyes wide with terror and her dusty cheeks streaked with tears. Only a year older than Kayce, Eva wasn't much of an outdoor girl. But she was smart and willing to learn.

And she's made it this long ...

There was a whimper of fear, and Kayce looked past Eva. Artem was twelve, though he acted ten and looked eight. The smallest of the three, he was wedged into the very back of the fissure where he was difficult to see.

"Hey, it's okay," Kayce whispered. "We're safe here. It's going to get loud, but we'll be all right. Just hold your hands over your ears and try to be quiet. Okay? *Shhhh ...*"

She saw the boy's hands reach up to his ears. As small as he was, Artem wasn't much help in a bind. But he tried hard to please and followed Kayce's every command to the letter.

Which is more than I can say about Ethan, she thought glumly.

Like Eva, Ethan was—had been—fifteen. Partly because he was older—but mostly because he was a boy—he'd decided he knew best whatever the circumstances and staunchly refused to listen to anyone else. But—

Well, it doesn't matter anymore, does it? Kayce thought. *He lasted—what? Two days? Serves him right ...*

She shook off the grim thought and once again peered into the open. The allosaur was still just out of sight, but the stench of rotting meat was strong, and she could hear the loose scree crunching beneath the animal's weight.

She tried to back farther into the cleft, but was already mashed up against Eva and had nowhere to go.

Relax! she ordered herself. *It can't reach us. It's gonna be damn scary, yeah. But it's not gonna get us.*

She remembered warning Artem that the attack was going to be loud and rolled her eyes at her own understatement. Dinosaurs roared for one reason, and that was to frighten other animals. And the louder they roared, the more terrifying they were.

And a monster like *Allosaurus*?

One of the most savage, most terrifying predators to ever prowl the planet?

She closed her eyes, steeling herself for the attack.

After it's over, I'll be lucky if my ears still work at all.

There was a clatter of rocks and Kayce opened her eyes. A bead of sweat trickled down her forehead as she focused on the shaft of sunlight slanting into the cleft. Motes of dust danced in the beam of light, as if there was no danger: as if everything was just fine and right in the world.

You're going to be okay, she assured herself. *Just stay calm—*

Over the rattle of rocks came a rumble: deep and resonant and extremely close.

It's growling! It knows we're close and it's growling!

Artem heard it too and began wheezing noisily, but Kayce knew the kid was trying his best to be brave and didn't try to shush him. She closed her eyes—marshaling her own strength—then reached down deep, searching for courage. And steadiness. And finally opened her eyes again and stared into the open.

Okay, come on, big guy. Give us your best shot. Show us what you've got—

A long gray snout eased into view, yellow teeth overlapping the pebbled jaws. The allosaur was looking straight ahead, and for a split second Kayce thought it might keep going, perhaps not realizing it had passed them.

But then the enormous head turned. A single eye peered into the cleft, blinking as the dinosaur spotted its prey. Kayce stared back, riveted by the overpowering sight. She knew—

she *knew*—the dinosaur couldn't reach her. But seeing the animal so close shredded her confidence. Her knees trembled and she fought the urge to scream.

The dinosaur glowered intently. And for several seconds stood as still as a rock. It almost seemed—

Without warning the allosaur lowered its head and bellowed, making noise louder than a howling jet engine. Shattering Kayce's ears and buckling her knees. A blast of hot, sour dinosaur breath hit her like a slap to the face, even as she screwed her eyes shut and tried to shrink away.

The animal bellowed again, the long snout at the very edge of the rocks, so close Kayce could have touched it. Eva and Artem screamed hysterically, Eva's mouth just behind Kayce's ear.

Kayce tried to force herself farther into the crevice, but Eva—suddenly distraught—began shoving back, fighting against her, pushing Kayce closer to the dinosaur.

"Eva! *Stop* it! Stop *pushing*!"

The dinosaur bellowed yet again—twisting its head and trying to force its jaws into the narrow gap—and Eva lost all control. She began flailing her arms, still screaming in terror.

The dinosaur roared and the noise hit Kayce like a hot steamy wind. She turned away as the dinosaur's yellow teeth snapped against the rocks, mere inches away. She tried to steel herself against the horror but—

"*Run!*" Eva began pounding her fists against Kayce's back and head and shoulders. "Kayce, *run*! It's going to *get* us! We've got to get *out* of here!"

Kayce shut her eyes as a gob of hot dinosaur spit struck her face, trying to keep her head turned away. "Eva, *stop*! Stop it! It's not going to—"

But Eva had snapped. Her eyes were wide, crazed, and filled with terror. She hammered her fists against Kayce, pushing and screaming and trying to force her way past.

"Eva, no! *Stop* it—"

Eva beat at Kayce's face, trying to drive her out of the way. Kayce ducked, struggling to dodge the girl's flying fists and fingernails. She tried to shove Eva back into the cleft, using her own body to keep the girl from bursting past.

Eva shrieked like a wild animal and Kayce wrapped her arms around the girl to hold her still. She tried to push the terrified girl back, but her shoes slipped on the loose rocks and both girls fell, Eva still flailing madly. Pounding Kayce with her fists. Kayce tried to turn her head, struggling to shield herself from the blows, but as she fell her legs splayed toward the dinosaur.

The allosaur saw its chance. It lunged and Kayce felt a tooth snag her shoe. With a scream of terror she jerked her knees up to her chest—

Eva suddenly had a rock in her hand. Kayce saw it coming and tried to duck but had no room. The rock struck the side of her head and a burst of blinding white light flashed behind her eyes. Her head swam and her limbs turned to rubber; hot bile filled her throat as her stomach bubbled, on the verge of throwing up.

Eva frantically clambered over her, and this time Kayce was powerless to—

"No ..."

Dazed and queasy—her face slick with blood—Kayce knew Eva didn't have a chance. She reached for the crazed girl, clutching at the leg of her jeans.

"Eva," she gasped. "No—"

With a terrified shriek, Eva jerked her leg free. Saw daylight ahead. And bolted from the cleft.

Horrified, nauseated, and barely able to see, Kayce rolled onto her elbows. She didn't know if the allosaur had looked away, or if Eva had somehow timed her escape just right. But the girl was suddenly past the dinosaur and sprinting for the trees.

Kayce's brain was still swimming, still hovering on the edge of consciousness. Blood streamed down her face. But she willed Eva to run ... to run as fast as she could.

Come on, she pleaded silently. *Come on, come on, come on—*

The dinosaur pounded up behind the fleeing girl. It didn't pause, didn't roar, didn't take time to study its prey. The huge head snapped down and the terrible jaws crashed shut. Kayce heard the crunch of bones and the crack of enormous yellow teeth slamming together.

The dinosaur lifted its head and Kayce saw Eva's legs dangling from the massive jaws. A red tennis shoe dropped to the ground as the girl kicked.

And then the dinosaur shook its head, whipping it violently from side to side. Shaking its prey and snapping—

Kayce's eyes rolled back in her head.

And all she knew was darkness.

1 Jack

Fourteen-year-old Jack Tyler pedaled onto the grass behind the high school, taking a shortcut across the field. A peewee football team was practicing on the far side and he grinned, remembering when he was that young and wearing a helmet and pads for the first time.

Such good times! Up from flag football and finally able to hit and tackle other kids!

The first week of practice, that's all everyone wanted to do: run as hard as they could and crash full blast into one another. The coaches knew that, of course, and made the most of it. They'd invented all kinds of drills in which players did nothing but hit and tackle one another.

The kids had to do it safely, of course. But once they'd learned the fundamentals—

Head up, shoulders even, eyes on the guy's numbers ... then hit 'im low, hit 'im hard, wrap 'im up!

—they attacked one another like maniacs.

As many times as they could.

And just as *hard* as they could.

One of Jack's favorite drills involved two players lying head-to-head on the grass. At the coach's whistle, they leaped to their feet and crashed into one another. Whichever player delivered the hardest hit advanced to the next round, and the game continued until only a single player remained.

Jack loved the drill ... and was so good that he'd won several times.

Yeah, just loved going one-on-one like that ...

Another favorite was fumble recovery. After calling out two, three, four, or perhaps even five players, the coach tossed the football onto the grass. The eager players then chased it down and dove upon it, each kid determined to regain the "fumble."

Jack looked back as the peewee coach blew his whistle and shouted.

"Everyone! Down to the fence and back! Go, go, *go!*"

Jack grinned.

Sprints.

Okay, that part wasn't so fun ...

He knew coaches had a thing for getting their kids in shape. But most of them didn't know the difference between effective conditioning and child abuse, and brutal practices often flirted with the line. After rough workouts it wasn't unusual to see players down on their hands and knees, puking their guts out on the grass.

But every one of us showed up the next day, anxious to do it all again!

Jack flicked his gears for better traction in the deep grass, stood up on his pedals to power himself over a small rise, and pedaled back onto the road. A half block ahead, an elderly man was just lifting a brown shopping bag from the back of a van. As the man turned, the bottom fell out of the bag and groceries spilled to the ground.

Oh, man!

Jack stood up on his bike and pedaled as fast as he could as the old man stooped to pick up his fares. Jack could tell the man had bad knees, or a bad back, or both: the guy was struggling to bend far enough to reach the ground.

Jack pumped even harder, then hopped off the bike as soon as he reached the van.

"Hey," he said, dropping his bike on the sidewalk. "Let me help you with that."

He filled his arms with cans, stood, and looked for somewhere to place them.

"H-here," the man croaked. "Just place them here, in the back of the van. T-thank you so m-much."

"Yeah, sure, no problem." Jack stepped toward the van. "Could you grab the door for me?"

"Y-yes ... yes, of c-course."

The old man opened the door partway, then moved aside, giving Jack just enough room to step past. Jack eased around and looked—

What the—

The old man abruptly shoved Jack from behind. Cans flew in all directions as Jack slammed into the bumper, and before he could recover the man grabbed his belt and legs and in a single powerful motion heaved him into the back of the vehicle. Another man was there waiting. As Jack struggled to regain his senses, the second man slammed him to the floor, jerked a canvas bag down over his head, and dropped on top of him, using his weight to keep Jack from moving.

"Ughhh," Jack stammered. He tried to breathe but only sucked folds of moldy canvas into his mouth. And the man was right on top of him—big and heavy as a bear—mashing his chest and keeping him from filling his lungs. Jack struggled to turn, tried kicking his legs, but—

Something jabbed him in the rear like a sharp, hot nail: every nerve in his body screamed as his butt burned like fire. He gasped in pain—tried to twist free—but—

His brain spun.

Became woozy—

—and that's all he knew.

*   *   *

Voices ...

He heard voices.

And vaguely understood that people—men—were talking somewhere nearby, though he couldn't make out the words.

He breathed in through his nose ... felt his brain spinning ... wondered what had happened.

The old guy.

Oh, yeah, he thought woozily. *Not nearly as old and feeble as he seemed.*

His brain was still muzzy—filled with fog as thick as steel wool—but a few disjointed cells were gradually beginning to fire again.

Filling in a few of the blanks.

Somebody took me.

But ... why?

He sensed that he was restrained. His arms and—he tried moving his feet—yeah, his legs were strapped down too. Tied to a cot or a bed or something.

The voices came again and he wanted to look ... to see who was speaking. To see where he was. And figure out what was going on.

At first he was too groggy to actually follow through. But as his brain began sparking, he finally managed to open a single eye.

Wha-what? A ... h-hospital?

The acrid smell of alcohol filled the room. And ... an unseen machine was emitting a soft *beep ... beep ... beep*. Jack could see monitors on stainless-steel stands beside him, tubes snaking down from bags of amber liquid. There were three other beds stationed along the wall, all of them empty, the sheets tucked in tightly.

Someone began speaking again—in a different room—and Jack concentrated on the voice. Listening for clues. Whomever was speaking was far enough away Jack couldn't make out the words. But the man's tone sounded relaxed and friendly.

Even though he knows I'm tied up in the next room?

He tested his arms by making fists.

Well, okay ... that worked.

He flexed his toes.

Okay. That worked too.

Moving as slowly as he could, he tried to lift his left arm. It moved, but only barely. Not even an inch. And he felt a belt or strap or something across his waist, holding him fast.

Being tied down scared him, but he forced himself to relax. And to remain still.

"So what about that redhead?" a raspy voice suddenly asked. The voice was clearer now. "Struttin' around like the king of the forest ..."

"Only to have that monster come bustin' outta the trees ... thing bit 'im in half like a raw carrot—"

"Kid screamed like a *girl*!"

The speakers laughed raucously.

"Seriously though, that was the best buncha squirts we've had in quite a while," one of the men finally continued. "I'll tell ya! Every single one of 'em beat the odds"—another quick laugh—"and *that* caused more'n a few headaches, tell you what!"

"And every one of them put up one *helluva* good fight."

" 'Cept for that first one. What'd she last ... forty-five minutes?"

"Oh, *right*, I'd forgotten! ... Now *that* was a gut-wrencher! Just a matter of being in the wrong place at the wrong time, I 'spose."

"Yeah, well, that's the name of the game, isn't it?"

There was the sound of footsteps—the squeak of rubber soles on a tile floor—and Jack closed his eyes as the walkers stepped closer. Jack felt them as they entered the room. Could hear them breathing, ... could even smell the rancid stink of body odor.

Don't move, he ordered himself. *Don't give yourself away.*

Someone bumped into the bed, and Jack felt an ache in his left arm ... along with an uncomfortable pressure inside his elbow. And realized, *They've got an IV in me! They're giving me drugs!*

The thought turned his stomach—made him want to fight against his restraints, to pull out the needle—but he forced himself to remain still.

"Okay," a voice said after a moment. Jack heard the scratch of a pen on paper. "Vitals look good. Think he's just about good to go."

Jack felt a bump, and then warm, gloved fingers touched his face and pulled his right eye open. A beam of light flashed across his face, so bright and startling he couldn't keep from flinching.

A man Jack had never seen before reeled back in surprise.

"What the—"

Jack thought quickly, knowing he'd given himself away. He began to mumble.

"Horph muffa duh ..."

"What the *hell*? Is he awake?"

"Huffa moph," Jack mumbled in a voice softer than a whisper. "Urfff ... mruph ..."

"What's he saying?"

"Not sure, but ... I don't think he's quite awake."

Jack had closed his eyes again, but now cracked them just enough to peer through his eyelashes. Two men in white lab coats were hovering over him. The nearest man—an ugly dude with inch-thick glasses, beaver-like teeth, and tufts of gray hair sprouting from his nostrils—leaned over and Jack mumbled, "Close ... closer ..."

"He's trying to say something: wants me closer."

The man bent at the waist, turning his head so that his ear was just above Jack's face.

"Closer," Jack whispered as softly as he could.

The man leaned in—

Jack snapped his head forward, fast as a cracking whip. He clamped his teeth on the man's ear, biting so hard that his teeth cracked together. Even as the man screamed, Jack wrenched his head to the side. He felt the ear tear, felt hot blood spurt across his face.

The man screeched like a cat being tortured with pliers. He jerked his head free, and Jack saw what was left of the guy's ear dangling from the side of his blood-smeared head. The man clamped a hand over the ruined ear, his white lab coat splotched red with blood.

The man gawked in disbelief ... but then the shock and surprise gave way to hot, fiery, unfettered fury.

Fury and ... madness.

Jack spat out a mouthful of blood and a chunk of ear against the guy's lab coat, then began thrashing against his restraints, fighting to free himself. He knew he'd gone too far and that his only hope was to get away.

The man's eyes boiled with rage, and without warning he raised a fist. Jack tried to turn his head, but there was nowhere to go and the fist crashed into his face. A light brighter than the sun flashed behind his eyes—

And that was that.

2 Artem

Hey.

Jack heard the voice.

Wondered idly where it came from.

Hey, come on.

Someone was shaking his shoulder, but his brain was too full of fog and haze and black widow-like cobwebs to make sense of it. He had a vague recollection of an ugly hairy-nosed creep in a blood-smeared coat—and ... something about an ear. But the memory was just a wisp, like the spidery remnants of a barely remembered dream.

Come on, man! We've gotta go!

There were more words, but Jack wasn't certain he really heard them. Thought they were simply part of a bad dream. Either way, the speaker sounded like a kid. Not some old coot, hairy nosed or otherwise.

His shoulder continued shaking.

"Come on, dude! We don't have *time* for this!"

Jack was beginning to believe it was an actual voice now, and not just something conjured up by his imagination. Someone was actually talking to him. Shaking his shoulder. Trying to wake him up.

He groaned, and stretched, mildly surprised that his arms moved.

"Okay," the voice said. "*Finally.* Now come on, you've gotta get up."

Jack groaned again, then finally cracked an eye and was startled to see—

Green.

Lots of green.

More green than he'd ever seen before.

He rubbed his fists into his eyes, then looked again. It took a moment for his vision to clear. But then the green resolved into leaves ... the leaves of impossibly tall trees that stretched high into a cloudless, powder-blue sky.

None of it registered.

He turned his head and spotted a worried but unfamiliar face peering down at him. It was ... a kid. A kid maybe ten years old.

"Oh, man," the kid said with obvious relief. "I didn't think you were gonna come out of it."

Jack blinked, and then blinked again, half expecting the trees, and the sky, and the strange kid to disappear.

But they didn't.

"Anyway, come on," the kid repeated anxiously. He tugged on Jack's arm, trying to pull him upright. "We've gotta go and, like, right now!"

Jack closed his eyes again. His brain was still too muddled to make sense of things. His mouth felt like it was full of sand, his muscles like limp strands of overcooked spaghetti. He wasn't going to move until—

A powerful roar suddenly shook the air, loud as a passing freight train, filled with heat and anger.

Jack bolted upright, his eyes wide as doorknobs.

"What the freak—"

"See?" The strange kid pulled forcefully on his arm. "Now come on! We've gotta get *outta* here! *Now!*"

The unseen animal roared again, bellowing with such force and madness that Jack was certain the very ground shook.

What the—

"Come *on!*" the boy insisted. He pulled desperately on Jack's arm, and this time Jack sat up, and then struggled to his feet. His legs were shaky and nearly buckled beneath his weight. But when the furious animal bellowed again—

It's getting closer!

—he forced them into action.

The young boy released his arm and began trotting into the trees. Not quite running, but moving fast enough to cover ground in a hurry. Jack's first dozen steps were shaky, but his brain and body were quickly recovering from whatever had befuddled them. And after a little stumbling his legs began to work in earnest.

He focused on catching up with the frightened boy. He was just beginning to gain a little ground when the kid turned and vanished into a patch of thick brush. Jack wondered where he'd gone, but then spotted a faint trail cutting through the foliage. He took the trail and after a moment spotted the boy creeping along. He caught up just as the kid turned and held his fingers to his lips—

"*Shhhh!*"

—before easing slowly ahead. The boy came to another trail, quickly looked both ways, then crossed the path and darted into the trees on the other side.

Jack's brain had finally cleared enough to realize he was in a forest unlike anything he'd ever seen. The trees were enormous, stretching more than a hundred feet into the sky. Many of them were pines—though they were strange in a way he couldn't quite identify—while others were broad, leafy hardwoods draped with curtains of hanging moss and vines. If not for the sweet-scented pines, he might have thought he'd somehow been dropped into a tropical rain forest.

After several minutes the young kid finally stopped beside a globular tree that sprouted limbs and branches in every direction like an enormous tumbleweed. He glanced past Jack into the timber behind them, then whispered: "Okay. We've gotta climb this tree. Be as quiet as you can, and climb as high as you can."

Jack looked up doubtfully. "Seriously? You want me to—"

Another roar shook the woods, even closer than before, and the boy looked at him with disbelieving eyes.

"Really?" he asked. "You're going to *argue* with me? Fine! Have it your way!"

Without another word, the boy grabbed for a branch and began to climb.

Jack took a quick look over his shoulder—heard the crunch of a heavy foot on a rotting log—and decided the kid was right.

Yeah, climb now, talk later.

He began to climb. There were enough branches to grab and stand upon, and the limbs were thick enough to support his weight. Coincidentally or not, the bright-green leaves were the size of dinner plates, thick and plentiful enough to hide both boys from the ground.

The young kid climbed halfway up the tree before stopping. He turned to face the trunk and then sat, straddling a thick branch. Jack climbed up to a limb just below him.

"Hey, sorry about—"

"*Shhhh*," the boy said. He pointed. "Sit so you're facing the trunk. So you can wrap your arms around it."

This time Jack did as he was told. He peered through the leaves toward the ground, then looked up at the kid. "Who're you?"

"Artem. Who're you?"

"My name's Jack." And then: "What the crap is going on?"

Artem shook his head and pointed. "Shhhh. It's coming. Don't move and try not to make any noise. If things get bad, wrap your arms around the trunk and hold on as tight as you can."

"But what—"

Crack!

A dry branch or log crunched in the woods and Jack's heart began to pound; his breathing became fast and hard. He could feel the blood thumping against his temples. He stared into the trees, then looked up at Artem.

"What is it?" he whispered. "What's coming?"

Artem shook his head grimly. "Just watch and see. It'll be easier that way."

"But—"

Artem slipped his hands around the tree trunk, then pointed his nose into the forest. "Just watch. And remember, we don't want it to know we're here, so try not to make any noise."

"But—"

"*Shhhh!*"

Jack shushed. And watched the trees. For several seconds nothing happened. But then he heard the rustle of leaves. Followed by the snap of a dry twig and the clack of a rock. A fly or a bee buzzed around his head, but he paid no attention. The air felt hot and still.

Jack realized that his hands were sweating, and he wiped his palms on his pants—first one and then the other.

And then finally saw something move. He'd been peering at the ground, but the movement was much higher. Like fifteen feet off the ground. He thought it might have been a bird, or, or—

A long crocodilian snout slowly emerged from the foliage, gray as ash, the jaws open and filled with yellow teeth.

Followed by an enormous head, a thick, muscular neck ... and then the rest of the body.

The animal was walking on two feet, its small arms curled against its chest. The thing was enormous, but despite its size it crept from the trees with the ease and grace of a cat.

Jack gasped in shock and horror.

It's ... it's ... it's a dinosaur!

His heart hammered in his chest.

His brain unable to accept what he was seeing.

"What the—"

"Shhhh!" Artem hissed, nudging Jack's shoulder with his shoe. "Don't make any noise!"

Jack couldn't tear his eyes away from the unbelievable sight to respond. He pushed aside a leafy branch for a better look—

A scream suddenly split the air—

"*Eeeeaiiigh!*"

—and the dinosaur snapped to attention. The great head whipped around, even as a second scream ripped through the forest.

"*Eeee—EEEEIIIGH!*"

The dinosaur growled with a deep, bold, powerful rumble. And then turned and thumped back into the trees the way it had come, its tail flicking gracefully through the air behind it.

Jack's jaw was hanging open. He gaped in astonishment, then turned to look up at Artem. To his surprise, the kid was grinning.

"What the—"

"It's okay," the boy whispered. "That scream? That was just Kayce."

"But—"

"She's drawing it away," Artem explained, still whispering. "So we can escape."

He chuckled softly.

"Works every ... well, *almost* every time."

He began climbing down the branches.

"Come on, let's get out of here before it comes back."

Jack was still too gobsmacked to do anything more than follow dumbly. He dropped through the branches and—once he was on the ground—took a step and nearly fell into a hole. When he looked, he was startled to see that the "hole" was actually an enormous three-toed track.

"Holy freak!" he shouted, all the surprise and shock and confusion suddenly gushing out in one explosive burst. "What the *hell* is going on?"

"You haven't figured it out yet?"

"Figured *what* out?" Jack jabbed a shaking finger toward the woods. "Some freakin' tyrannosaurus comes storming from the trees—"

"It was an allosaurus."

"*What?*"

"It was an *allosaurus*."

"A ... a what?"

"An allosaurus."

"There's a freakin' *difference*?"

"If it was chewing off your face you probably wouldn't notice, I guess. And you probably wouldn't care a whole lot but, yeah. There's a difference. And—anyway—there are no real tyrannosaurs here. Won't be for another sixty million years."

The kid waved a hand.

"Look, I know you've got a million questions. Everyone always does. But it'll be better if you just wait. Kayce's better at explaining things."

"Kayce? Who's Kayce?"

"She's ... look, you'll meet her soon enough. But right now, we've gotta get out of here. You know, while we still can. Okay?"

Jack nodded dumbly, the barrage of surreal information too overwhelming and unbelievable to fully grasp. Artem took off through the trees following a faint trail. He seemed so sure of himself that Jack followed without question. But after everything he'd seen, and heard, he was now eyeing the forest more carefully than ever.

And more warily.

These trees aren't just different, he thought, looking up and around. *They're ... primitive. They're prehistoric. They're—*

There was a rustle in the brush. Jack looked down as a pair of two-legged lizards the size of turkeys darted across the trail between him and Artem, one chasing the other. He froze in surprise, then called out: "Hey! Did you *see* that?"

Artem turned quizzically. "What?"

Jack pointed. "*There!* Two—I don't know!—Iguanas or something just ran past! On two legs!"

Artem rolled his eyes as if that was the dumbest thing he'd ever heard. "Get used to it. They're all over the place. Thick as mosquitoes and twice as pesky."

"But ... what—"

"Look, there's a lot going on. I get it. I've been there. But it'll be better if you just wait to hear it from Kayce. Okay?" And then, when Jack hesitated: "Trust me. We've done this before. We're getting it figured out. And it's always better if you hear it from Kayce. So for now, just go with it. No matter what you see or what you hear, just go with it."

"But—"

Artem opened his mouth and this time Jack answered with him: "Wait to hear it from Kayce."

Artem grinned, though there was no humor in it.

"I had my doubts," the boy said, "but you're catching on. You might just make it here."

3 Revelations

They continued creeping through the trees. Jack was already curious about the variety of strange vegetation that filled the woods. But now that he'd had a taste of the creatures wandering about, he became laser-focused on his surroundings, listening as much as watching. Alert for ... for ...

Heck, for whatever's there!

He kept an eye on Artem, too, and quickly noticed that the boy moved through the trees like a natural woodsman. It hadn't struck him before, but he realized the boy's head was always moving—his eyes sweeping left and right and up and down and back and forth—as he scanned the woods.

Watching for obstacles.

Searching for danger.

Hardly making a sound as he hiked.

Kid's been doing this a while, Jack thought. *Whatever "this" is ...*

An animal screamed in the nearby trees with such a blood-curdling cry that Jack's knees turned to jelly. Artem glanced briefly in the direction of the screeching creature before returning his attention to the trail.

Holy crap! Jack thought as he searched the trees for some sight of the ungodly animal. *Kid hears a noise like that and doesn't give it a second look? What the hell!*

He kept staring in the direction of the blood-chilling shriek, terrified of spotting the creature that made it. But almost instantly something roared from the opposite direction. And suddenly it was all too much.

He cleared his throat.

"Hey, Artem—"

The kid turned and glared. "*Dude!* You got ears, or what? I *know* you've got a million questions. So did I. So does everybody. But I can't answer 'em all out here. So get over it. Okay? We're almost there, and once we hook up with Kayce she'll tell you everything you wanna know. So can you just hold on for a bit?"

Jack blinked. He wasn't used to being told off by a kid.

Or having some ten-year-old treat me like a blooming idiot.

He felt a rush of anger—and indignation—but common sense quickly took over. He tipped his head.

"I'm sorry," he whispered. "There's just so much to take in, y'know? It's a little overwhelming."

Artem seemed to relax. His shoulders sagged and he blew out his breath. "Yeah, I get it. I'm still not used to it. But just hang on a little longer. Okay? We're almost there."

"Okay, yeah ... I can do that."

Artem nodded and was about to continue down the path, but then turned and gave Jack another look.

"Word of advice, though?"

"Sure. Anything."

"Don't act like this around Kayce. She's been through a lot and—well—she doesn't have a lot of patience. You make her mad and she's likely to just leave you out here. And, um ..."

"Yeah?"

"Out here? By yourself?" The boy shook his head. "You won't last a day."

"No?"

Artem shrugged sadly. "No one ever has."

Several minutes passed.

Jack didn't think Artem was deliberately trying to mix him up as they hiked, but he quickly became so disoriented he had no idea which direction they were going. If he'd needed to return to where Artem had found him—or to the tree where they'd seen the allosaurus—he wouldn't have known which way to start.

But Artem didn't seem the least bit confused. He cut through the woods like he'd done it a hundred times. Like he knew exactly what he was doing and exactly where he was going. He only stopped once, when they came to another trail. The boy peered cautiously up and down the path, then gestured for Jack.

"Look," he said, pointing at the ground.

Jack looked. Almost beneath his feet was an enormous track thirty inches long and probably eighteen wide, the toes widely splayed. There were indentations at the end of each toe, which Jack realized were made by heavy, pointed claws.

And it's fresh, Jack thought, eyeing the sharp, crisp edges. He felt a chill that sank all the way to the bone. *Probably just a few minutes old!*

"Is that—"

Artem nodded. "An allosaurus. One of the big ones."

Jack gaped. "You mean that thing we saw *wasn't* a big one?"

Artem shook his head. "Not really, no. It was a male, for one thing—they're not as big as the females—and it wasn't full grown. It was just a kid, like ... a teenager."

Jack stared slack-jawed, suddenly lost for words. Artem took another look up and down the path to be sure the coast was clear, then crossed the trail and headed back into the trees.

Jack took a final look at the incredible track, and then followed quietly.

Jack lost track of how long they hiked. Haunted by the onslaught of strange sights—not to mention the shrieks, screeches, and screams of phantastic birds and animals—his brain was whirling in a thousand different directions. And he was surprised when Artem stopped beside a jumble of large boulders.

"Okay," Artem announced. "Here we are."

"Here we are what?"

Artem pointed to a pair of tree limbs leaning against the boulders. Several smaller limbs had been lashed across them to form a makeshift ladder, the first sign of anything manmade Jack had seen.

"Go ahead. Climb on up."

Jack did as he was told, and Artem followed as soon as he reached the top.

"Kinda obvious, but we call these 'The Boulders,' " Artem announced. He pointed. "There's a hollow between the rocks over there. Nothing big can get inside, so if you're ever on the run, it makes a good hiding place."

He sat on the edge of the rocks and gestured for Jack to join him.

"We've got other hiding spots here and there. You've gotta keep track of where they all are, 'cause when you're on the run it's easy to get confused."

"Remember where *they* are? I have no idea where *we* are!"

"Yeah, well, you'll figure it out soon enough."

"So what are we doing?" Jack sat beside Artem, dangling his legs over the edge of the boulder.

"Waiting for Kayce."

Jack rolled his eyes—

Just who the heck is this Kayce?

—then said: "Look, help me out a little. Tell me what's going on."

"It'll really be better—"

"If I hear it from Kayce. Yeah, I know already. But c'mon ... give me *something*. What's going on?"

Artem looked at Jack for a moment, then shrugged. "Okay. But listen: don't start asking a buncha questions. Just kinda let it all soak in. Once you've got the big picture, the little things'll start making sense."

"Fine."

"Okay. You know we're a long way from home, right?"

Jack looked up as a large animal—

Another allosaur?

—roared in the forest. "Obviously. But just where in the heck—"

"Our best guess is that we're a hundred fifty million years back in time."

"*What*—"

"You *saw* that allosaurus, right? How much more proof do you need? And, anyway, here we are. We were sent here deliberately. And no one expects us to survive."

4 The Game

Jack was too stunned to respond.

"This is the thing," Artem explained. "Back in our own time, people figured a way to travel into the past. Only there's no way back. People can *get* here, but what's the point? Once they're here, they're stuck. Forever. Because there's just no way to get home again."

He swatted at a fly-like bug circling his ear.

"So what do you do? There's no way to profit from a one-way trip to nowhere so ... they came up with a game."

"A *game?*"

"A sick, twisted, perverted game. They kidnap bunches of kids and send 'em back. Usually ten at a time, and almost always teenagers. Just so that people with more money than brains can bet on them."

"*Bet?*"

"Uh-huh. It's obviously hard to survive in a place like this. So they wager on who'll get killed first, who'll last longest ... stuff like that. And they wager on how certain kids'll get it. They might bet that one kid'll be eaten by an allosaur, another by dilophosaurs. Like that. That sort of thing's hard to predict, obviously. So anyone who gets it right wins a buttload of cash."

Jack's brain was reeling, thinking Artem had to be spinning fairy tales.

Like some sort of tasteless, repulsive, unbelievable joke.

"So you're saying we've been sent here to *die*?"

'That's *exactly* what I'm saying. People don't just *think* we're gonna die, they're *counting* on it. Hoping for it. Actually betting on it." He nodded grimly. "And when someone *does* get killed, or eaten, or ... *whatever*, some lucky butthole back home wins a whole pile of money."

Jack struggled to swallow a painful lump that had suddenly risen into his throat.

"I'm sorry," he said. "But do you know how *stupid* that sounds?"

" 'Course I do. But"—Artem gestured as a tremendous roar shattered the forest, followed by a flurry of terrified squeals—"do you have a better explanation for that?"

Jack didn't. But—

"Why kids? Why teenagers?"

"I don't know. But ... I guess kids don't last as long as grownups. And the sooner we're all gone, the sooner they can send in another bunch and start all over again."

He seemed to hesitate.

"What?" Jack asked.

"Well, I don't know this for sure, but ..."

"*What?*"

"I think there must be some sort of thrill in watching a kid die."

"Good crud ..."

"Believe me, I know. Anyway, you're about to get all your questions answered."

"Why's that?"

Artem pointed with his nose. "Kayce's here."

Jack had already formed a mental image of the mysterious "Kayce," the girl who had all the answers. He pictured a hairy, rough-n-tumble, muscle-bound jungle woman able to play tackle football without a helmet or pads. An Amazonian able to bench-press three times her weight, wrestle alligators, and sprint through the forest with the speed of a frightened cheetah.

All while wearing a sixty-pound backpack and couple of ammo belts strapped across her chest.

He followed Artem's gaze and saw the brush rustle, and then a girl stepped into the open ... a girl as normal as any he'd ever seen. Four or five inches shorter than Jack, she had an intense, focused gaze and brown pony-tailed hair that trailed from the back of a baseball cap all the way to her waist. Her clothes were well worn and in need of a wash, but were otherwise ordinary.

Even from the top of the rock, Jack could see an enormous scab just above her right ear.

Artem waved—

"Hey, Watermelon!" he called.

—and then—ignoring the makeshift ladder—hopped off the boulder and ran to meet her. Jack too hopped off the rock, landing badly and dropping to his knees. He rose quickly, dusted off his jeans, and walked over to join the other two.

Kayce gave Artem a quick side hug and said, "I told you to knock of that 'Watermelon' crap."

"Yeah, yeah, whatever." The boy turned and nodded at Jack. "Anyway, here's the new kid."

Kayce turned a severe, penetrating gaze on Jack, and Jack felt himself being sized up. Thoroughly. Brutally. The girl looked him up and down as if trying to decide whether he was worth wasting her time on—

Like she's choosing players for a game of dodgeball and I'm the skinniest kid standing against the wall.

—her harsh eyes lingering on his bruised face.

Kayce scrunched her nose a little—apparently not impressed with what she saw—and asked, "What the hell makes *you* so frackin' special?"

5 Kayce

Jack blinked and said, "Huh?"

Kayce was still looking him over with the same expression she'd give a boil on somebody's butt. "They've never sent a lone kid before. Everyone always come in groups. So why you? Why now? What's the freakin' deal?"

Jack blinked again, put off at being treated so abruptly. He felt his blood heating up, but said: "Look, I have no idea what's going on. I don't know where the hell I am or what the hell I'm doing here."

He nodded at Artem.

"He said you'd answer *my* questions."

Kayce turned to Artem. "How much have you told him?"

"Just the basics. I kept telling him to wait for you, but ... he kept pestering me."

"I believe it." And then to Jack: "What happened to your eye?"

"My eye?"

"It's black and blue and practically swollen shut. And your face and shirt are covered with blood. You trip on a shoelace?"

Jack reached up to his eye, winced when he touched the tender bruise, then glanced down and for the first time noticed the dried blood stains on his shirt.

Oh, yeah ...

"I, um, sorta ... *resisted*."

Kayce's left eyebrow went up a little. "Really? That's a first. What'd you do?"

"Bit some guy's ear off."

She looked skeptical, but asked, "Big guy with buck teeth and Coke-bottle glasses?"

"And just one ear, now."

Kayce exchanged glances with Artem, and both of them grinned.

"Wish I could've seen *that*—"

"No kidding," Artem agreed. "That guy's one sick dude: doesn't even trim his nose hair."

"That *is* a sick dude—"

"A sick dude with one ear," Jack added.

"Hmmmm," Kayce said thoughtfully. "I wonder if that's why he sent you back by yourself."

"What do you mean?"

"You pissed 'im off." She reached out to touch a spot of dried blood on his shirt. "Made him so mad that he dumped you in the mail just to get rid of you."

Jack nodded at Kayce. "Looks like you've done some resisting yourself."

"What are you talking about?"

He flicked a hand. "You've got a scab the size of a dollar bill on the side of your head."

She reached up and touched the crusted blood with such nonchalance that Jack knew she no longer thought about it.

"Um, no," she said. "This was something else. One of the other girls did this."

"Seriously? What happened?"

"Hit me with a rock. Just about thirty seconds before a freakin' allosaur bit her in half."

"Holy hell."

"No kidding—"

Jack shook his head like he was trying to clear it of cobwebs, then looked from Kayce to Artem and back to Kayce again. "Look ... I hate to act like the village idiot, but just what the hell is going on? What's this all about?"

"All right, I'm gonna give you the quick version. We'll fill in the gaps later. But just so you stop bugging us, here's the story.

"First, yeah, we're about 150 million years back in time. Kids get sent here eight or ten at a time and rich people wager on long each of us lasts: you know, who goes first, who goes last, what kind of animal gets us ... stuff like that. It's a game they call Dinosaur Run. And it always involves kids, because we aren't supposed to last as long as, say, some Navy SEAL trained in wilderness survival."

"Yeah, Artem told me all that. The quicker you're all gone, the quicker they can send in the next batch of victims. But, well, how do they know what's going on? The people back home, I mean."

Kayce gestured. "There're cameras in the trees. Radio monitors, stuff like that. Once in a while they'll send in a coupla goons to adjust the cameras, tag a few animals, move things around a little."

"Why would anyone do that? Artem said they can't get back again, right?"

"They're not *told* they're not going back. They come thinking they're gonna get paid a buttload of cash to hang a couple of cameras. So why not? Hell, they think they're gonna have a little fun, see a few dinosaurs, earn a truckload of money, and still be home in time for dinner. Who *wouldn't* sign up for a gig like that?"

"So they're just ... *abandoned* here?"

"Worse than that. Guys in charge don't want a buncha goobers interfering with their precious game, so the goons aren't just left to rot, but they're drugged—"

"*Drugged?*"

Kayce nodded. "Drugged, poisoned, something. I don't know how it works. But they're given some slow-acting toxin. Probably told it's malaria vaccine or leech repellent or something. So they come, do their work, and—after about three days if the dinosaurs haven't gotten 'em—they go into seizures and die."

"You've gotta be kidding me."

"I'm not. And these seizures? Trust me when I say they're ugly. They last for hours and they're agonizing." She pulled a face. "So when the goons die? They die screaming."

"It's a *bad* way to go," Artem agreed with a nod. "It's actually better if the dinosaurs get them."

"But why in the *hell* would anyone *do* that to them?" Jack asked incredulously.

"Because the people in charge are lowlifes who don't give a damn. The guys they send back are gomers nobody cares about and who nobody's ever gonna miss. And since they can't have these idiots interfering with their perverted game, they make sure they're not around long enough to cause problems."

"Tell him about the hunters," Artem suggested.

"Hunters?"

Kayce nodded. "Yeah. Most kids don't last more than a few days here. But Artem and I have been here nearly a year now. And we've not only outlived our welcome, but we've been helping out the other kids, too. Totally messes up the point spread. So every once in a while they send back guys to get rid of us."

"To hunt us down," Artem expanded. "To hunt us down and snuff us out."

Jack felt the skin on the back of his neck begin to crawl. "You're kidding."

"I'm not," Kayce said, as Artem nodded vigorously. "Six different times now. Guys with high-powered rifles, scopes, camouflaged clothes. The whole works. They're pretty good, too. Last guy came really close to ... well, the kid and I just made it by the skin of our teeth."

Artem (nodding furiously): "If he hadn't stumbled into that pack of dilophosaurs ..."

Kayce nodded grimly, and the two of them bumped fists.

"Holy crap." Jack shook his head at the madness of it. "How do these guys find you?"

Kayce and Artem exchanged somber glances, then Kayce reached for Jack's right shoulder. She pressed her fingers around for a moment like a chiropractor searching for a particular nerve, then pinched the skin.

"Yeow!" The sudden jolt of pain was fleeting but intense, and Jack instinctively jerked away. "Hey—"

"Hold still," Kayce ordered. She took Jack's left hand and raised the fingers to his shoulder where he felt a lump, just beneath the skin. For some reason the spot was tender. "You feel that?"

"Yes ..."

"It's a tracking chip. Every kid has one implanted before they're sent here."

"A *tracking* chip? W-why?"

Kayce shrugged matter-of-factly. "Couple reasons. The first is so they can keep track of us—"

"Which means there's no way to hide from the freakin' hunters," Artem added. "They've got monitors that zero in on the implants like Homer Simpson after a jelly doughnut. They find you no matter where you are."

"That's right," Kayce agreed with a nod. "And, you know, they've tagged a lot of the big dinosaurs, too. The really big ones are territorial and don't wander around a lot. Anyway, they've got sensors and cameras and crap set up here and there, and when you get close—either you or a dinosaur—the sensors pick it up and turn on the cameras. You know ... to record the action."

"Good crap." Jack was still fingering the tender spot—the tracking implant—on his shoulder. But then: "So how do you stay away from these ... hunters?"

Kayce and Artem once again exchanged glances, then Kayce took Artem by the arm, spun him around, and pulled back the collar of his shirt. There was an ugly scar just to the side of his neck.

It took a moment for Jack to catch on, but then his eyes widened in horror.

"No ... you didn't ..."

"Yes, we did." She patted a sheathed knife on her belt ... a knife the size of a samurai sword. "I cut out Artem's, and then he cut out mine."

"Holy hell ..."

"Didn't have any choice," Artem explained. "Otherwise, they would have gotten us a long time ago."

Jack had no idea how to respond, so he just shook his head.

"Anyway," Kayce went on, "the kid and I have made such a nuisance of ourselves that the fine people back home are desperate to get rid of us. ... And, well, that's what the hunters are for."

"But these hunters all had seizures and died?"

"A couple of them did, yeah."

"And what happened to the others?"

"Dinosaurs," Kayce said matter-of-factly.

"Dinosaurs killed 'em?"

"Snapped 'em up, chewed 'em down, crapped 'em back out again. The guy that walked into the dilophosaurs? He ... well, the animals tore him to shreds. *Literally* tore him to shreds."

"Holy buckets," Jack said, fighting off a wave of chills. And after a few awkward seconds: "How do you know all this stuff? About the game and everything."

"Well, there's another type of person who shows up from time to time."

"And what type is that?"

"Once in a while someone cheats at the game ... like maybe they stiff the gang, or try to get out of paying their debts." She nodded solemnly. "Believe me, you *don't* wanna do that—"

"No kidding," Artem added. "You screw with these guys and there's only one punishment."

"You get sent here?"

"Uh-huh. And they don't waste poison on guys being punished. They're not typically outdoor types anyway, so there's no reason to think they might last very long. They're desperate for our help, so they're really talkative ... and they've told us what's going on."

"They were really mad at the last guy," Kayce added. "Sent him back naked."

"*Naked?*"

"They wanted him to suffer," she explained. "Wanted to make things as miserable as possible for him."

She looked up as some large dinosaur moaned mournfully in the distance.

"You know, it's one thing to send a guy back to die. But to send him here naked like that ..."

"Good crud."

"He was making threats," Artem said. "Like, 'Give me a percentage of the profit or I'll go to the police.' So they were, like, *really* mad at him."

"I guess." Jack turned back to Kayce. "So ... how have you two managed to last as long as you have?"

Kayce was about to speak, but Artem beat her to the punch. "Two things," he said.

"Which are?"

"First"—he pointed at Kayce—"she's really smart."

"Yeah, I get that. And the other thing?"

"The other thing is—and this is important—I always do *exactly* what she tells me."

Jack looked at Kayce, who nodded solemnly.

"That's the secret," she agreed.

5 Attack

Kayce looked up at the sun. "Well, if we wanna make it back before dark, we need to get started. The others will be getting anxious."

"Back where?"

"To our current campsite. Still seven other kids there, and I don't like being away too long."

"Seven—"

"Seven out of the last ten they sent back. So, you gonna come with us?"

"Do I have a choice?"

"Of course you have a choice. But … if you want to live, well, you'd better come."

Stell reeling from the onslaught of unbelievable information, Jack couldn't do anything more than make a weak after-you gesture. "Let's go."

Jack's brain was spinning—whirling—filled with so much fuzz and fog and unanswerable questions he struggled to walk straight.

He had a hard time believing that Kayce's story was real, and not just some crazy, horrifying nightmare. But he'd seen the allosaur. And heard the roars of terrifying, unimaginable creatures. And there was no denying that while the trees, and plants, and smells of the prehistoric forest were similar to those back home, they were distinctly alien.

Like these pine trees. I know they're pines, but ... they're unlike any I've ever seen. They're taller, and bushier, and have longer needles. And they smell—he closed his eyes and inhaled—*they actually smell ... greener ... than the pines back home.*

Kayce abruptly stopped and Artem froze in his tracks behind her. Jack stopped too, wondering what was going on. Kayce lifted her nose as if she was sniffing the air.

Jack watched for a second, then said, "What's going—"

Artem whirled around and mashed a finger against his lips.

"*Shhhh!*" he hissed. "Don't make any noise!"

The severity of the boy's voice instantly convinced Jack not to argue. He began looking left and right, trying to see what—

Kayce turned her head just enough to speak to Artem without taking her eyes off the trees ahead.

"The rocks," she said in a whisper so soft Jack barely heard her. "Take"—she looked at Jack—"what's your name?"

"Jack."

"Take Jake—"

"*Jack!*"

"—take *Jack* to the rocks and hunker down. Stay there until you're sure it's safe, then take the old way back to camp. I'll lead this sucker away and meet you there."

"You got it," Artem replied in a voice even softer than Kayce's.

The boy turned and looked at Jack. He once again mashed a finger against his lips—

Shhhh!

—then crooked a finger.

Follow me!

Jack still didn't know what was happening. He gave Kayce a final glance—she was staring into the trees with the focus of a lioness preparing to pounce—then followed as Artem left the trail and began picking his way through the trees. He felt a chill that had nothing to do with the temperature. And realized he was worried, even though he didn't know exactly what had Kayce and Artem so uptight.

Artem came to an immense pile of dinosaur dung blocking the way and eased around it. Jack was about to follow, but then took a second look and stopped. The fresh manure—already buzzing with flies—was filled with white slivers.

Bone slivers.

Holy buckets, he thought, staring. *What kind of place is this?*

Artem suddenly realized that Jack was no longer following. He turned and walked quickly backward.

"Hey, we don't have *time* for this!"

Jack ignored the rebuke, pointing instead to the pile of dung. "Have you *seen* this?"

"Yeah. Like a thousand times." He flicked a hand. "That's not even from one of the big ones. Now come on—"

Before he could finish, an earsplitting roar shook the forest. Jack whirled around, his jaw dropping and his blood turning to ice. He stared into the trees, then turned as Artem grabbed his arm and jerked.

"Dude, come *on*! We've got to get out of here—"

A second deafening roar blasted the woods, so loud and terrifying that flocks of startled birds exploded from the trees.

"—and we've got to go *now*!"

Jack resisted, still staring into the timber. Artem tugged again, then kicked him hard in the shin.

"*Ow!* What the—"

"Come *on*!" Artem hissed. "We've got to get *out* of here!"

Jack hesitated another second, but when the unseen dinosaur bellowed a third time—with such anger and fury he could actually feel the heat—he gave in and turned to follow. He'd only taken a dozen steps before a sharp *crack* popped through the muggy air: the sound of a tree snapping in half.

Artem looked back with fear in his eyes.

"Oh, crap, it's coming after us." And then to Jack: "We've gotta make a run for it. Don't stop, don't look back, don't waste time asking questions. Got it? Come on!"

Dropping all pretense, the kid turned and tore through the trees, blasting through the timber like his hair was on fire and his butt was catching. Jack hesitated a split second—too surprised for his brain to keep up—then ran after him.

Artem was small enough to shoot through the brush like a frightened rabbit. Jack wasn't all that much bigger, but nevertheless struggled to punch his way through the vines and limbs and prickly branches that clawed and clutched and clasped at his arms and legs like long bony fingers. Within seconds he was chuffing for breath, his heart hammering and sweat running down his face.

Artem, meanwhile, showed no signs of stopping. Or slowing. He ripped through the forest at top speed, and though Jack considered himself athletic—

Heck, I'm one of the fastest kids in the eighth grade!

—the smaller kid was flat outrunning him.

He's ... fast, he thought as his legs began to burn.

A distant, faraway part of his mind told him the boy was just more experienced in the forest. And that he was used to dodging rocks and roots and branches as he dashed through the trees.

Which ... explains—

He winced as a springy limb lashed his face like the slap of an open hand

—*why he can chug so fast through these frackin' trees!*

Jack was quickly panting like a winded hound, his lungs and legs flaming—

Artem abruptly turned, bolting into a patch of prickly berry-laden bushes. Jack turned to follow and almost instantly cracked his head against a thick, low-hanging branch. Stars flashed before his eyes, but he gritted his teeth and forced himself—

A loud chuff came from the trees behind him ... the sound of a large animal exhaling.

Holy hell ...

Jack was making enough noise that he could no longer hear Artem. But the cracks, crunches, and snaps of some gawdawful creature crashing through the woods behind him were unmistakable.

Artem obviously heard them too. As fast as he was running, he actually increased speed, opening an even greater lead over Jack.

Jack lowered his head, pumping his arms and legs—

From out of nowhere, a long-haired boy flashed from the trees and crossed the trail, right between Jack and Artem. Jack yelped in surprise—

"*Aaaah!*"

—catching nothing but a fleeting impression of wide eyes and a horrified expression as the kid streaked through the trees. He knew from a single glance the kid was freaked out of his mind.

Artem suddenly came running back, shouting at the fleeing boy.

"Travis! Hey!"

The long-haired kid didn't look back, didn't slow down, didn't stop. Actually picked up speed as he plowed through the trees.

Artem sucked in his breath as the strange kid vanished into the timber. "Oh, crap ..."

Jack ran up beside him, wiping the sweat from his eyes. "Who ... who's that ..."

"He's—"

A horrifying roar shook the forest, and Jack knew the unseen dinosaur was still coming. Artem grabbed Jack's arm and pulled.

"Come on!"

The boy took off again, dropping his head and running as hard as he could. Jack paused just long enough for a deep breath, then charged after him. A second roar thundered through the woods—just behind the nearest trees—and Jack knew the agitated animal was mere seconds from catching them. He lowered his head and pounded through the brush—

An exposed root snagged his shoe and held fast. With a cry of surprise, he dropped like a rock, landing face first in the dirt. He tried to regain his feet but stumbled, and instead of trying again turned and scrabbled sideways into the brush. A fallen tree lay just ahead and he skittered around the roots to the far side of the trunk where he pressed himself tight against the rotting wood and lay still.

The next instant an enormous animal burst from the trees. Jack's face was flat against the dirt, but he had just enough of a view to see what was happening.

The animal was a dinosaur. An ... *allosaur* ... maybe the same one he'd seen earlier. The animal's jaws were open and lined with teeth, thick yellow foam dripping from the corners. The dinosaur whipped its head from side to side, then started into the trees the way Artem had run—

There was a horrified scream from the right—from the direction the long-haired kid had gone—and the dinosaur snapped around. It lowered its head and bellowed—

Jack cringed, thinking the noise would shatter his ears.

—then thumped into the trees toward it.

Jack was panting for breath and abruptly realized his entire body was shaking. He tried to push himself up with his hands but his muscles had turned to rubber and flopped him back to the ground. He struggled and was finally able to lift his head enough to look in the direction the dinosaur had run—

A terrified scream cut through the air—

"*Aaaaaiiigh!*"

—followed by a tremendous roar. There was a crack loud as a gunshot—the sound of a tree snapping in half—followed by a strangled cry—

"*Aaaaaii—*"

—that ended as abruptly as it began.

Jack could no longer see the dinosaur, but he could hear muffled pops and crunches as the animal thrashed through the brush.

No, no, no, he thought as he pictured the long-haired kid. *No ...*

Even though he couldn't see more than a few yards into the timber, he had no doubt what had happened. He had no idea who the frightened kid was.

Or where he'd come from.

But ... it's all over now ...

5 Lost ...

For several long minutes Jack simply lay beside the log, his body shaking, his muscles quivering like jelly. He could hear animals slinking through the woods around him, though the allosaur had gone silent.

It's either stopped moving, or it's finished ... eating ... and has snuck away again.

He didn't know how long he lay there. It might have been a few seconds or half an hour. He had no idea. But in time he pushed himself up and shifted his legs so that he was sitting with his back against the fallen tree. His head was spinning and his stomach bubbling. Some deep, faraway part of his brain was telling him there was something wrong with the air—

Either too much or too little oxygen to breathe right.

—but he didn't waste time worrying about it. He glanced to his left and right—didn't see anything threatening—then leaned his head back and closed his eyes, trying to settle his nerves. He'd once been on a school ski trip when the bus driver lost control on an icy road. The bus had careened down the steep canyon road completely out of control before it crashed through a guardrail, flew over an embankment, and finally tipped onto its side.

No one had been seriously injured. But the terrifying turns, spins, and skids—not to mention the wild swaying, and bouncing—scrambled Jack's equilibrium, leaving him dizzy, shaky, and sick to his stomach.

But I didn't feel half as sick as I do now, he thought miserably.

He placed a hand on his stomach, feeling it turn and churn like a bubbling cauldron. He longed for a sip of something cool—

Like a shot of Coke, or Dr Pepper.

—to ease the nausea. But he no sooner had the thought than a horrifying shriek erupted from the trees, and he whipped his head around to look.

That's not *human*, he thought. *That's ... an animal!*

Remembering the kind of creatures prowling the prehistoric forest forced him back to the moment. Using the log for support, he struggled to his feet, deciding that his muscles—while not at 100%—were now at least steady enough to get him around.

He looked in the direction he'd last seen Artem and took several steps that way before stopping for a look back. The allosaur had flattened the brush as it charged after the long-haired kid, and Jack felt nausea coiling through his stomach like an icy-cold snake.

Crap! I don't wanna look, but ... if there's a chance that kid's still there somewhere—maybe lying hurt, or injured—I've gotta try to find him.

He stood uncertainly for a moment—terrified of what he might find—then took another look all around, sucked in a lungful of the thick, syrupy air—and began following the allosaur's trail.

Can't believe I'm doing this, he thought anxiously. *Following a freakin' dinosaur ...*

He thought back to what Kayce and Artem had told him about ... all this.

The dinosaurs.

The twisted "game."

The freakin' idiots back home who got their jollies by wagering on kids being killed and ... eaten.

As crazy and terrifying and unbelievable as it all seemed, he hadn't once disbelieved any of it.

But then again, here I am. I've seen the kids. I've seen the dinosaurs. I've seen frickin' animals that haven't existed for a hundred million years. I couldn't believe it any more if the evidence jumped up and bit me on the butt.

His stomach boiled and roiled—on the verge of spewing everywhere—as he crept through the timber. But not really because of what he was doing. He didn't understand it at first, but after a moment realized it was because he was ... lost.

Not just that he didn't know where he was, which he didn't.

But because he didn't know what to *do*.

Or what to *think*.

He'd been dropped unwarned and unprepared into an alien world. A world in which he didn't know the rules. Where he didn't know what to do or which way to go. And was only following the path of some monstrous dinosaur now because it seemed like the right thing to do.

Something rustled in the brush ahead and he stopped and crouched, preparing to run. And after a moment the brush rustled again.

But whatever's there isn't very big. Certainly not the size of an allosaur.

Even so, he didn't relax, knowing an animal didn't have to be the size of an allosaurus to be dangerous. He kept still, and after a moment spotted a chicken-sized lizard scurrying through the brush with something dangling from its mouth. He didn't know what the creature was, but it was running on two legs and looked like an animal he'd be smart to avoid.

He waited until the chicken/lizard had vanished into the trees, then continued along the trail of mashed and broken brush. He didn't have much hope of actually finding anything or ... any*body*. But he knew he'd always worry if he didn't try.

There was more rustling ahead and he stopped again, worried that perhaps the allosaur was still around. He listened carefully and finally decided the crunches and crackles were from several small animals rather than one big one. He glanced around, checked to be sure nothing was sneaking up behind him, then stepped carefully forward.

There was a sudden flurry of high-pitched squeaks and squeals as a pair of small animals began fighting. Jack stopped and listened, but the unseen animals quickly settled their differences and became quiet again. He hesitated and then took another step—

The woods thinned just ahead. He strained for a look into the clearing and spotted a pair of small dinosaurs scampering about.

But what—

He took another step—brushing against a leafy fern—and felt something wet on his hand. He looked—

Blood!

He stared, horrified, at the red smear, then noticed that the entire leaf was spattered with blood.

Holy crud ...

The icy snake in his stomach wriggled and writhed, his heart pounding so hard it could feel the blood throbbing in his ears. He peered ahead and spotted a shoe in the grass. He made a quick scan of the trees, then crept toward it. The grass and brush had been mashed flat, splotches of fresh blood splashed everywhere.

He leaned over to pick up the shoe—

A bone—jagged as a broken stick and still partially covered in bloody flesh—jutted from inside.

Hot bile boiled up in Jack's throat as he dropped to his knees. His stomach churned, and he clamped a hand over his mouth to keep from throwing up.

There was a loud *cheep*, and he looked over to see a mass of gore in the brush just ahead—part of an arm, and a hand—and then a cat-sized dinosaur ran past with what looked like a length of gut dangling from its jaws.

Jack's stomach lurched and he spewed violently into the brush. Throwing up again and again, unable to stop, totally sickened by the awful sights.

He finally staggered to his feet, clamped his hand back over his bile-drenched mouth, and stumbled away as fast as he could.

6 ... and Found

He wasn't certain how long he wandered. It felt like hours, but might have only been ten or fifteen minutes. He wasn't keeping track and he wasn't paying attention to anything around him. Was staggering blindly through the woods, trying to rid himself of the appalling images of gore and death. His body was completely on autopilot, and he stumbled through the trees with no idea of where he was or where he was going or what animals were lurking about.

The forest floor began to rise, becoming steeper, and he finally stopped for a look around.

Good, crud, he thought. *No idea where I am.*

He climbed to a prominent moss-covered rock and then sat so he could look out over the forest.

Jeez ...

Everything Kayce and Artem had told him still seemed impossible. Incomprehensible. Too fantastic to believe. But the roars and bellows of large animals continually shaking the forest were undeniable.

Unlike anything he'd ever heard, unlike anything that existed in a normal world. And so alien it was almost impossible to picture the creatures making them.

A deep, seldom-visited part of his soul wanted to cry. And he might have if he hadn't been so sick. But he closed his eyes and dropped his head, his shoulders shaking and his eyes welling with tears. He might have lost all control, but some small forest animal suddenly chittered in alarm and he looked up—

What the—

Something was moving in the woods below him. He coiled instinctively, loading his legs and preparing to run ... but then saw the baseball cap.

Kayce.

The girl was walking slowly, and carefully, glancing frequently at the ground without ever really taking her eyes from the surrounding trees. She seemed to be following the same trail as Jack, perhaps even following his tracks.

She crept closer, stopped and studied the ground for a moment, then lifted her head and began scanning the trees. Jack lifted a hand and she spotted him right away. She cast a quick look around, then climbed up the hill and sat on the rock beside him.

"Hey."

"Hey," he said.

"You okay?"

"No. Not really."

"I guess you must've found Travis, huh? What was left of him?"

"If that's who it was, yeah."

She blew a lungful of air out through her teeth. "Yeah, that had to suck. 'Specially on your first day."

"What happened?"

"Not sure yet. He must've left camp for some reason, but I can't believe he'd be that stupid. I mean, going into the woods alone isn't such a good idea."

Jack just nodded.

"Look," she said. "I could spend an hour trying to make you feel better about all this. But the fact is that nothing's gonna help. The brutal truth is that your old life is over with. Period. And yeah, I know what a shock that is: we've all been through it. But the sooner you accept the fact that you're here—and that you're never going home again—and start dealing with that, the better off you're gonna be."

She softened her tone a little.

"I'm sorry to be so blunt. But every kid here goes through exactly the same thing. Some kids never learn to cope, and they don't last long. Simple truth."

"What happens to them?"

"Some freak out and become easy prey. You know, for the dinosaurs. Others just give up. They quit trying and become careless and make mistakes ... and then, you know, end up like Travis. We've had a couple of kids just snap and run screaming into the forest." She reached up to brush a bug or a twig or something from her hair. "We never see them again."

She shrugged.

"There's a fact of life that applies here as much as it does back home. You have to make the best of things, whatever your circumstances. You can't wait for everything to be just fine and dandy and free of problems to make a go of things. You can't wait until your life's perfect before deciding to be happy. Or to be productive."

She tossed her head.

"Everybody's got problems. Everybody. And yeah, ours are a little more dramatic than most. But you can learn to deal with them. You can decide to fret and mope and cry until some dinosaur takes a bite of your ass, or you can put your best foot forward. Make the most of what you've still got."

She gave him a look that seemed to penetrate all the way to the bone.

"So I guess the question is, am I gonna be able to count on you? Or are you gonna flake out and become just another problem for the rest of us?"

Jack looked at her sourly. Apart from everything else, her brusqueness was off-putting.

"Or ... what?" he asked. "You gonna just leave me to the dinosaurs?"

She didn't even blink. "That's an option. But it's entirely up to you, cowboy."

Jack hesitated and she added: "The key to surviving here is to forget everything you've lost. Quit dwelling on your old life. Then just live, and love, and work, and fight like every day is your last. 'Cause it just might be."

"Love?"

"Well, in your own way, whatever that is. Anyway, you think you can do that?"

He gave her a dour look. "I don't have any choice, do I?"

"Not really. Not if you want to live more than a few hours."

He blew out his breath. And let his shoulders slump in resignation. And then said: "Yeah. You can count on me."

"Are you sure?" Her tone suggested that she wasn't entirely convinced.

"Yes." And then with a shrug: "That little brainwashed kid—Artem?—told me you're the only reason he's still alive."

She lifted a shoulder in a barely perceptible shrug. "He's not wrong about that." She tipped her head. "When he first got here, I didn't think he was going to last a day. I mean, he *is* just a little kid! But"—she sighed—"he did everything I told him. And he's not only lasted, but now? Heck, if anything ever happens to him I might just give in myself. Go looking for the biggest, meanest, dinosaur in the forest and say, 'Chow down, buddy!' "

She tapped a fingernail against her teeth, then stood and pointed into the forest.

"Ready to go?"

"Ready or not."

"Okay. Let's get back before it gets dark."

They'd only hiked a short distance before they heard frantic crackling in the brush ahead. Kayce instantly motioned for Jack to get down, then dropped into a crouch and stared intently into the trees. The crackling became more frantic, and Jack knew that whatever was out there was coming closer.

He watched for a moment, then whispered. "What is it?"

"It's not a dinosaur," Kayce whispered without turning her head.

"How do you know?"

"I know."

The running creature came closer, directly toward Jack and Kayce. Jack wanted to turn and run—to get as far away from whatever-was-coming as he could—but Kayce remained calm, and still, as she watched. The sound of running continued, and now Jack could hear sharp chuffs of breath: the sound of a winded animal ... one that had been running long and hard and fast.

Kayce crouched a little lower, loading her legs, then leaped just as something appeared from the vines and leaves. The fleeing creature was a girl, a few inches taller than Kayce. Kayce grabbed her around the waist, clamped a hand over her mouth to keep her from screaming, and pulled her sharply to the ground.

Jack only caught a quick glance as the girl dropped, but saw enormous eyes filled with fright and flooding tears.

Kayce was already trying to calm her.

"Shhhh, shhhh, shhhh," she whispered. "It's okay. I've got you. Shhhh."

The sobbing girl struggled for a moment before realizing she wasn't about to be eaten. Kayce removed her hand from the girl's mouth—

There was the sound of pounding feet—more crackling brush—and a second figure appeared from the trees, this one a boy, running hard. Running so fast he almost crashed into them before he realized anyone was there.

The boy jerked to a stop, his startled eyes flicking from person to person. Jack wasn't certain but thought the boy's eyes widened in fear when he spotted Kayce. But then the kid whirled around and tore back down the trail the way he'd come.

What the—

Kayce watched the boy vanish into the timber, then turned around and Jack was shocked by the transformation. Her face was suddenly hard as steel, sharp as an axe, and flushed with anger. Her jaw set like a steel trap, she looked into the crying girl's eyes.

Something seemed to pass between the two girls.

Kayce's face became even harder, looking as if it had been chipped from stone.

"Did Josh—"

The girl nodded. "And Travis. They were ... they tried ..."

Kayce's lips tightened. Turned white. And then in a voice as soft as snowflakes but with the power of thunder, she said, "I'll take care of this."

She turned and leveled a finger at Jack. "Stay here," she ordered. "Don't move and"—she pointed toward the girl—"do *not* touch her."

She hugged the girl quickly, whispered something Jack couldn't hear, then hopped to her feet and raced into the brush.

Jack was too bewildered to understand what was happening. He stared into the trees after Kayce, then looked at the sobbing girl, noticing for the first time that her clothes had been torn.

Oh, crap, he thought as he figured it out. *No wonder Kayce told me not to touch her.*

The girl knelt in the dirt, staring after Kayce with her arms wrapped around herself as if she was cold. After a moment she half turned, spotted Jack crouching in the brush behind her, and flinched in surprised. She was so startled it was several seconds before she realized she didn't know him.

"Who're you?"

"Jack. I just got here." And then: "Is there anything I can do—"

"*No!*" the word came out in a harsh, hostile hiss.

Jack held his hands up, as if to show that he wasn't carrying a weapon. "Hey, look, I'm safe. I just want—"

"Just stay the hell away from me. You got that—"

There was a sudden scream from the trees, followed by an anguished howl. Jack's heart sank as he flashed back to the screams he'd heard when Travis ...

His arms erupted in goosebumps, and the skin along his spine began to crawl. Struggling to understand what was happening, he glanced at the trembling girl, who was holding herself even more tightly.

The howl of agony continued for a moment before morphing into pitiful cries and pleas.

Jeez, what have I gotten myself into?

Several minutes passed, and then he heard the rustle of leaves and caught glimpses of someone creeping back down the trail.

Kayce.

He stood as the pony-tailed girl walked up. She looked down at the other girl, nodded once, and then looked at Jack.

"Ready to go?"

"No, what?" He shook his head like he was shaking it free of cobwebs. "Wait—what just happened?"

Kayce shook her head. "We'll talk about it later—"

"No!" Jack stammered. "W-what—" He shook his head again. "Look, I know I'm the new guy, but what the *hell*? What's going on—"

"I broke his leg," Kayce said simply.

"You ... wait, *what*?"

"I broke his leg." She glanced over at the traumatized girl, then stepped close to Jack and lowered her voice. "You know what was happening here, right? You've heard that little talk about the birds and the bees?"

"Yeah, I think so. Know what was happening, I mean. But still—"

"Look. Any kid willing to ... well, to do what Josh was doing wouldn't hesitate to bash your head in with a rock just to get an extra fish for breakfast. Trust me, we've seen it before and it's always the same. We've learned from experience and we don't give second chances. Not anymore. And *that*"—she waved a hand into the trees in the direction of the pathetic, agonized cries—"is the only way to deal with something like this. The *only* way. There's no way any kid can act like that and expect to stay part of the group."

"So what's gonna happen to him—"

"What do you *think's* gonna happen? He's got a broken leg. He's not going anywhere and ... well, the forest is a dangerous place."

Jack didn't reply. He was too stunned—too completely gobsmacked—to react. The running kid—

Josh, was it?

—tried to ... have his way ... with the distraught girl. So Kayce had broken his leg.

And left him for the dinosaurs.

As calmy as if she was simply throwing out the trash.

Which, in her mind, was probably exactly what she was doing.

Kayce leaned in and whispered. "Like I said, we'll talk about it later. For now, let's just try to make it back before it gets dark.

Kayce led the way through the forest, the flustered girl—Jack heard Kayce call her "Janice"—close on her heels. And while Kayce kept a sharp eye on the trees—turning her head this way and that as she watched and listened for signs of danger—she hiked at a brisk pace.

Girl's in a serious hurry, Jack thought, struggling to keep up. As fast as the pace was, it wasn't nearly as rigorous as a typical football workout. But Jack was quickly huffing for breath.

Gotta ... be ... the air or something, he thought. *Definitely different from what I'm used to ...*

He wiped a sleeve across his forehead, surprised by how profusely he was sweating.

Like ... bullets ...

On the other hand, struggling to keep up with the stern, pony-tailed girl kept his mind from ... from ... well, from *everything*. It kept him from dwelling on the onslaught of unbelievable information. And it was—mercifully—giving him time to adjust to the shock of it all.

An animal bellowed in the trees—

Something big, Jack thought nervously. He peered into the trees. *And most likely hungry and loaded with teeth!*

—but Kayce scarcely looked in its direction before giving the forest another careful scan.

Freakin' huge animal stomping around and she doesn't seem to care, Jack thought in disbelief. *Who* is *she?*

Jack lost track of how long they hiked. His brain was so occupied—so overwhelmed by the barrage of bizarre, impossible-to-believe revelations—that hours could have passed without his realizing it. But eventually Kayce stopped and seemed to hesitate. And then turned to Janice.

"Go on ahead. We'll be right behind you."

Janice nodded and skulked down the trail, then Kayce turned to Jack.

"What is it?" Jack asked.

Kayce frowned. "I just want to make sure you're ready for this."

"Ready for what?"

"Well, you've gotta understand that this isn't like football camp. Or cheerleading camp or chess camp or whatever else you might be thinking. After what everyone's been through here—what we're all *going* through—everyone's got glass half-empty attitudes. And you've gotta be ready for that."

"You don't seem that way. Neither does Artem."

She almost smiled. "No, we've pretty much come to terms with things, so we're both glass half-full. All the way. I guess"—she scrunched her nose as she searched for the right words, and Jack sensed she was confiding in him: perhaps even confiding in a way she didn't attempt with the others—"I guess I'm just hoping you won't let the downer attitudes get to you."

Jack glanced ahead, trying to get a glimpse of what was there, then lifted his hands.

"Hey, if you're glass half-full, I'm nine-tenths."

She half-smiled. "Okay, nine-tenths, let's do it." She held up a finger. "Just remember to watch yourself. Out here, pessimism is a disease that can kill you as fast as the dinosaurs. And it's contagious."

She tapped a finger against his chest.

"Very, *very* contagious."

"I get'cha." He puffed out his chest and gestured. "After you, boss."

She led the way, and after a moment stepped into a clearing flanked on the right by a steep, rocky cliff. Jack had steeled himself for what was coming, but nothing could have prepared him for the misery gathered in the small open space.

Good crud, he thought. *Kayce wasn't kidding. If anything, she understated.*

Janice was sitting on a jagged rock, being consoled by two girls. In the way of teenage girls everywhere, they had their arms wrapped around one another as they sobbed. Two boys were sitting on a log that someone had dragged in from the trees. Jack glanced around and after a moment spotted Artem perched on a tree branch over the clearing.

Kayce had said the kids were all good looking—

Jeez, they make the models in Teen Vogue *seem dull as dishwater.*

—though their clothes were dirty and—in many cases—torn and tattered. But their striking attractiveness was overpowered by their haunted expressions.

To a person, the kids' eyes were sunken and troubled, empty as fathomless pits. Filled with despair so dark and deep the misery radiated into their faces. The girls soothing Janice cast frequent, vile looks at the boys who, in turn, kept their heads turned, apparently shaken by what Travis and Josh had attempted.

And angry to have been betrayed by two of their own.

Kayce looked once around the clearing as if taking roll—making sure everyone (with the exception of Travis and Josh) was still there and everything the way she'd left it—then jerked a thumb at Jack.

"We've got some good news," she announced. "It wasn't a hunter, after all. They just sent us another kid. Jake."

"Jack."

She gave Jack a sour look, then pointed.

"That's Megan and Natalie and ... Janice, of course." She turned and gestured toward the boys. "And that's Colton, and Tim and"—she pointed into the tree—"you already know Tarzan the Jungle Squirt."

Jack gave a noncommittal wave. He wasn't certain what he should do, but Tim spoke up.

"Where're Josh and Travis?"

"Dinosaurs," Kayce replied, not quite telling the whole story.

The boys flinched, but didn't seem extremely surprised or rattled. Colton flicked a hand at Jack. "Why's he alone? Is he the only one to come through?"

Jack had to force himself not to react. Colton's voice was as precise and cultured as an English aristocrat. But his refined, wealthy, educated manner seemed completely at odds with his tattered clothes and dirt-smudged face.

"I don't know," Kayce said. "I'm as surprised as you are."

"Are they changing the rules?" This from Natalie, a striking dark-haired girl who appeared Latina.

"Don't know," Kayce repeated. "It's never happened before and I'm as confused as you are."

She turned back to Jack and pointed. "If you're thirsty, there's a fresh water seep just around the cliff there"—she turned and gestured down the hill—"and the bathroom's that way."

"The, um, *bathroom*?"

"There're no stalls, if that's what you're wondering. Pick a good bush and enjoy yourself."

"But be considerate and cover it with dirt!" Megan snapped. She had light hair that hung almost to her elbows, and despite the circumstances it appeared she still tended to it.

Or at least tries to ...

With a flash of irritation, she threw a pine cone that scored a hit on Tim's ear. "I stepped in one of Tim's turds and nearly puked."

"It wasn't mine, you stupid bitch, " Tim grumbled, firing back a cone of his own; he missed, which prompted Megan to flash a nasty gesture.

"It was so!"

"Was *not*—"

Kayce: "Enough already!" She subjected everyone to a harsh, *I'm-tired-of-hearing-it* glare, then turned to Jack. "But yeah, be considerate."

Artem, from the tree: "There's a stick there to lean across the path. You know, so no one else walks up while you're busy."

Kayce: "And don't go too far. The hill's steep enough that not a lot of big animals come wandering around. But you never know."

Kayce glanced around, then turned back to Jack. "Hungry?"

The question caught him by surprise. For the past few hours—

God, has it only been that long?

—food had been the last thing on his mind. But now that she'd mentioned it ...

"Well, yeah," he said. "I guess I am. A little bit."

Kayce looked up at Artem, who nodded and then swung down from the tree and crooked a finger at Jack.

"C'mon."

Feeling like an unwelcome visitor, Jack followed the boy out of the clearing in the direction of the water seep. The trail followed the cliff, eventually coming to a mossy patch where water trickled from the rocks and into a small pool before streaming downhill.

Artem stepped over the pool and lifted a plate-sized stone from a pile of rocks.

"Rocks keep everything cool," the boy explained. He reached into a recess and removed a bit of cloth, which he unwrapped to reveal several slabs of thin, pink meat.

"Fish," he said. And then, when Jack hesitated: "Uh, are you okay eating it raw?"

"Raw?"

"You get to used to it. But"—he glanced back into the rocks, then removed another bundle—"here's some we cooked last night."

He unwrapped the bundle.

"It's a little burnt, but still ..."

Jack picked out a piece of charred meat, frowned, then took an experimental bite. The most-blackened portions, it turned out, were actually the tastiest.

"Go ahead," Artem urged. "Eat as much as you want."

Jack nodded and took the bundle; actually having something in his mouth—he hesitated to think of it as "food"—reminded him of how hungry he actually was, and he ate ravenously. Artem, meanwhile, nibbled at a piece of raw fish.

"Where'd you get the fish?" Jack asked between bites.

Artem gestured vaguely. "We built a dam in a stream down the hill. Fish can get in, but then can't get back out again. Makes 'em easy to catch."

"Is this all you eat?"

"No. Sometimes we find fresh dinosaur kills. Usually gotta fight off a few scavengers for them, but if you're fast you can carve off a coupla nice steaks before something big comes along and chases you off."

"Do you eat that raw too?"

"Sometimes."

"Why?"

The boy spit out a slender fish bone. "Building fires isn't always a good idea. During the day people can see the smoke, and that's never a good thing. Hunters, remember? And at night, a lot of animals are attracted to the light."

"They're not afraid of the fire?"

"Not as much as you'd think. For one thing, they don't have a lot of experience with it. And when you're fifteen or twenty feet tall, some kid with a homemade torch isn't all that intimidating."

"Huh." Jack glanced back toward the clearing, then bit into another chunk of blackened meat. "So let me ask you: is everyone always so gloomy?"

The boy gave him an odd look. "You remember why you're here, right? You know what's going on?"

"Yeah. Kinda, sorta."

"Kids here don't have a lot of hope. No reason to be happy. A good day is when we don't, um, *lose* anyone. And today? We lost two. They were both idiots, sure. But still."

He shrugged.

"Anyway, to answer your question, don't expect any campfire sing-alongs. What you saw is about as cheerful as things get. Sort of our version of Wacky Wednesday."

Crap, Jack thought, chewing into another chunk of blackened fish.

He had a thought.

"You have any weapons? You know, to protect yourself from dinosaurs? Or ... hunters?"

"Kayce's got that Godzilla-rated knife—you saw that, right?—and we've got a couple of rifles. We've taken a few pistols and things from hunters after ... well, you know. But Kayce keeps everything stashed away somewhere. Hidden. *I* don't even know where it all is."

Jack stopped in mid-nibble to stare incredulously. "What? *Why?*"

Artem seemed hesitant to explain, but finally shrugged, apparently deciding there was no need to keep anything secret. "Three reasons, I guess."

"Which are?"

"Main thing is, we're just kids, and none of us knows anything about being a commando. We start shooting and we're as likely to kill ourselves as some dinosaur."

Well, yeah, I guess that makes sense. "What else?"

"The guys who bring the guns aren't supposed to last long. Their being here messes things up, right? Interferes with the freakin' game? So they're given ammunition, but most of it doesn't actually work."

"*What?*"

"Yeah. They're given a lot of bullets, which gives them confidence, right? But only the first dozen rounds or so actually fire. Nothing else works."

"But that's *stupid*! Why would anyone have ammunition that doesn't work?"

"Think about it. They send guys back to adjust the cameras, or to hunt down Kayce and get rid of her. So they give whoever it is enough ammunition to feel safe and secure. But once the guy realizes he ain't going home again, they don't want him shooting up every dinosaur in sight. So yeah, they give him a lot of ammunition. But most of it's fake. Besides, they know *we* might end up with some of it, and they obviously don't want *that*, right?"

Good crap ...

Jack thought over the new information for a minute, then said, "So what's the third reason?"

Artem looked back evenly. "You've seen everyone," he said, flicking a hand toward the clearing. "Would *you* trust any of them with a gun?"

Jack blew out his breath, then shook his head. "Still doesn't make sense to have guns and not use them."

"You'll understand once you've been here a while," Artem replied patiently. "Remember Travis and Josh? The guys chasing Janice? What if *they'd* had guns? Or what if someone just lost their mind in the middle of the night? Even without guns, kids sometimes go nuts. And when that happens, it's bad enough when all they've got to fight with are rocks and sticks."

"Huh."

"And, um, I guess there's actually another thing, too."

"Yeah? What's that?"

"You've seen the animals here. They're pretty stout. Shooting at them just tends to make them mad."

Jack shook his head at the stupidity of it all, then looked at Artem. The boy was nibbling his raw fish like a Cub Scout on a fresh cob of corn.

Like eating raw fish is the most natural thing in the world ...

"So, how old are you?"

"Twelve," the boy said with a hint of defiance. "And yeah, yeah, I look eight, I know. I hear it all the time."

"I was actually thinking ten."

"Yeah?" The kid seemed pleased. "Sweet."

He tossed away what was left of his fish. "Have you had enough?"

"Yeah, I think so."

"Then come on ... let's get back to camp."

7 Night Fright

The moon eventually came up, a quarter moon that looked like a sliver of rich butter as it rose over the forest. There were stars, too, that twinkled and shimmered more brightly than anything Jack had ever seen at home—

Probably 'cause there aren't any lights around, and no pollution in the sky.

—though Jack didn't recognize any constellations.

He was exhausted—physically, mentally, and emotionally—but knew he'd never be able to sleep.

Not after a day like this ...

The sound of a soft snore drifted across the clearing.

Don't know how, but someone's getting some sleep, anyway, he thought. *But then, they've had time to adjust to everything.*

He reached a hand up to his face and rubbed his eyes.

And felt his stomach sink. Felt his jaw tremble. And felt ...

Don't ... cry, he ordered himself.

Gotta hold it together.

And after several miserable seconds: *Jeez ... shed a tear in front of this bunch? They'll never let you live it down.*

He clenched his teeth to keep his jaw from trembling, but still felt an enormous lump rising painfully in his throat—

Crunch.

The sound drifted from the trees as softly as a whisper so faint and subtle that Jack wondered if he'd imagined it.

He closed his eyes and listened carefully. The nighttime forest was far from quiet, of course. Legions of cricket-like bugs hummed and chittered all around. Leaves rustled in an unfelt breeze as night birds flitted through the blackness. A small animal hooted in the distance.

Snap.

He opened his eyes and peered into the darkness. Like before, the sound was soft.

And I know it wasn't my imagination.

He looked around the clearing, then rose to his feet and crept toward Artem's tree. He paused as someone stirred restlessly in their sleep, then stepped lightly to avoid making noise and waking anyone.

He looked up when he reached Artem's tree and was wondering how to—

"Hey, Jack. You okay?" Artem's voice floated down from the canopy of leaves.

"Yeah. Um, I think I heard something."

"Oh? Like what?"

"Just a couple of noises. Really soft. Like some animal stepping on dry twigs or leaves or something. Maybe trying to sneak up on us."

"Something big?"

"Not *real* big. Not like an allosaur, I don't think. But I don't know." Even as he spoke, Jack felt suddenly foolish. After all, he hadn't heard anything but a couple of snaps in the woods. Sounds that might not have been anything more than trees shifting beneath their own weight. He mentally kicked himself, wishing he'd waited to find out for sure what was going on—

There was a rustle of swishing leaves and branches, and Artem's face poked from the foliage.

"Where did you hear it?"

"Hey, listen," Jack said apologetically. "It's not like I *know* something's out there. I just heard—"

"It's okay," Artem assured him. "Kayce would rather have a hundred false alarms than risk having a single animal sneak up on us, y'know? It's one of the reasons she's still alive—"

A blood-curdling shriek abruptly cut through the darkness. Jack whirled around just as something dark flashed from the trees. There was a scream, a shriek like the end of the world, the sound of animals tearing through the grass.

Jack snatched up a stick from the ground and raised it like a baseball bat. There was a horrendous shriek from behind and he turned just as a screeching nightmare leaped—

Jack was swinging his bat, even as Artem screamed, "*Look out!*"

—and felt the wood connect. The springing animal screeched in pain—

Keeee!

—and lunged away.

One of the girls was screaming on the far side of the clearing and Jack rushed toward her, spotting someone lying in the dirt—another of the girls—a pair of animals the size of German Shepherds crouching over her. Jack wasn't even thinking—was operating entirely by reflex—as he clenched his teeth and swung as hard as he could. The stick cracked over an animal's back and shattered into a thousand pieces.

The animal screeched and buckled and then bolted away. Jack instantly kicked at the second animal, which turned, hissed, and flashed a set of claws ... and then bounded back into the darkness.

Chase spun around and spotted another creature, this one leaping at Artem's tree, trying to reach—

Artem!

Without thinking about what he was doing, Jack bolted back across the clearing. There were screams and shouts from every direction—blood-curdling shrieks, screeches, and cries ... the sounds more horrible than anything Jack had ever heard. But he shut them all out, focused only upon the creature attacking his friend.

Artem screamed—

"*Aaaaaiiigh!*"

—and Jack saw the creature swinging below the tree, its jaws and claws clamped upon something. And then he caught a glimpse of Artem.

It's got his leg!

Jack set his teeth as he reached the tree and kicked as hard as he could. His shoe slammed into the creature's side, folding the animal in half like a soggy taco. The creature screeched in pain and rage, but quickly regained its feet and sprang back into the woods.

Jack watched to be sure it was gone, then looked anxiously up into the tree.

"Artem! Are you okay?"

Nothing.

"Artem? *Artem!* Are you okay?"

"Y-yeah. I'm okay."

"Did it get you?"

"No, I ... I think I'm—"

Something abruptly slammed into Jack from behind, knocking him flat on his face. He felt the burn of claws slashing across his side and screamed—

"*Aaaaaiiigh!*"

—as the animal bit down, snagging its teeth in his belt. Jack was stunned, but a deep part of his brain told him he was mere seconds from being torn apart and his arms and legs were already struggling to escape. He rammed an elbow back as hard as he could—felt it connect with something solid, possibly the side of the creature's head—then flipped onto his back.

The stunned dinosaur hissed, crouched, and sprang at Jack's face. Jack screamed again, but his left hand closed around a rock and he slammed it as hard as he could against the animal's head. The dinosaur screeched, but leaped back to its feet and tried again. With jaws wide and forearms outstretched, it leaped—

Artem dropped from the tree with a horrendous cry—

"*Ayyyyyyy!*"

—landing on top of the animal and crushing it to the ground.

"Artem!"

Knowing the boy would be killed, Jack leaped to his feet and dove. He hit the smaller boy broadside, knocking him away—

"*Oof!*"

—then dropped on top of the thrashing, slashing, snapping creature. A sharp claw sliced across his hip, but he ignored the pain and wrapped his arms around the animal and squeezed as hard as he could.

The animal screeched, practically in his ear—

Cheeeeeee!

—and twisted its head, lunging at Jack's face.

Jack turned his head away from the snapping jaws, gritted his teeth, and grabbed the back of the creature's head.

The animal thrashed more violently than ever—legs, claws, and jaws a terrifying blur of energy—but Jack got a grip on the back of the creature's neck and slammed its head against the ground. And then again and again. And again, until the animal was no longer fighting back.

He finally rolled to his knees, kicked the limp creature away in disgust, then turned to look for Artem.

The boy was standing just behind him.

"Hoe-lee *crap!*" the kid gushed. "I can't believe you just *did* that!"

Jack nodded, then turned to scan the clearing. There was just enough moonlight to make out shapes and outlines, but it seemed the attack was over and the last of the screeching creatures gone.

Kayce suddenly appeared from the gloom, carrying a thick branch like a club.

"You two okay?"

"Five by five," Jack said.

"What—"

"We're okay," Jack said. He sucked in a huge lungful of air. "You?"

"I'm fine, but"—she seemed to be shaking her head—"but they got Janice. And Colton's missing, so ... they probably got him, too."

Jack gave the campsite a closer look. On the far side— where he'd broken a club over the back of one of the creatures—a body was lying motionless—

So, Janice, probably.

—and even in the gloom it was obvious she'd been torn open. The three remaining survivors—Natalie, Megan, and Tim—were huddled together a short distance away.

Jack turned away and looked at Artem.

"Let me see your leg."

"Huh?"

"Your leg! Let me see it!"

"Hey, I'm fine," the boy said, drawing away.

"Dude, that thing had its teeth in you. Now let me look—"

"Let 'im look," Kayce ordered.

Artem hesitated another second, then leaned over and pulled up his right pant leg.

"Nice try," Jack said, kneeling in front of him. "But that's not the one I need to see."

He reached down and pulled up the left pant leg himself, spotting ribbons of fresh blood trickling down the boy's calves before finding the actual slashes and gashes.

"Whew, you're one lucky kid," he said. "Another second and that thing would've taken your leg clean off."

He peered a little closer, gauging the severity of the wounds, then glanced up at Kayce.

"I guess you don't have a first aid kit? Any bandages or anything?"

Kayce spread her hands. "What you see is what you've got."

Jack sucked air through his teeth, then pointed to the knife on Kayce's belt. "Give me your knife."

"What?"

"You heard me. Give me your knife. Or do you want Boy Wonder to bleed to death?"

Kayce reluctantly unsheathed the scalpel-sharp knife—a commando blade long and sharp enough to turn the most grizzled Navy SEAL green with envy—as Artem stammered, "W-what are you g-gonna do?"

"I'm not gonna hurt you," Jack assured him. "But we've gotta stop this bleeding while you've still got a little blood left to save."

He helped Artem over to a nearby log, had him sit, and then placed one of the boy's hands over the worst of the wounds.

"Hold that right there for a minute."

Artem did as he was told, and Jack strode across the clearing to where Janice lay still. She'd been horribly mutilated by the animals and the coppery smell of fresh blood was still strong in the air.

Jeez, you poor kid, Jack thought as he knelt beside her. *Your last day on this planet sure was a miserable one, but ... well, I hope you can find a little peace now.*

Trying not to think about what he was doing, he used Kayce's knife to slash several strips of cloth from the girl's shirt, then several more from her torn blue jeans. Tearing up her clothes further exposed the girl's gruesome wounds, and Jack had to choke down the bile, forcing himself to concentrate on his task.

Finally, he strode back to Kayce and Artem.

"Okay, bud," he said, once again kneeling in front of the boy. "Let's see that leg."

He used folded pieces of Janice's blood-smeared shirt to cover the worst of the gashes, then secured them with strips of blue denim that he knotted neatly around the boy's leg. Finally, he eased Artem's pant leg down over the makeshift bandages.

"Okay, bud." He slapped the boy on the knee. "You're practically good as new."

"What about you?"

"What about me?"

Artem reached over and flicked Jack's shirt. "You're bleeding like a mother."

Jack looked. Parallel tears crossed his shirt, which was soaked wet over his belly.

"What the—"

It took a moment, but then he remembered being slashed.

Doesn't really hurt though ...

He lifted his shirt, surprised to see a gash running horizontally from one side of his belly to the other.

"Ay, yi, yi—"

"Freakin' buckets—" Artem exclaimed. He instantly took charge. "Here, hand me that cloth."

He took what was left of Jack's makeshift bandages and quickly dressed Jack's belly, just the way Jack had done.

"Wow, you catch on fast," Jack said.

"Had a good teacher. Where'd you get the cloth?"

"I, um, borrowed it from Janice."

Artem stopped work for a moment, and when he continued it was a little less enthusiastically.

"Look, you were bleeding," Jack explained. "And I didn't know what else to do."

"Yeah, I know. It's just ..."

"Hard. Yeah, I get it. But ... try not to think about it."

Kayce had left to check on the other survivors, but walked back just as Artem was tying off Jack's bandage. "You told me you were okay."

"I thought I was."

Kayce inspected the bandage, then looked at Artem. "You did that?"

"Uh-huh."

"Strong work."

"How're the others?" Jack asked, as Artem beamed. "They okay?"

"A few cuts and scratches, but nothing serious. But up here"—she tapped her head—"they're totally messed up. But that's understandable. They were right there when Janice and Colton, um ..."

"Yeah. I get it."

"Anyway, we've gotta get outta here now. All this fresh blood is going to attract scavengers. And the thing is, a lot of the bigger animals would rather steal meat than hunt it. So a few of them might come snooping around too. Believe me, you don't wanna be around if that happens."

"What're we going to do about Janice? And—you know—Colton?"

"Nothing we *can* do," Kayce replied bluntly. And then, before Jack could protest: "Think about it. We don't know where Colton—even if he still *is*—and we don't have any tools to bury Janice. And even if we did, a two-ton animal could uncover her with just two sweeps of its claws. So what's the point? Besides, we'd be swarmed by hungry scavengers before we were halfway done."

She lifted her hands.

"I know what you're thinking. Really, I do. But we've been through this—hell, more times than I can count now—and believe me, there's nothing we can do. For them, anyway. And in the meantime, *we've* got to get clear ... and the sooner the better."

Jack peered into the woods. "Not to sound critical, but is that safe? Wandering around in the middle of the night?"

"No, it's not. Most of the time it would be incredibly stupid. But"—she blew out her breath—"with the smell of blood in the air, sticking around here would be even worse."

She lifted a hand, then pointed as some animal screeched hungrily in the trees nearby

"See? It's already starting."

She looked back and forth between Jack and Artem.

"And the two of you smelling like butchered corn-fed beef isn't going to help. I mean, you know that when sharks smell blood in the water—"

"They come running? Um, swimming?"

She nodded. "And if anything, dinosaurs are worse." She waved a hand around the clearing. "And with this much blood splattered around ..."

"Yeah, I get it."

"Too bad we've gotta leave," Artem whispered wistfully. "This was one of the best camping spots we've had."

"I know," Kayce said, giving the boy a quick side-hug. "And we might be back again. Someday. But in the meantime, we'll be okay. We'll find another place."

"You got someplace in mind?" Jack asked.

Kayce looked at Artem. "What do you think about trying the chatterwoods?"

Artem looked up for a moment, thinking, then nodded. "Yeah, that's a good idea. Be scary getting there in the dark, but I don't have a better suggestion."

"The chatterwoods?" Jack asked.

"You'll have to see 'em to understand." She turned back to Artem. "Be quite a hike getting there—"

"But we can do it," Artem assured her.

"—and we'll be fairly close to another stream there, so we'll have water."

She looked back over her shoulder—making sure she wouldn't be overheard—then whispered: "Like I said, those three over there are pretty messed up. Like, right on the edge of wigging out. We'll have to keep an eye on them."

"Not a problem," Artem assured her.

She turned to Jack, who shrugged.

"I'm still the new kid," he said. "But whatever you need, just name it."

She nodded. "Thanks." And then: "Be right back."

She walked back to the other survivors.

"So what are these kids like?" Jack asked quietly.

"The girls aren't so bad," Artem replied. "It's not like they're wonder women or anything, but they mostly do what they're asked and they don't cause a lot of problems."

He lowered his voice a notch.

"I don't want to sound rude, but ..."

"What?"

"Well, I hate to say it, but I've been here a little while now and, well, kids like that don't usually last long."

"Good crud," Jack answered, understanding what the boy was saying. But then: "What about Tim? What's he like?"

"Tim's an ass," Artem said, practically hissing the words. "Total jerkwad. I hate to see anyone killed by a dinosaur, I really do. I mean no one deserves that, right? But if anyone did, well ..."

"A real Tony-bro, huh?"

"A what?"

"You've never heard that joke? Kid tells his teacher that his name is Tony. And the teacher says, 'Cool: you're named after two parts of the body—toe and knee.' And Tony says, 'So's my brother Butthead.' "

Artem had just been drawing in a breath, but suddenly began laughing ... laughing so hard he began to choke. He doubled over, choking and sputtering and struggling to breathe, and Jack had to pound him on the back to settle him down.

Kayce walked back over and glared. "What's wrong?"

"Nothing," Jack insisted as Artem struggled to catch his breath. "I just told him a joke."

"You're telling *jokes*? *Now?*"

"Uh, yeah, that wasn't appropriate. Sorry."

Kayce watched Artem for a moment—the kid was still struggling to breathe—then said to Jack: "I've known the kid for nearly a year and I can count on one hand the number of times I've seen him smile. And I've *never* seen him laugh."

She play-punched Jack in the arm as Artem clamped a hand across his chest and finally began breathing normally again.

"So if you know any more jokes, keep 'em coming." And after a quick glance at the other survivors: "Come on, let's go."

They joined Tim, Megan, and Natalie, and Kayce once again took charge.

"Not gonna sugar-coat anything," she announced. "But you know what things're like in the dark, and this is gonna be damn tough. I'll go first; Megan, Natalie, and Tim, you guys follow."

She looked at Jack.

"You okay bringing up the rear?"

"Sure."

"And Artem, you stick with him."

" 'Kay."

She thought for a moment, then took Jack by the arm and led him a few feet away.

"Look," she whispered. "Artem's good in the woods: he knows the sounds and rhythms of the forest and can usually sense when something's wrong or out of place. So listen to him. Listen to everything he tells you."

"I can do that."

"I mean it ... if he tells you to run, you take off like a friggin' rocket."

"I can do that."

She hesitated before going on. "Kid's a real pain in the ass, I know. But he's the closest thing I have to family, so I need you to watch out for him."

"I can do that too."

Artem had walked over and she ruffled the boy's hair and told him: "Keep the new guy outta trouble."

"I will. Don't worry."

"I always worry."

She play-punched Jack again, and Jack realized that despite his newbie status, he'd just been given an important assignment. A position of trust. And responsibility.

Which she denied Megan, Natalie, and Tim.

Artem looked up at Jack and said, "If anything happens, try to stay with me."

Jack nodded. "You've got it."

"I'm serious. I mean, you see me running for my life?"

"Uh-huh?"

"Best thing you can do is try to keep up."

This is one *dour bunch of kids*, Jack thought as Kayce led the way through the black forest. He couldn't help remembering what Kayce had said about Artem. That not only did the kid rarely smile, but that he never laughed.

What an awful way to live, he thought, giving the kid a quick look.

On the other hand, he understood the kid's attitude completely.

Kids were sent here to die, he thought, still trying to come to grips with that awful reality himself. And then realized he was subconsciously separating himself from the rest of the group.

I keep thinking "they" *were sent here to die; not* "we."

He shook his head clear, then tried to concentrate on the hums and patterns of the nighttime forest.

He already knew the forest was a noisy place, even at night. There were birds, bugs, bats, mammals, and—yeah—even dinosaurs, that mostly hunted and fed at night. Some were nocturnal because the darkness offered a measure of safety. But there were also animals that specialized in hunting night feeders. And so the darkness was filled with hums, chirps, flits, chitters, and chatters unique to nighttime.

Jack was already completely mixed up, turned around, and disoriented in the prehistoric forest. And hiking in the darkness just made things worse. He not only had no idea where he was going, but wouldn't have been able to find his way back to the last campsite with a map, compass, and trail of breadcrumbs to follow. Kayce, on the other hand, seemed to know exactly what she was doing and where she was going. She strode through the woods like a woman on a mission, as surely as if she was following a marked, paved, well-lighted trail.

And if she's just faking it, she's fooling everyone.

The group hiked slowly, but steadily, and seemed to be making good time. And while Jack had a difficult time hiking as stealthily as Artem, the group as a whole seemed to be moving quietly.

The one exception was Tim.

The kid stepped on so many sticks and twigs and crunching leaves that Jack was certain he was doing it on purpose. Kayce looked back several times, and Jack sensed her annoyance. But when Tim stepped on a stick that popped through the darkness like a gunshot, Kayce finally lost her temper.

"Can you at least *try* to be quiet?"

"It's not me," Tim snapped insolently. He jerked a thumb over his shoulder. "It's Artem ... he makes more noise than a herd of frackin' elephants."

"Shut up, Tim!" Artem shot back.

"Who're you telling to shut up, you little turd?"

Tim took a step toward Artem, who defiantly threw his shoulders back, determined to stand his ground.

Jack quickly stepped between the two, daring the bigger kid to make a move. But Artem wasn't ready to let things go.

"Hey, Tim," the younger kid taunted from behind Jack. "Tell us about your brother."

"My brother?"

"Yeah ... we heard you had a brother named Tony!"

"W-*what*?"

Jack nearly snorted, but before either of the boys could respond, Kayce was there. And even though she was much smaller than Tim, it was clear she not only intimidated the snotty kid, but actually frightened him.

"Do—you—*mind*?" she hissed. "We've got to be *quiet* out here!"

"Sorry, Kayce," Artem whispered, though Jack was sure Kayce knew Artem wasn't the problem.

"Just keep it quiet back here," Kayce hissed again; Jack sensed enough vehemence in her voice that had he not already been hiking as quietly as he could, he certainly would have started.

She stalked back to the head of the column, and as soon as she started again through the trees, Tim gave Artem a final shot.

"Little prick!" he rasped, carefully lowering his voice to keep Kayce from hearing. "Second I find you alone I'm gonna pull your damn—"

Jack leveled a finger to let Tim know he wasn't going to tolerate any bullying. He took a single step—

There was no warning. Before Jack realized what was happening, a shadow blacker than night and big as a house lunged from the foliage. An enormous head snapped down, and there was a flash of yellow teeth as the powerful jaws slammed together.

Tim had just enough time to begin to scream—

"*Aaaaaii*—gugh, gugh—"

—before the surprised cry became an anguished gurgle ... and then stopped altogether.

Jack stood transfixed as the great head rose above the brush, parts of the other boy dangling from its jaws. The animal shook its head from side to side—jets of hot blood whipped across Jack's face—then tossed its head back and ground its teeth together.

Jack heard the crunch of bones as the dinosaur chewed down its prize.

Jack turned to run as one of the girls screamed from the trail ahead. The black dinosaur whirled around and its muscular tail slammed Jack just above the waist, flinging him head-over-heels into the brush. The impact drove the wind from his lungs, but he had enough presence of mind to know he had to put some distance between himself and the dinosaur. Still reeling in shock and horror, he scuttled through the brush on his hands and knees—

The dinosaur was suddenly back again, smashing through the thicket. A heavy foot slammed into the ground, just missing Jack's head. He instinctively curled into a ball, knowing he was seconds from either being snapped up like Tim or mashed into a blob of goo.

Something wet and slippery dropped onto the back of his neck and he shivered, but tried to hold as still as he could.

The dinosaur surged past, shaking the ground with every thunderous step. Jack was frozen in shock and terror, but suddenly felt something tugging on his arm. He reeled away, then realized it was Artem, pulling him in the opposite direction. He rolled onto his hands and knees, rose to his feet, then followed as Artem tore back down the trail the way they'd come—

Jack tried to keep up, but Artem abruptly turned, leaving the trail and plowing straight into the foliage. Jack charged after him, but was instantly struggling against tangles of branches and vines that whipped at his face and arms, tripping over snarled roots that clutched at his shoes.

The younger boy ran full-out for several minutes, then finally slowed and stopped. He lifted his eyes—looking this way and that—then stepped back to Jack, who was bent over his knees and chuffing for breath.

"I t-think we're okay," the boy whispered through chattering teeth. "At least n-nothing seems to be—"

He took a closer look.

"W-what happened to you?"

Jack looked up, still breathing fast and hard from the surprise and terror of their close call, not to mention the mad sprint through the trees. "W-wha—what are you talking about?"

Artem reached out and touched Jack's cheek. "You're covered with blood. Where did it get you?"

"W-what?" Jack looked down, realizing his shirt was covered with fresh blood, which appeared black in the dim moonlight. He reached up, touched his cheek, and stared stupidly at his fingers for a moment before remembering.

"Uh, y-yeah," he stammered as his stomach lurched. "This isn't me. It's ... from Tim."

"You sure? You're not hurt?"

"No, no, I'm sure. I'm fine."

Artem looked at him for another moment, then nodded.

"Now you know what it's like around here," he said. "The reason everyone's always so glum. You just never who's gonna be next. Or when it's gonna be you."

Jack didn't know how to respond, but Artem wasn't finished.

"That might've been me back there," he said in a voice softer than a whisper. His voice cracked. "If you hadn't stepped between us—"

"Could've been either one of us," Jack clarified. He sucked in a huge lungful of air, then scanned the dark woods behind them. "So ... whadda we do now?"

"Keep going."

"What about Kayce? And the others?"

"Well, if they got away they'll head for the chatterwoods. No way to know who's made it 'til we get there."

"Think Kayce's okay?"

"Who knows? But ... she's been in worse jams than this. And she has a way about her. She should be okay."

Jack remembered something. "Did I, um , hear you call her 'Watermelon' once?"

"Yeah, I do that sometimes." He nodded. "She hates it, though."

"Why do you do it?"

" 'Cause she's *like* a watermelon. She keeps, like, this hard shell around her. But on the inside? She's soft and—she'd kill me for saying this—she's actually kinda sweet."

"Yeah. I think I can see that." And then, after several seconds: "But Tim—"

"Forget Tim," the boy said softly, and gently, as if he'd never had a harsh thought for the other boy. "He's gone. There's nothing we could have done for him. And there's nothing we can do for him now, so ... well, there's just no sense in even thinking about it."

"How long did you say you've been here?"

"Almost a year, I guess. Why?"

"I don't know. It's just ... I don't know. I don't mean to sound critical, but it's hard to believe how callous everyone's become. I mean, a kid was just *killed*! And you're telling me not to worry about it."

"Yeah, well, it's something you need to get used to," Artem said. " 'Cause you're one of us now."

8 Night in the Tree

Artem turned, about to start back into the trees.

"Wait," Jack whispered, taking his arm.

Artem turned. "What?"

"I guess you know where we're going, right?"

"Yeah. Not as well as Kayce, but yeah." And then, after a moment's thought: "But it might be smart to climb a tree and wait for daylight. You know, just to be sure we don't get lost."

He glanced up—as if checking the stars—then turned back to Jack.

"What do you think?"

"No idea," Jack said. "I'm still the new kid. You're the boss."

"You're different from most guys."

"How so?"

"Most of the guys who end up here've got huge egos. They never listen to me."

Jack shrugged. "Yeah, well, maybe I know something they don't."

"What's that?"

"So far, you're the only thing that's keeping me from being killed."

They continued hiking, though Artem was no longer watching for danger as much as looking for a suitable shelter. After several minutes he stopped and pointed toward a tree shaped like a tumbleweed, similar to the one they'd climbed earlier.

"What do you think of that?"

"Looks good to me."

Artem glanced around, and Jack could tell he was worried.

"I'd rather keep going," the boy confided after a moment. "I mean, I don't want Kayce worrying about us. But, um ..."

"What?"

The boy blew out his breath. "Well, two things. The first is that hiking around in the dark is crazy stupid. The animals *all* see better in the dark than we do, and we could walk right into some hungry tricycloplots. I mean, it would be crapping us out before we even knew we'd been eaten."

Jack smiled at the imagery of the boy's speech. "And what's the other thing?"

"Well, I hate to admit it, but it would be easy to get lost out here in the dark. I mean, I'm *pretty* sure I know where we're going, but it's hard to tell. And if I *do* get mixed up, then ..."

He left the rest unsaid.

"Huh," Jack answered. And after a moment's thought: "What would Kayce tell you?"

Artem didn't snort, but he came close. "No question ... she'd tell me to get my butt up the tree."

Jack spread his hands. "Well, then?"

"Okay. Tree it is."

Jack didn't think there was any way he could possibly get any sleep in the top of a tree, no matter what the circumstances. But it had been a long day. A tough day. And he was exhausted ... wrung out mentally, emotionally, and physically. And before he knew it—

He woke with a start.

And was so disoriented that he slipped and nearly fell out of the tree. He just managed to grab hold of a branch before dropping off the limb he'd been sleeping on.

Holy buckets, he thought as he tried to settle his nerves and catch his breath. He glanced toward the ground and felt his stomach drop, realizing how close he'd come to falling.

Jeez, as if I don't have enough problems ...

He looked around, trying to orient himself. The sun wasn't up yet, but it was light enough to see. It took several seconds for his brain to catch up, but then things once again began sparking and falling into place.

The trees.
The mulch-scented forest.
The thick, syrupy air.

The dinosaurs ...

He looked deep into the trees as it all came rushing back.

Some ungodly creature screeched with such an unearthly cry that chills began crawling up Jack's spine like the legs of enormous, hairy spiders. He looked deep into the trees and it all came rushing back.

Ay, yi, yi!

He looked over to where Artem had his legs draped over a thick branch. The boy was leaning against the trunk with his arms folded across his chest, looking as at home in the tree as Tarzan in his favorite jungle hammock.

As if he was tucked safe and sound in his own bed, in his own home, snuggled up in piles of warm homemade quilts. ... Man, what a way to live ...

He reached up and touched his eye. It was still sore and puffy where the hairy-nosed, goggle-eyed, one-eared creep had clobbered him—

Stupid jerk!

—but he didn't have any trouble seeing through it.

He reached up and felt the spot on his shoulder where they'd implanted the tracking device. The whole concept of being tracked was sick. But just *feeling* the vile lump beneath his skin was unnerving. And he couldn't help remembering sci-fi TV shows and movies about space aliens that placed probes in their victims.

He remembered how Kayce and Artem had sliced out the implants from one another, and felt his stomach do a quick flip.

Yeah, I'd like to get this thing cut outta me, too, but—

He pictured Kayce carving into his shoulder with the wicked dragon-slaying machete she carried.

—I bet that'd hurt like hell!

He stretched out on his branch, hearing his joints creaking and cracking like dry corn flakes being crushed with a spoon, then took a deep breath. There was definitely more oxygen in the air than he was used to breathing and he felt a rush of dizziness.

He twisted on his perch—

A twig snapped in the trees and he froze, then peered through the leaves, straining for a glimpse of whatever was coming. His heart rose into his throat as he pictured another allosaurus creeping toward them. He tried to slow his breathing, but his lungs were pumping about as fast as his heart.

He stared—

The leaves rustled and a large animal emerged from the shadows. The creature wasn't as large as an allosaurus, but it was walking on two legs. Jack caught his breath, worried that it might come after him, but after the dinosaur had stepped fully into view it sniffed at a prickly bush and then began nibbling on the leaves.

Jack relaxed.

"We think it's called ankylopollexia," a voice whispered.

Jack turned his head. Artem hadn't moved an inch from the way Jack had first seen him, though the kid's eyes were now open.

"They look scary," the boy continued softly. "Especially when they've got their arms out like boogeymen in some monster movie. But they're harmless. If we waved our arms and made a little noise, that guy'd take off like a frightened rabbit."

"How do you know what it is?"

"Don't really. Most of the time we just guess. But the guys who come to adjust the cameras sometimes tag certain animals so the sensors can pick them up, and they carry identification cards with pictures. And some of the kids know a little about dinosaurs. And sometimes we just make up names."

"Huh."

He watched the ankywhateverthefreakitwas chew on the tender leaves. Once it swallowed, it used its forearms to pull one of the branches closer to its mouth. He looked back to Artem.

"Do you cut the implants out of everyone who comes here?"

"No. Just me and Kayce."

"How come you don't do it to everyone?"

"Couple reasons."

"Which are?"

"Most kids won't let us, for one thing." He patted away a fierce yawn. "They know it's gonna hurt like hell—and they're right about that—and who wants to go through that? I mean, hell, it's *surgery,* but with no scalpel, no painkiller, and no laughing gas. Just Kayce and that freakin' stegosaur-sticker she calls a knife."

Jack shuddered. "You do make it sound pretty awful."

"It's not something you wanna go through twice, that's for sure."

"Huh." And then: "So what else?"

"What else what?"

"What's the other reason you don't cut 'em out of everyone?"

Artem quickly became somber again. For a moment he seemed to be thinking, choosing his words, then said, "Most kids just aren't around long enough for it to matter."

Jack pondered that for a moment, then asked, "So, you cut out Kayce's implant?"

"Uh, huh."

"What was *that* like?"

"Scared the crap outta me."

Jack looked over as the ankyloplots—

Or whatever the dang thing's called!

—crunched down a mouthful of green leaves, then turned back to Artem. "How so?"

"Well, jeez, man! I was actually cutting into her! All this icky red stuff, blood running everywhere ..." He shuddered. "When she cut mine out, I screamed like a girl and I'm not ashamed to admit it. I mean, it hurt like *hell*!"

He shook his head.

"But when I dug out Kayce's, she barely flinched. Just sat there and hummed and hawed like I was painting her toenails."

"You're a brave kid," Jack said, sincerely impressed. "Not just for getting yours cut out, but for daring to go after Kayce's."

"I'm just glad it's over with."

The ankylofreakosaur glanced up at the boys—they weren't even pretending to be quiet anymore—but didn't seem concerned about them.

"So let me ask you something else," Jack said.

"Go ahead."

"People who've set up this sick game have got tracking devices and monitors and cameras and crap, right?"

"Yeah."

"And they keep sending hunters after you and Kayce."

"Uh, huh."

Jack waved a hand. "So why do you stick around? I mean, why not take off? Get as far away from here as you can?"

Artem rolled his eyes, then flicked a hand. "You know what's ten miles that way? Dinosaurs. Or"—he flicked his hand in the opposite direction—"ten miles that way? More dinosaurs. There's nowhere you can go to get away from them. I mean, seriously ... *nowhere!*"

"But what about the hunters?"

'They're a problem," Artem admitted. "But Kayce's got this thing about trying to help the other kids who get dumped here. It seems pretty pointless sometimes, but she thinks it's important to try."

"She have a reason?"

"Oh, probably just 'cause that's the way she is and, you know, it's the right thing to do ..."

"And?"

"And partly because it's a way of getting back at those buttheads who sent us here. I mean, anything to mess 'em up, right?"

He grinned.

"But if it helps, you can think of it this way: if we *had* left and gotten out of here?"

"Yeah?"

"Well, you'd be nothing but a pile of green steaming allosaur crap by now."

9 Torvosaur Trouble

Artem yawned, then glanced up at the sky. The sun still wasn't quite up, but it was certainly on its way and life in the forest was in full swing. Birds squawked, bugs chittered, and small animals scurried through the underbrush. Larger dinosaurs—animals that Jack hadn't seen yet—moaned and trumpeted in the distance.

Sound like freakin' foghorns, Jack thought idly. *Things've gotta be huge!*

Artem looked idly over the trees as some predator roared in a way that undoubtedly scared hell out of everything within half a mile, then stretched and said: "So, what'cha think? Ready to get going? Find Kayce again?"

"Get going while the getting's good?"

Artem nodded. "Let's do it."

As the boys clambered down from the tree, the ankylothinger looked up—half-chewed limbs poking from both sides of its mouth—snorted in surprise, then scampered back into the safety of the brush.

"Y'see?" Artem asked. "Thing looks like it'd eat you for breakfast, but it's really no more dangerous than a funny-looking deer."

"I still wouldn't get close," Jack said. "Back home, more people are killed by ordinary deer than by sharks."

"Seriously?"

"Absolutely."

"Oh-*kay*," Artem said. "From now on I'm keeping my distance."

He looked up and around as if searching for landmarks, then pointed into the trees.

"I think it's this way."

Artem led the way as they hiked through the forest, carefully watching the trees for signs of danger or ambush. Jack followed a few steps behind, keeping an eye out over his shoulder for anything trying to sneak up from behind.

Can't believe this place is real, Jack thought as he hiked.

He'd always known there were dinosaurs, of course. But even though he'd seen pictures, and fossils, and museum reconstructions, actual prehistoric animals had always been a vague, nebulous concept.

Kinda like the back side of the moon. I know it's there, but I'm never gonna see it and it has no impact on my life so ... what the heck?

But now here he was, in a forest colored in a million different shades of green and brown. The timber ranged from immense, oddly-shaped pines to fragrant palm-like trees with thick woody trunks and eerie hanging vines, the ground covered with tall, sweeping ferns that provided cover for all kinds of weird cat-sized dinosaurs and odd furry rodents.

When a large animal roared deep in the woods, Jack glanced briefly in its direction, then turned away—

Good crap! he thought as he realized what he'd just done. *Now I'm doing it! Frickin' monster roars in the trees and I don't give it a second thought!*

It rattled him to think he was already becoming so used to the terrifying sounds that he no longer gave them his full attention.

I've gotta stop that and I've gotta stop it right now, he thought, resolving to pay more attention. *I don't and one of those monsters is gonna sneak up and bite me in half ... just like Tim.*

He began peering even more carefully into the woods, making certain to check beneath the ferns and the tops of trees for anything that might be lurking there.

Now that the sun was fully up—beams of sunlight slanting warmly through the thick canopy of leaves—Artem had an easier time finding his way through the forest. He now knew for sure where he was, and where he was going, and it wasn't long before he turned and said: "Almost there. But first"—he pulled aside the leaf of an enormous fern to reveal the way ahead—"we have a slight obstacle."

Jack looked and spotted a river cutting through the forest. "Is this where you catch your fish?"

"What? Oh, heck no! We usually fish in a stream a little closer to that last camp. The water there's not quite so fast as this."

Jack nodded. As rivers went, it didn't seem so formidable. It was probably nine or ten feet wide and maybe waist deep.

With, maybe, a few deeper pools ...

"There's not, like, any kid-eating fish swimming around, are there?"

Artem actually chuckled. "Yeah, that would really be the frosting on the cake, wouldn't it?" He shook his head. "But no ... or, at least we've never run into any. Thirsty?"

"Oh, yeah."

"Well, here's your chance to fill up."

The boys checked up and down the riverbanks for threats. A group of fat animals with tiny heads were splashing through the water upstream, and Jack instantly recognized the double rows of diamond-shaped plates along their backs, as well as the heavily spiked tails.

Artem gave them a quick, unconcerned glance.

"Are those stegosaurs?" Jack whispered.

Artem took another look. "Um, no, but that's a good guess. We're not sure, but we think they're called dacentrurus."

"Dacentra*what*?"

"Dah-SENT-rah-roos," Artem repeated. "Yeah, it's a goofy name. Probably ought to call 'em ... oh, what the heck? Just call 'em stegosaurs if you want."

"I guess there's a difference?"

Artem bobbed his head from side to side. "Not much, but dacentroos are actually a little taller and they've got bigger butts. You'll see stegosaurs sooner or later—assuming you're around for a couple of days—and you'll see. The two look enough alike to be kissing cousins, but if you look closely you can tell they're not the same."

"But you're not worried about them?"

Artem scoffed. "They're not as timid as that ankylopollexia. But they're only dangerous when they feel threatened. You see the tail spikes, right?"

"Oh, yeah."

"So you never want to startle one from behind. Dacentrurus means 'tail full of spikes,' and those points aren't just for show. They're deadly, and the dacentroos know how to use them." He looked up at Jack. "I once saw a dead allosaur that had one of those spikes broken off right in the middle of its gut."

"Sheesh. That'd hurt like a mother."

"No kidding. Come on."

They walked down to the river's edge and knelt in the grass. The dacentrurus were still frolicking in the water upstream, along with several weird lizard/ostrich-looking creatures—

If ostriches had claws and teeth!

—and Jack wondered briefly about the wisdom of drinking water downstream of them. But thirst quickly overcame caution—

Beggers can't be choosers!

—and dunked his face in the rushing water.

Oh, that tastes good! he thought, drinking freely.

He drank until he was full, and then plunged his entire head underwater. When he came back up for air, he shook his head like a dripping German shepherd just out of the pond, then turned to Artem.

"Oh, man ... that's just what I needed."

"Yeah, it's nice. We know where there's a pool fed by hot springs, and it's pretty sweet if you ever get homesick for a hot bath. It smells pretty nasty, though, and you smell like sulfur for the next few days, but ... it's worth it."

Jack shook his hair again—water droplets flying everywhere—then glanced around. Just dipping his head in the cold water had instantly revived him—made him feel more than a hundred percent better—and cleaned the taste of sand and steel wool from his mouth.

He sat back on the grass and listened to the strange cries, cackles, and calls that filled the prehistoric forest.

Sounds like a zoo, he thought, amazed by all the noise. The dacentrurus made deep, hooting grunts as they frolicked about, and big, distant, unseen animals were trumpeting like elephants. Above everything else were high-pitched shrieks and squeals like you might hear from a troop of frantic monkeys.

But I seriously doubt these're monkeys.

He wasn't certain, but thought the only mammals that existed at this point in time were small.

Like rats and mice and voles.

As he listened, the shrieks and screeches increased in intensity, and then suddenly began to fade, many of the nearby animals becoming silent. One of the dacentrurus snorted in alarm, and Jack glanced over to see the plated, spike-tailed animals climb from the river and begin filing into the far trees.

Artem's right, he thought idly as the animals rumbled away. *They do have big butts ...*

"Oh, crap," Artem whispered as he watched the departing animals.

Jack looked over, surprised to see lines of worry creasing the boy's face. "What?"

"Can't you feel it?" Artem asked.

"Feel what?"

"Wait for it ..."

Jack frowned, then looked around, wondering what had the boy on edge this time. One minute earlier he'd been enjoying the freshness of the cool, rushing water but ...

The warm air suddenly seemed thick, and heavy, and oppressive, the sense of foreboding magnified by the relative silence of the woods.

Jeez, no wonder all the dacentrojobbers took off ...

He glanced again at Artem, who was peering intently into the woods.

"What is it?" Jack asked, knowing he needed to whisper.

"I'm not sure yet. But"—the boy lifted a finger, paused, and then pointed to the right—"it'll be coming from over there."

"How do you know?"

" 'Cause the dacentroos all went the other way." He gave Jack a meaningful look. "They might have wicked tails, but they're not stupid—"

Boom ...

Artem snapped his head around as Jack looked into the trees.

Boom ...

Jack heard the sound—

Like the thump of an enormous bass drum ...

—and felt the ground tremble beneath him.

Boom—crack!

This time the sound was followed by the crunch of a rotting log, or perhaps a small tree being snapped in half.

"Crap," Artem repeated. The boy looked anxiously in all directions, then pointed into the river. "Hurry! Get into the water!"

"Wait," Jack said, even as Artem splashed into the current. He didn't know what was coming, but realized it was scary enough that it had Artem on the run ... and that it was almost upon them. "Couldn't we run—"

"No time," Artem hissed. He crawled back to the edge of the bank and lifted his head just free of the cold water. "Hurry and get in here."

Jack wasn't certain they were doing the right thing, but remembered Kayce telling him to listen to the boy. He splashed into the water, then turned to hug the bank beside the smaller kid.

"What is it?" he asked again. "Another allosaurus?"

"I don't think so," Artem whispered grimly. "I don't think we're gonna be that lucky."

Jack felt his stomach turn.

Something scarier than an allosaur? What the crap!

He peered over the edge of the riverbank even as—

Boom ... ca-runch—boom—snap!

The approaching animal was thumping closer, knocking down small trees and bulldozing whatever brush was in its way. There were cracks, crackles, and pops that Jack recognized as the sound of woody underbrush crunching beneath the weight of heavy feet.

There came a sound like distant thunder and Jack glanced into the sky before realizing: *No ... that's not thunder! That's a growl!*

Without turning his head, he whispered, "What are you thinking?"

"From the amount of noise it's making, I think it's a torvosaur."

"Torvosaur?"

"Big suckers. And nasty."

"Bigger than allosaurs?"

"Oh, yeah." Artem slid deeper into the river until his eyes were just barely above the edge of the bank. "They're not as common as allosaurs here—we're a little out of their usual territory—but what they lack in numbers they make up for in attitude. And meanness. I mean, allosaurs kill to eat. And I don't know for sure, but sometimes I think torvosaurs kill just for the fun of it—"

He stopped and pulled himself closer to the bank. Jack looked up to see the treetops rustling ... and then—with the brush crackling all around—an animal thumped from the woods.

Jack caught his breath.

The torvosaur had the same basic shape of the allosaurs he'd encountered, but most of the similarities ended there. The animal was the color of a new penny, but with black, zebra-like stripes. Larger than the allosaurs he'd seen, it was long as a school bus and eight or nine feet high at the hips. It walked on its toes—each heavy foot sinking deep into the soft soil—with its long, narrow head low to the ground and its tail flicking high in the air behind it.

Jack's chest began to ache and he realized he was holding his breath. He eased closer to the riverbank.

The dinosaur thumped to the edge of the river, then turned to nip at its hindquarters, as if trying to rid itself of an annoying fly or mosquito. One of its small forearms reached up to scratch its ear, and then the animal turned to look up and down the river.

"Holy buckets," Jack whispered without realizing he was speaking.

"*Shhhh!*" Artem hissed in a voice so low Jack barely heard him.

Jack just nodded. Even though the dinosaur was several yards upstream, he could smell the stench of sour garbage and spoiled meat hanging over the animal like a thick, rancid fog. There was a raspy buzz in the air, which he realized came from a cloud of black flies droning over the animal's head.

The torvosaur stood still for a moment, then dropped its nose to the ground and began sweeping it left and right.

Probably checking to see what other animals are in the neighborhood.

The animal took a step to the side—Jack saw the soft earth smoosh up around its toes—and again swept its nose over the ground. Despite his fear, Jack was captivated—almost hypnotized—by the sight of the massive dinosaur. He could see muscles rippling beneath the striped, copper-colored skin and was amazed by how smoothly and easily the animal moved.

Like a five-ton cat.

The torvosaur's jaws closed as it once again lowered its nose, but then opened slightly when it next lifted its head, revealing rows of sharp, yellow teeth.

Man, that's the most incredible animal I've ever seen!

He now knew why the dacentrurus left the river.

Yeah, they might get lucky with one of those wicked tail spikes. But I'd still put my money on this monster.

Despite the circumstances, the thought of betting reminded him why he was there, and he felt chills that sank all the way to the bone. And he suddenly had a sense of what might be happening back home, 150 million years in the future.

There might be cameras on us right here, right now, watching our every move. And with that dinosaur standing there—almost on top of us—the players might be going crazy, betting piles of money on whether Artem and I get out of here. And if not, which one of us gets snapped up first ...

Another thought hit him, an old joke about two backpackers who encountered a furious grizzly bear. When the bear charged, one of the hikers calmly removed his heavy boots and replaced them with running shoes from his pack.

"Are you *crazy*?" the second man shouted. "You can't outrun a bear!"

"Don't have to outrun the bear," the first hiker said as he turned and raced into the woods. "I only have to outrun *you*!"

Yeah, it was funny at the time, but—

Jack glanced at Artem through the corner of his eye, wondering what he'd do if the torvosaur found them.

Could I ditch him? Could I leave him to the dinosaur ... just to save myself?

He didn't think so—he didn't *want* to think so—but it was one of those things you could never know until it actually happened. Even so, he eased a little closer to the boy—until their shoulders were touching—just as a way of keeping track of him—

A nearby animal screeched in the trees, snapping Jack from his thoughts. He turned his head, then shot a look at the torvosaur. The dinosaur had come to attention and was staring intently into the forest.

Jack's heart pounded as he wondered what was going on. Wondering if the dinosaur would leave, or continue whatever it was doing. He wanted to ask Artem, but before he could the dinosaur growled. Watching it, Jack sensed the animal was showing contempt for the lesser creature in the trees.

The torvosaur growled again with a rumble that was deep and ominous and terrifying, then lifted its head. It sniffed the air, and then thumped forward and splashed into the river.

Jack slid even deeper into the water—immersing himself until only his nose and eyes were showing—and saw Artem do the same.

The torvosaur sniffed at the river, then lowered its snout straight into the current and began sucking in water. Jack and Artem were clearly visible from where the dinosaur was standing: all it had to do was look—

"Don't move," Artem whispered, his voice barely audible.

"Yeah, no kidding."

Jack shivered, and only partially because he was immersed in cold water. He didn't know how well dinosaurs saw—or smelled—but knew both boys were in plain sight. Only partially hidden by the rippling current.

And with nowhere to hide ...

10 The River

The torvosaur was still sucking in water, and Jack was amazed by how much it was able to drink. For more than a minute it stood motionless, its snout deep in the current. It wasn't until another unseen predator roared in the trees that it lifted its head and peered toward the sound.

Come on, Jack thought. *Go check it out. Go see what's out there ...*

The animal growled, then abruptly dropped its head and bellowed, roaring with such ferocity that Jack's blood turned to ice. He had to fight a crushing urge to leap from the water and run for his life.

The torvosaur roared again and Jack turned his head and closed his eyes, trying to shield himself from the earsplitting noise. The dinosaur took a single step—

Jack felt the impact of the heavy foot through the river bottom.

—then splashed through the middle of the river, straight toward the two boys.

Jeez oh jeez oh jeez oh jeez ...

Jack tried to remain still, but his entire body was shaking, trembling, and even bouncing as the dinosaur splashed closer. He closed his eyes—as if that might prevent the dinosaur from seeing him—then wrenched them open again, needing to know what was happening.

He heard a sound like a whistle and realized it was Artem, the boy so terrified he'd begun to wheeze.

Calm down, he thought, silently willing the kid to quiet himself; both boys had sunk as low into the water as they could get without drowning. *Thing's gonna hear you ...*

The dinosaur splashed through the water until it was a mere yard or two from Jack and then suddenly stopped. The animal lowered its head and bellowed, nearly shattering Jack's ears.

He winced in pain, and terror, fully expecting the animal's jaws to snap down—

The torvosaur bellowed again, and Jack struggled not to scream. The sound penetrated all the way to the bone, biting into his nerves like high-speed drills. And over the animal's roar came a shrill, high-pitched cry. Jack's senses were so overloaded it was several seconds before he realized it was Artem.

He twisted his head, wanting to tell the boy to calm down, terrified the dinosaur would spot him. He tried to reach out—

The boy abruptly exploded from the water and scrambled onto the grassy bank on all fours. Screaming hysterically, he tried to get to his feet, slipped, and scurried toward the trees on his hands and knees like a four-foot beetle.

Jack shouted, "Artem, *no!*"

But it was too late. The boy was scuttling for the trees as fast as he could go. The torvosaur turned, spotted the fleeing boy, and roared furiously.

And then burst from the water.

"*No!*"

Without thinking, Jack leaped to his feet and shot from the river. He ran dripping through the grass, directly into the dinosaur's line of sight.

"Hey!"

He shouted as loud as he could, waving his arms to attract the animal's attention.

"Hey! Over here"—he waved his arms frantically—"I'm over *here!*"

The torvosaur turned and bellowed, just as Artem scrambled into the brush and disappeared.

Jack didn't waste a second. He spun and ran back for the river. He leaped when he was still six feet from the bank and hit the water with a splash. He ducked beneath the surface and swam back to the near shore and mashed himself tight against the bank just as the dinosaur crashed into the river after him. Jack's head was still underwater, but he felt the animal hit the water.

The dinosaur roared—the sound muffled by the rushing water—and Jack held as still as he could, knowing the animal was mere feet away.

The torvosaur splashed back and forth as it searched for him. Jack felt the impact of the dinosaur's feet on the river bottom, as well as the rush of pressure waves that lifted and heaved him against the rocks again and again. His chest began to burn from lack of air, but he didn't dare lift his head above the surface to breathe.

Hold on, he thought desperately. *Just ... hold on ... just for another second ... just for another ...*

He heard the dinosaur bellow—knew it was trying to frighten him into showing himself—and felt it surge past, mere inches away. As soon as the animal passed, he lifted his head, gulped down a quick breath of air, and once again ducked beneath the surface.

The torvosaur bellowed again, and again, the roars muted by the water but terrifying all the same. Jack's eyes were closed—he couldn't see a thing—but he felt the water gush as the monstrous animal thrashed about, growing impatient and frustrated as it searched for its prey.

Jack's lungs began to burn and he clenched his teeth, and his fists, trying to hold on. The dinosaur stormed past, swung around and splashed upstream; Jack clutched at roots poking up from the river bottom to keep from being swept into the current.

His lungs were flaming—ready to burst—but the dinosaur splashed past once again and the rush of water lifted Jack from the bottom and into the air. He tried to gulp down a lungful of air—swallowed a mouthful of water instead and nearly choked—then inhaled a shot of air just before he splashed back into the water. He swept his hands through the current, grabbed onto a tangle of roots, and held on as tight as he could.

The torvosaur continued thrashing through the river, certain its prey was there. It surged past and a heavy claw snagged Jack's pant leg, pulling him away from the bank and into the current.

Jack struggled to free himself, even as the dinosaur splashed forward, unknowingly dragging Jack along with it. His hands were jerked from the roots and the torvosaur was unknowingly hauling him through the water. His head, chest, arms, and legs bumped over the rocks on the river bottom, battering him mercilessly as the dinosaur dragged him along. His head cracked against a submerged rock—a flash of white light burst behind his eyes—and his mouth opened and filled with water—

The dinosaur abruptly turned, hesitated, and then splashed back the way it had come. But in that moment Jack's head bobbed above the surface. He gulped down a lungful of half air/half water, choked, and then pulled his leg free.

The torvosaur kept going and Jack crawled toward the nearest bank. His lungs were on fire—partly from lack of air and partly from the cold river water he sucked down his windpipe—his entire body pulped. pummeled, pommeled, and punched.

Pounded to mush.

His brain was spinning, and it was several long seconds before it settled down and finally began working again.

And finally realized the dinosaur was no longer splashing around.

He opened his eyes and spotted the torvosaur a short distance away. It had climbed from the river and was standing near the trees, its nose up in the air as if testing the breeze.

Holy buckets, Jack thought wearily. *I t-thought I was a g-gonner.* And after another look at the dinosaur: *I'm n-not safe yet ...*

He watched the torvosaur for nearly a minute—

Why's it just s-standing *there?*

—then carefully scanned the woods behind him.

Don't k-know where Artem's g-gone, but ... at least the d-dinosaur didn't get him.

The basking torvosaur abruptly snorted, convulsing with a booming reptilian sneeze, and Jack began to tremble. Now that the dinosaur seemed to have lost interest in him—giving him a moment to collect his thoughts—the enormity of the past several minutes began to sink in.

The way he'd stupidly lunged out of the river to distract the dinosaur.

Then fled terrified back into the water.

Playing an insane game of hide'n-seek with an enraged, five-ton predator.

I can't believe I just did that!

The trembles became shakes, and only partly because he was still immersed in the chilly water.

Speaking of which:

I've gotta get outta here ... before I get hypothermia.

He glanced again at the dinosaur, which was still standing near the trees and facing the other way. It seemed to be enjoying the warmth of the sun after its splash through the frigid water, and didn't look like it was in any hurry to leave.

Good crud, come on! Jack thought miserably. His entire body was now shaking from the cold, his teeth beginning to chatter. *D-don't know how much l-longer I can h-handle this—*

Psssst!

Jack wrapped his arms around his chest in an effort to keep himself warm, thinking he'd just heard something.

Psssst!

The sound came again and Jack glanced back, spotting a flicker of movement in the brush. He was shaking so violently from the cold it was hard to focus ... but after a moment he spotted a pair of eyes peering at him from the foliage.

Ar-Ar-Artem?

The boy pushed his face through the leaves, held a finger to his lips—*Shhhh!*—then patted the air, apparently telling Jack not to move.

Yeah, no k-kidding, Jack thought dismally. *You come in here and freeze your b-b-butt off!*

He glanced toward the torvosaur, but the animal was still standing contently in the warm sunlight. Its head was up as it sampled the air and listened to the wild chatter of animals in the forest.

Psssst!

Jack turned his head; Artem waited until he was looking, then moved his arms like he was clawing at the air.

Jack's teeth chattered violently as he wondered, *W-what the c-crap?*

Artem mimed clawing for another moment, pointed at Jack, pointed downstream, and then once again clawed at the air.

What the ... oh! He's telling me to swim downstream!

Jack looked back at the dinosaur—the animal was peering into the woods in the direction of some distant animal roaring like the biggest lion in the forest—then turned to Artem and nodded.

The dinosaur tossed its head as if shaking off flies, then reached a hand up to scratch its ear. Jack watched nervously, took several deep breaths, then stretched out in the cold water and pushed himself into the current. The water caught him and right away carried him headfirst into the middle of the channel like a chunk of old wood. He used his hands to paddle along, keeping his nose and mouth just out of the water. The river curved around a jumble of boulders—and then a stand of pines—and just that fast he was out of the torvosaur's line of sight.

Finally!

He pushed himself to the nearest bank, clawed his way out of the water, and plopped spread-eagle on the grass.

Holy buckets! he thought. *T-thought I was gonna die!*

His arms and legs felt like rubber, and he knew that if the torvosaur suddenly burst from the woods, he wouldn't have the strength to run. His head hurt where it had been slammed against a rock in the river and—

There was a rustle in the brush and he tensed, expecting a dinosaur ... but it was just Artem, creeping from the foliage. The boy looked all around, saw no sign of danger, and tiptoed toward Jack.

"Hey," the kid whispered, kneeling in the grass beside him. "You okay?"

Jack struggled to find enough breath to respond. "Y-yeah. I ... t-think so."

Artem looked him up and down—didn't notice anything broken, bloody, or missing—and nodded. "You just saved my bacon."

"Yeah, well—"

"I mean, I've never seen anyone do that before! Risk yourself, I mean. I ... I can't believe you did that!"

"Yeah, well, without you I'd be lost ... wouldn't be able to find my own elbow, let alone the chatterwoods."

Artem grinned, then asked, "Can you walk?"

"I think so. In a bit. But ... I need a minute to catch my breath." He lifted a hand to his temple, then asked, "My head look okay?"

"You've got a huge bruise, if that's what you're talking about." He reached down and touched the side of Jack's head. "Goes good with your black eye, though."

"Ohhhh, that's just great."

"Least it's not bleeding."

"Well, that *is* good news." He lay back and tried to catch his breath, then finally said, "Okay, help me up."

Artem took his arm and pulled as Jack tried to get his feet beneath him. His muscles felt weak and rubbery, and his first couple of steps were as wobbly as a newborn calf's.

"Oh, crud," he said. "Nothing wants to work: I hope we don't have a long way to go."

"No, we're pretty close. And you'll loosen up once you start moving around. Everything'll start working again."

Jack took a few more steps and felt a little steadier. "Okay, I think you're right. My legs feel like wet noodles, but I don't think—"

There was an earsplitting roar, and the torvosaur blasted from the trees in an explosion of cracking limbs and branches.

Artem screamed—

"*Aaaaaiiigh!*"

—and bolted for the trees. Jack turned to follow, then abruptly spun in a different direction. His legs felt numb—like they'd been shot full of Novocain—but he forced them into action and stumbled toward a chestnut-like tree just ahead.

There was a powerful thump—the impact of a heavy foot slamming the ground—and the shudder nearly knocked Jack off his feet. He regained his balance and darted behind the tree, intending to keep it between himself and the charging dinosaur. In his terror, he was hoping—

The dinosaur slammed into the trunk, which snapped like an old matchstick. The tree crashed down, knocking Jack to the ground beneath it. A thick branch cracked the back of his head as snarled limbs and branches flattened him like an enormous fly swatter.

The torvosaur was still rushing forward; it ran right over the tree—smashing through the limbs—believing its prey was still going the same way. The animal's weight crushed Jack even deeper into the soft earth, mashing his chest, ribs, arms, and legs. A heavy foot slammed through the limbs beside Jack's head in an explosion of splintering wood. Dry branches snapped, cracked, and popped around his ears like firecrackers.

The dinosaur continued forward, and a clawed foot snagged a springy branch, pulling it forward. Just as the limb was about to break, it slipped free and snapped back, striking Jack in the face—

And that's all he knew.

11 The Chatterwoods

Jack.

Jack heard his name, but his brain was too muddled to make any sense of it. His entire body felt whipped and drained ... as hollow as a discarded straw.

"*Jack!*"

He recognized Artem's voice ... and through the fog and the pain and the confusion remembered—

That freakin' dinosaur!

He tried to speak, but nothing came out but garbled, unintelligible sounds.

"Morphrup?"

"Hey, are you still alive?"

He felt Artem gently patting his face.

"C'mon, dude, wake up, will ya?"

Jack clenched his eyes, then breathed in through his nose, filled his lungs, and finally opened a single eyelid. Artem was kneeling above him, looking anxious.

"Hey."

The single word came out sounding more like a husky croak than actual English.

Artem managed a half smile. "Jeez, dude! You scared the *crap* outta me!"

"Yeah"—it was the same bullfrog voice as before—"um ... where's the dinosaur?"

Artem flicked a hand. "It kept going. Probably didn't realize you were stuck beneath the tree."

"Jeez." Jack tried to move, but was pinned by heavy limbs and branches that held him as tightly as a fly in a spiderweb. He gave it another try but stopped almost instantly, discouraged not only by the flattened tree, but by an explosion of aches and pains that shot through him like shards of broken glass. "Ohhhh. ... I almost wish it *had* gotten me ... might have hurt less."

"I know the feeling—"

There came a roar from the trees: not from the torvosaur, Jack thought, but from something equally nasty and in just as bad a mood. He began struggling in earnest.

"Come on, help me out of here."

With Artem's help, he pushed through the tangled branches and finally managed to extricate himself.

"Are you hurt?" Artem asked, brushing dirt and leaves from Jack's sopping, river-soaked clothes.

"Feel like crap. But no, I don't think I'm hurt." He reached up and touched the new bruise on his head. "How's this thing looking?"

Artem glanced up, shrugged, then continued plucking twigs and leaves from Jack's clothes. "I've seen worse."

"Where—" Jack started to ask before stopping himself. He remembered Travis—and Tim—and realized Artem must have indeed seen some pretty horrible things.

Compared to that, a mere bruise isn't anything to be whining about ... even if that frickin' rock did come within a whisker of bashing my brains out!

"We're just about there," Artem announced a short time later. They'd been hiking slowly but steadily since leaving the river. "The chatterwoods."

Jack was anxious to see exactly what inspired a name like "chatterwoods," and why Kayce and Artem believed they'd be safe there. And he didn't have long to wait. Artem pushed ahead for another minute, then pulled aside a leafy fern.

"That's them," Artem said in a low voice. He pointed toward a cluster of thick, snarled, scrub-like trees. "We call 'em 'chatterwoods' 'cause you can't move through 'em without making a heckuva racket. Nothing can sneak in without you knowing all about it, and the brambles are so thick nothing really tries."

Jack wasn't sure what to make of them. The usual forest trees had been cleared in a circle sixty or seventy yards across.

It looked like there had once been a short-lived fire there—burning down the hardwoods—with thick brush and brambles growing up in the void. Jack knew that a large determined animal—an angry allosaurus, for instance—could crash through the thicket if it wanted. But it was equally clear that few ever tried. The brush seemed impenetrable.

Artem pursed his lips.

"You gotta be careful of the thorns, though. The branches are thick with them, and they're not only sharp as hell, but they secrete some sorta toxin. If they scratch you, you're likely to get infected, and if one breaks off in you ... well, you don't want that to happen."

"Because ..."

"Because it'll make you sicker'n hell. And you'll be screaming your guts out while the rest of us hold you down and Kayce cuts the thing out of you with that brontosaur-butchering knife of hers." He nodded firmly. "Believe me, I've seen it. And by the time it's over, you'll be wishing one of the damn dinosaurs got you first."

"Oh-*kay*," Jack said slowly. Artem's salty language was jarring, and hearing it from such a young kid gave it an even more powerful kick. "Note to self: watch out for thorns."

Artem grinned, though there was no humor in it. "I tried to warn this kid named Jason about them—"

"And he didn't listen?"

"What do you think? He went bustin' through the branches like he was all that, just to prove he didn't have to listen to me."

"And—"

"I hate to gloat ..."

"Yeah, yeah, I get it. What happened?"

"A thorn came up through the bottom of his shoe—they're *really* sharp—and the tip broke off in his foot. He didn't tell anyone, and by the time Kayce figured it out his foot was almost black. His ankle and calf were swollen up like balloons and the infection went all the way to the knee. And when Kayce dug out the thorn?"

"Yeah?"

"He screamed like a girl."

"Ay, yi, yi," Jack said, eyeing the chatterwoods reluctantly. "Are you really sure we ought to go in there?"

"Unless you'd rather stay out here with the dinosaurs."

"No, no, but ... you lead the way."

"Just be careful," Artem advised. "Go slow, take your time, and watch where you put your arms and feet, and you'll be fine."

He shrugged.

"Besides, we'll only be here for a little while. Just long enough to rest and for Kayce to decide what we're gonna do next."

"Okay, then," Jack replied. He waved. "Lead on."

Artem walked to the edge of the brambles, poked around, and after a moment squeezed through a break in the foliage. Jack eyed the tangled branches suspiciously—searching for the dreaded thorns—

Don't see anything ...

—and then followed.

He was instantly fighting through jumbles of prickly twigs, limbs, and branches, picking them from his shirt and pants to keep them from tearing his clothes. The brush was extremely dry, and it crunched and crackled as he struggled along.

Holy buckets, he thought, plucking a bristly twig from his shirt. *No way to get through this crap.*

He grimaced as powder-dry leaves munched noisily beneath his shoes.

Sure makes a good alarm system, though. No way anything could sneak in here without making more noise than the local marching band.

Artem stopped just ahead, waited until Jack caught up, then reached out, took hold of a branch, and pulled it toward him.

"See it?"

Jack looked and spotted a sharp, sickle-shaped thorn about an inch-and-a-half long. "That's it?"

"That's it," Artem said, carefully releasing the branch. "It doesn't look all that dangerous, but it's worse than a snakebite."

"Yeah ... wait, *what*? Snakebite? You got snakes here too?"

Artem gave him a look that instantly made him feel stupid for asking. "Seriously? We're in a world ruled by reptiles and you don't think there might be a few snakes slithering around?"

"Uh, just never thought of it." He glanced around, as if thinking one of the slithering serpents might be slinking up behind him. "Ay, yi, yi ..."

"Yeah, well, when you've got three-ton lizards with eight-inch teeth breathing down your neck, a seven-foot snake doesn't seem all that scary."

"Seven ... you said seven-foot *snakes*?" Jack asked.

"And you might not actually classify them as snakes," Artem conceded. "Some of them have these tiny legs, even though they're kinda useless."

He shrugged.

"The other thing is that they mostly hunt at night. You find 'em during the day once in a while—you might, you know, kick over an old log and find one curled up underneath—but they're mostly nocturnal."

"That's terrifying," Jack said, still glancing nervously around.

"You'll get used to it," Artem assured him. "Trust me ... after you've been here a while—you know, assuming you last that long—you figure out you can't be scared of everything. You start to pick and choose what to worry about."

"Criminy," Jack muttered. "You're not making me feel any better."

Artem turned and crept forward, following the meager trail. Jack gave the poisonous thorn a final glance before following, twisting and contorting his body as he struggled to avoid the knotted, prickly branches. He spotted several more thorns as he hiked, but was encouraged by the fact they were not nearly as plentiful as they could have been.

He felt a tug and looked to see his shirt sleeve snagged on a branch.

Good crud ...

It took several seconds to free himself, and when he looked up again, Artem had vanished into the matted brush ahead. He fought off a moment of panic and forced himself to relax.

Not much of a trail, but it's the only one here so it's not like I'm gonna get lost ...

He crept ahead, and after several seconds came to a clearing.

"Hey, slowpoke," Artem called cheerfully. He was standing beside Kayce, who was looking back with a speculative expression. Megan was sitting cross-legged on the ground, Natalie stretched out on her side as if asleep. "Good to see you made it."

"Yeah," Jack replied. "Just trying to avoid the thorns."

Kayce continued peering at him, and after a moment he realized she was inspecting the bruise on his head.

"Have a little trouble?" she asked.

"You should have seen it!" Artem gushed. He quickly told her all about their night in the tree, followed by both torvosaur attacks, talking faster and faster as he warmed to the story—

"... andthedamnthingjustcameoutof*nowhere* ..."

—but slowed as he described how Jack risked his life to distract the dinosaur, allowing Artem to escape.

Kayce listened carefully, glancing at Jack from time to time. Her expression changed—and softened—as Artem emphasized in his typically colorful way that he'd be nothing but chewed-up bone and gristle if not for Jack.

"So, yeah," Artem concluded sincerely. "He saved my backside. Totally."

Kayce gave Jack another thoughtful look, then nodded.

"Thanks," she said simply. And then to Artem: "Looks like they sent us a winner."

Jack shook his arms—his clothes were still damp, though drying quickly—then sat on a large rock. "So what's the plan?"

Kayce waved a hand. "For now, we're just gonna take a little time to decompress. Been through a lot, obviously, and we need to let some of the stress bleed off. We'll need to think about finding something to eat, eventually, but for now, just kick back and try to relax a little."

"Fine by me," Jack said.

Kayce leaned close to Artem and the two of them whispered back and forth. After several seconds, Artem nodded, then walked over and sat beside Jack.

"Everything okay?" Jack asked quietly. "Kayce seems a little uptight. She worried about something?"

"No, no, it's not that," Artem assured him. He looked over to make sure Kayce was looking the other way. "She was just a little surprised. You know, about the way you looked after me. Like I told you, kids don't usually do that here. Don't usually think of anyone but themselves."

His voice dropped another notch.

"Especially around me."

"You're serious about that?" Jack's voice was as soft and low as Artem's. "The other kids being mean to you?"

"Serious as a heart attack."

"Well, you don't have to worry about that with me."

"Yeah, I've figured that out already."

"And trust me ... any kid who goes after you will have to go through me first."

Artem smiled, though Jack could still see the sadness in his eyes.

"Thanks."

Jack was feeling hungry: his stomach actually rumbled as he talked with Artem. But he hadn't had a restful night. And the stress and strain of the past few days was taking its toll. That, combined with the warmth of the buttery sun, had his eyelids drooping.

"Ah, man. I've gotta lie down for a minute."

"Sure, go ahead. The rest of us aren't going anywhere."

Jack eased his butt from the rock and onto the ground. He had to move a couple of sharp sticks beneath him, but was then able to stretch out comfortably.

He closed his eyes, but then cracked one open again to peer up at Artem.

"I hate to be rude," he said apologetically. "But I'm dead tired. I'm afraid I'm gonna fall asleep on my feet ... or my butt."

"No worries," the boy replied. He grinned. "The first rule of survival here is: Drink every chance you get, pee every chance you get, and sleep every chance you get ... 'cuz you never know when you're gonna get another chance."

And then: "Don't worry. Anything happens, I'll let you know."

12 Plan B

"Hey ..."

Jack felt a shoe digging him rudely in the side.

"Hey, Sleeping Beauty ... wake up."

He cracked an eye, winced in the bright sunlight, then lifted a hand to shade his eyes. The shoe once again dug into his bruised, tender ribs.

"Come on, get up. Something's happening."

The shoe dug once more into his side. He knew it wasn't Artem or Kayce—

Gotta be one of those stupid girls.

—and when the shoe came in again he grabbed it with his nearest hand, yanked hard, and dropped whoever it was onto her butt.

"*Hey—*"

"Don't kick me," Jack snapped. He grimaced in the dazzling sunlight, then struggled to sit up, wincing as his knotted muscles creaked and groaned. Megan was glaring at him from the ground as Natalie peered into the brambles on the far side of the clearing. Kayce and Artem were nowhere in sight.

"You don't have to be an ass about it—"

"You don't have to kick me, either." He struggled to his feet. "Where're Kayce and Artem?"

"There's something moving outside the brambles," Natalie called. "They went for a look."

"Something like ... something *big*?"

"You think they'd waste their time checking out something *small*?"

"Judas Priest," Jack groaned. "Is it just coincidence that everyone here has an attitude? Or is that something you pick up from eating raw fish?"

"Har, har."

Megan picked herself up and dusted herself off, still blasting Jack with icy glares. Jack didn't know her well enough to be certain, but thought she considered herself superior because she'd been here longer.

Like a high school senior picking on a newbie freshman, even when the freshman is bigger, smarter, and better looking!

He turned away—showing his disinterest—then looked up as an ominous, deep-pitched snarl came from outside the brambles. As Natalie had suggested, the unseen animal sounded big.

Certainly big enough to smash its way in here ...

"See?" Natalie asked.

"Ay, yi, yi," Jack whispered to himself. And then: "Are we like, *safe*, here?"

"Kayce said we should be, but that's why she went to look. Just to be certain Godzilla is just snooping around and not looking for a way in."

Jack nodded, but without confidence. The animal growled, the sound deep and resonant like a rumble of distant thunder.

Or like the purr of a hungry, five-ton lion!

As tough and impenetrable as the chatterwoods originally looked, they suddenly didn't seem so secure anymore—

A leaf crunched and Jack looked over to see Kayce and Artem sneaking back through the branches. Artem instantly crept to Jack's side, looking apprehensive.

"We might have a problem," Kayce announced softly. She jerked a thumb back over her shoulder. "There's a freakin' huge torvosaur out there, and it must've gotten a whiff of us. It's sniffing around like it's looking for a way in."

"It's not the same one we saw," Artem whispered to Jack. "It's bigger, and it's got a huge scar across its face."

"What are we gonna do?" Megan asked. Despite her earlier insolence, she'd wrapped her arms around herself and Jack knew she was worried. Even as he watched, she cast a glance over her shoulder in the direction of the snarling dinosaur.

Which is understandable ... five kids've been killed in just the past few hours ...

"Let's just sit tight," Kayce suggested.

"Can it get in here?" Natalie asked.

"It's a five-ton dinosaur," Megan snarked. "If it wants in, a few sticks and thorns aren't going to stop it."

"Megan's right," Kayce agreed, ignoring the snooty tone. "It can get in if it wants to bad enough. But nothing's ever tried before, so ... just relax."

Jack was amazed by how calm she seemed, and he realized again why everyone looked to her for leadership.

And why she's lasted so long ... especially when no one else has. And then: *Artem's right: she* is *like a watermelon.*

The torvosaur crunched over a rotting log and Jack felt chills creeping up his spine like enormous hairy-legged spiders. The dinosaur was no more than thirty yards away, and the prickly, thorny, tangled brambles now seemed about as secure as so much wet tissue paper.

Especially against a ten-thousand-pound monster.

The dinosaur growled—a little more loudly now and (Jack thought) with a touch of impatience—and there was a crunch of dry brush, as if the animal was testing the scrub, searching for the easiest way in.

Megan began trembling anxiously, breathing so fast she was almost wheezing, and Natalie edged closer to give her a little support. Jack felt a touch and turned to see that Artem was standing beside him, so close their elbows were touching. Jack put an arm around the boy's shoulders and felt him shudder.

Kayce, too, had begun looking around as if searching for another option.

She's worried, he realized. *Place has always been safe, but ... she's never seen an animal make a real effort to get inside, either.*

Jack felt tremors through the ground as the torvosaur plodded around the brambles, the sound of snapping, crackling limbs and leaves pinpointing the animal's location. The dinosaur had been moving from left to right, but it stopped, growled loudly, and then turned and began moving the other way, apparently unhappy it couldn't find a way in.

Megan was wheezing so loudly now that Jack began to worry the dinosaur might hear and decide to attack. Kayce stepped over and took the girl's hand, trying to calm her. Artem was leaning against Jack now, seeking comfort from his older friend.

Jack looked at Kayce: the pony-tailed girl met his eyes and he raised an eyebrow, asking, *We gonna be okay in here?*

She tilted her head and lifted a shoulder in a subtle gesture that Jack took to mean, *I don't know.*

She glanced in the direction of the growling dinosaur, then whispered just loudly enough for everyone to hear.

"I've never seen a dinosaur try to get in here. But this one seems to have a bee up its butt. And it doesn't seem to be giving up, so let's try sneaking out the back. With a little luck we can be gone before it figures out we've hit the road."

"The back?" Jack asked.

She pointed with her nose. "That way. It's a tight squeeze, but if we're careful we can make it." She looked left and right, then turned in the direction of the snarling torvosaur. She listened for a moment, released Megan's hand, and pointed. "A little farther to the left and it'll be exactly opposite the way we're heading. As soon as it gets there, we'll go."

She waited until the animal had thumped as far to the left as it seemed determined to go—it began crunching against the thick, tangled branches of the chatterwoods—then stepped toward the edge of the brambles and motioned for the others to join her.

"Come on, let's go."

She glanced again in the direction of the growling dinosaur—

Jack couldn't actually see the animal, though he could see the tops of the brambles shaking and weaving.

—then turned sideways and eased onto a faint trail. Megan and Natalie followed, with Artem just behind and Jack bringing up the rear. Kayce took a half-dozen steps, then turned and pointed toward a menacing thorn.

"Watch out for thorns," she whispered.

Yeah, no kidding, Jack thought, remembering Artem's description of the kid with the black leg.

He looked back over his shoulder as the torvosaur rumbled in frustration.

Think we're getting out of here just in time ...

Kayce was able to slink through the brambles with the ease of a cat. Artem was almost as skilled, though Megan and

Natalie were about as stealthy as popping firecrackers. If there was a protruding branch, they snagged it; if there was a dry stick in the path, they stepped on it; if there were dry leaves, they crunched them beneath their shoes. Jack wasn't nearly as practiced as either Kayce or Artem, but he had experience in the woods.

And I don't make half the noise as those two bozos, he thought, worried they were going to give the whole group away. He couldn't remember exactly, but didn't think they'd been nearly as obnoxious earlier. Before Tim—

Well, earlier, anyway.

He turned his head and listened: the torvosaur was still on the far side of the chatterwoods, sounding more agitated than ever ...

Megan or Natalie—Jack wasn't certain which—stepped on a pile of dead leaves, which crunched like Rice Krispies beneath her shoe. Kayce turned her head with an irritated *Shhhh!*, and even from several feet back Jack sensed her aggravation.

Jeez, it's almost like those two are trying *to be difficult*, he thought. He couldn't believe the girls were deliberately trying to be obnoxious. *Especially with a thirty-foot dinosaur sniffing after us!*

But unless they were simply too frightened and rattled to be stealthy, he couldn't imagine why they were making so much noise.

On the other hand—

Maybe I'm just being overly sensitive ...

His left pant leg became snagged, and when he reached down to free himself was horrified to see that he hadn't been caught by a branch, but by one of the poisonous thorns.

Ay, yi, yi, he thought as his heart pounded. *Another inch and it would have had me.*

Despite the fear and worry he already felt because of the agitated torvosaur, he began to shake, realizing how close he'd come to being scratched. And the fact it had happened without the roars and screams that occurred during a dinosaur attack somehow made the experience even more frightening.

He began puffing in and out, trying to steady himself, then gingerly pinched the fabric of his trousers, worked it back and forth, and finally eased it free of the poisonous thorn.

Holy buckets, he thought as he pushed the thorn-wielding branch gently away. *Gotta be careful!*

The others, by now, had gotten ahead of him. Watching carefully for more thorns, he eased ahead, trying to catch up. And after a moment saw the brambles beginning to clear. He spotted daylight, stepped over a pile of dry leaves, and finally walked into the open.

Kayce was standing beside the trail, checking the woods ahead as Megan and Natalie—

An earsplitting roar shook the forest, so loud and close Jack's heart dropped. He snapped his head around, spotting a torvosaur standing just inside the nearby trees. The dinosaur blended so well with the foliage no one had seen it. The animal took a step toward them, dropped its head, and bellowed with terrifying ferocity.

Jack's knees buckled, nearly dropping him to the ground. But even in his terror realized the animal's face wasn't scarred, meaning that it wasn't the same animal that had chased them from the brambles.

Megan and Natalie screamed hysterically. Without warning, Natalie turned and bolted back toward the chatterwoods, Megan just behind her.

"*No!*" Kayce screamed. "Not that way!" And then, as the girls blasted toward Jack: "They can't go back in there! *Stop them!*"

Natalie had already shot past, but Jack lunged and got a handful of Megan's shirt and tried to pull her to a stop. With a frantic scream the girl whirled around, swinging a closed fist that struck Jack on the side of the head.

Jack winced and ducked and tried to hold on, but Megan wrenched herself free and bolted into the brambles. Without thinking, Jack ran after her. Limbs and branches and poisonous thorns scratched and tore at him as he ran, running as hard as—

He burst into the clearing, just a step or two behind Megan. Natalie was already on the far side, about to race onto one of the meager paths leading back to the outside.

"Natalie, *no!*"

Even as he yelled, he saw the brambles shake and tremble and knew all the noise and commotion had finally spurred the scar-faced torvosaur into making its move.

"Natalie, *no!*"

The agitated dinosaur bellowed—its enormous head now visible over the brambles—and Natalie realized her mistake. She spun around and collided with Megan and both girls fell to the ground. They thrashed in a tangle of flailing arms and legs before Megan freed herself and began scrambling away on all fours—

The torvosaur burst from the thicket, its jaws open in an evil reptilian grin, and a faraway part of Jack's brain noted an ugly scar bisecting its face.

Natalie looked up and screamed, then curled into a ball and clamped her arms around her head. The torvosaur was right there—

Right there!

—but its head was up, its eyes locked on Megan as the girl scuttled frantically for safety. It lurched forward and a heavy foot slammed down on Natalie. Jack felt the impact—heard the sickening crunch of breaking bones—and saw jets of blood spray the nearby leaves and branches.

But the torvosaur didn't notice, its eyes still locked on Megan. Frozen to the ground, Jack stared in horror. In a single terrifying motion the dinosaur dropped its shoulders, snapped it jaws, and lifted its head again.

Megan screamed, her head and arms and legs protruding from opposite sides of the torvosaur's mouth. The animal paused for a split second, then bit down and began whipping its head savagely from side to side. Megan screamed—

"Aaaaaiii—"

—the strangled cry turning to a sickening gurgle before ending altogether.

Jack tore his eyes away, then looked again as the dinosaur turned and thumped back through the brambles, holding its prize in its jaws. His heart was pounding and he realized he was wheezing, his breaths coming so fast and hard they weren't actually filling his lungs, leaving him dizzy. He put a hand out to support himself and was surprised to realize he'd fallen to his knees.

He dropped his head and closed his eyes and concentrated on slowing his breathing. His stomach bubbled and his mouth was sour, but after a moment his head began to clear. He looked behind him. Kayce and Artem were nowhere in sight, but he could still hear the second torvosaur growling outside the brambles.

Jeez oh jeez oh jeez oh jeez ...

Still on his hands and knees, he started back out of the brambles—toward Kayce and Artem—then changed his mind.

He glanced toward Natalie.

I don't wanna look, but ...

He remembered the horror of finding what was left of Travis.

Shuddered at the thought of what he might find now.

But I can't just leave without making certain she's actually ... gone.

It took nearly a minute to steel himself, but then he crept forward on his hands and knees. If he'd been standing, he would have had a better angle and wouldn't have needed to get too close. But down on the ground he couldn't see much until he actually reached what was left of the unfortunate girl.

Holy crap, he thought miserably.

There was no question the girl was gone. Her body had been crushed, though her eyes were still open—

The eyes blinked.

And shifted, staring blankly into space.

Bloody hell ...

Jack crept closer and gingerly took the girl's hand, which was limp and cold. The eyes flicked toward him.

"Hey, it's okay," he whispered, not knowing what else to say. "Just relax."

He patted the cold hand.

"You're gonna be okay."

She's dead, he thought, horrified. *She just doesn't know it yet.*

"Just relax," he repeated, continuing to pat the soft, clammy hand. "Just relax ... and think of nice things."

The eyes blinked again, appearing confused as they peered at him. He wasn't certain if Natalie could see him, or hear him, or if she was even aware that he was there.

"Can you feel the sun?" he asked, struggling to sound comforting. "It feels good on your skin, doesn't it—"

The eyes blinked.

Then glazed over.

And after another moment Jack realized she was gone.

He screwed his eyes shut—struggling to fight back the tears ... and the horror. Knowing it was useless to think about it.

There was a rustle of brush, and he turned to see Kayce and Artem creeping into the clearing. He quickly waved them back, warning them not to come any closer. He glanced once toward the brambles—one of the torvosaurs was thumping around just outside the thicket—then crawled toward his friends.

"We heard screams," Kayce whispered matter-of-factly.

"Megan," Jack whispered simply.

"And Natalie?"

Jack gestured vaguely. "She's gone too."

Kayce didn't react. Her face was so expressionless it could have been chipped from stone, but her eyes were filled with anguish. Artem was shaking, and Jack sensed it was because of what had happened to the unfortunate girls and not in fear for himself.

Jack realized that he was shaking himself, but steadied himself enough to ask, "What now?"

"They were the last of the group," Kayce reported calmly. "The game's over."

Jack wasn't sure what that meant. "So ..."

"The game's over," Kayce repeated. "Last kid's gone so ... time for the losers to weep and wail and grind their teeth, and for the winners to collect their cash."

"And then what?"

Kayce shrugged matter-of-factly. "Then they'll round up another batch of kids and send them back. And then start another game."

13 Time Travel

They stopped for the night near a jumble of dark, mossy, jagged boulders. The rocks didn't provide anywhere for three people to hide together. But they were filled with nooks, cracks, crannies, and crevasses deep enough for single occupants to avoid the jaws and claws of large animals.

Kayce eyed the boulders skeptically, then turned to Artem. "You gonna sleep in a tree?"

The boy nodded and pointed. "That one right there."

"What about you?" she asked Jack.

"Um, I guess I haven't really thought about it. Any suggestions?"

"Well, monkey boy likes his trees obviously—"

Artem grinned proudly, wearing his goofy quirk like a badge of honor.

"—but I've never developed a feel for them. I mean, one wrong move in the middle of the night and you fall forty feet." She pointed. "I kinda like sitting with my back against the rocks."

"You can actually sleep like that?"

"I can sleep standing up." And then, as Artem nodded vigorously: "After you've been here a while, you find out there's a lot of dumb things you can do when you really need to."

She paused and peered into Jack's eyes, recognizing the confusion, worry, and anguish building inside him. And knew from experience he'd eventually explode if he continued trying to hold it all in.

"Look," she said, "we might as well talk about it. You've been through a lot these past two days. We all have. But the best thing you can do is try to learn and move on. Nothing you do will bring any of those kids back, and you can drive yourself crazy worrying about it. So don't. Don't even start. Forget everything that's happened. Just concentrate on the here and the now. Focus on just staying alive until morning."

"And in the morning?"

"And in the morning you concentrate on making it until tomorrow night. And then making it to the next morning again. Forget the big picture and just take things one friggin' day at a time. And if that's too tough, just take things hour by hour, or even minute by minute."

Jack nodded, looking from Kayce to Artem and back to Kayce again, and suddenly felt a lump rising painfully in his throat. And before he knew it gushed, "God, I don't want to end up like those other kids ..."

"Neither do we," Kayce assured him. "Neither do we."

"So let's don't," Artem suggested resolutely. "You watch our backs and we'll watch yours."

Jack tried to grin, failed, but then nodded his agreement. "Okay ... sounds like a plan."

Kayce went into the forest, and a short time later returned with several green apple-like fruits.

"Dinner," she said simply, tossing a couple to Artem and a few more to Jack. And then, speaking to Jack: "We could catch a couple of iguanas if you've got a craving for protein ..."

"Iguanas?" Jack bit into one of the "apples," which tasted like a soft, sweet, succulent pear.

Juicy as fresh watermelon ...

"Well, we don't know what they actually are, but they look like iguanas"—she lifted her shoulders as if asking who-the-heck cares—"so, you know ..."

She bit into an apple/pear of her own, and from their expressions, Jack knew the fruit wasn't anything new to either of his friends.

Probably eat 'em all the time. And then, as he took another bite, savoring the sweet juice: *And they probably taste a whole lot better than raw iguana.*

"So let me ask you," Jack said, polishing off his first apple/pear and starting on the second. "Why is this a one-way trip? I mean, if they can get people here, why can't they get anyone home again?"

Kayce and Artem exchanged glances and Kayce nodded, giving Artem the go-ahead to respond. The boy said, "You *saw* the size of the machine—"

Jack: "Actually I didn't. Guy punched me out, and the next thing I knew I was here. I didn't see *anything*."

Artem: "Oh, yeah. Well, it's a freakin' big machine—"

Kayce: "They call it a Time Displacement Device."

Artem, with a nod: "Right ... the Time Displacement Device. Anyway, it's the size of a bus. And I guess it's *possible* they could transport one back here—"

Kayce: "But even if they did, there's no way they could power the damn thing. I mean, it's not like there's anywhere to plug it in."

Artem, with another nod: "That's right. So anyway, that's why. They can—and do—send people here. But there's no way to reach through the wormhole and yank them back out again."

Jack: "The wormhole?"

Artem: "It's just an expression. No one we've ever talked to actually knows how the thing works. Just that it *does* work."

The boy frowned for a moment, carefully choosing his words before continuing.

"It's kind of like a guy throwing rocks in a lake. He can throw in as many as he wants, but since there's no one in the lake to throw them back ..."

"Sheesh."

"And if you wanna know the truth," Artem continued softly, almost sadly: "I don't think I'd *want* to go back."

Jack and Kayce gaped incredulously.

"Why the hell not?" Kayce asked.

"Well, I'd love to go home again. Of course I would. Seriously. I mean, I *do* but I don't."

"What the crap are you talking about?" Jack asked, thinking that maybe the boy had spent a little too long in the sun.

"Well, you gotta understand that teleportation isn't like jumping on an airplane, flying to Hawaii, and then hopping back off again. You see, your body isn't actually being transported through the wormhole. Only the blueprints."

Jack (again): "What the crap are you talking about?"

Artem: "Okay, look: the Time Displacement Device can't actually send your body through time. So instead, it makes a *copy* of you. It basically looks you over, makes a blueprint, then vaporizes your body and recreates it somewhere else. But here's the thing—"

He lifted a finger.

"—whenever you make a copy of something, the copy is never *exactly* the same as the original. Things get smudged and blurred, for instance. Some of the fine details get lost. And then when you make a *copy* of a copy—"

"You magnify those mistakes?"

"Right," Artem said with a nod.

"Wait," Kayce said, rubbing her eyes. "You're saying that we're not our original selves? That we're ... *copies*?"

"And *flawed* copies at that. So if there *was* a way to get back home again, we'd essentially be *copies* of copies ... and with even more mistakes and smudges than we have now."

He turned to Jack.

"You'll see what I mean soon enough. Most kids—when they get here—notice that they've forgotten things. Like maybe a memory was shifting places in their brain when they were copied. So the information was lost. And some kids notice that maybe they don't run as fast as they used to. Or that they don't see as well. Or hear as well. Or maybe their joints hurt when they never did before."

Jack shuddered. He'd already noticed that his joints seemed somewhat stiff, but thought it was just the result of frantic running, and swimming, and sleeping in trees. He felt chills, and the thought that his body had been altered—possibly even damaged in ways he didn't understand and hadn't yet noticed—was unsettling. As was the knowledge that going home—if that ever became possible—would magnify those alterations. Making them even worse.

Artem's right, he thought. *As much as I want to, maybe I don't really want to go back either.*

They brooded over Artem's disturbing revelation for several minutes—

Gawd, we're damned if we do, and damned if we don't ...

—and then Jack remembered something.

"You told me earlier there was something else about how people get chosen for this friggin' game."

Kayce scrunched her nose, and Jack realized he'd touched a nerve. The girl suddenly seemed so uncomfortable he thought that perhaps she wouldn't answer. But then she sighed.

"They say that across the United States, a kid goes missing every forty seconds," she said. "Which is around 800,000 a year."

"Yeah, I've heard that."

"Many of them are never seen again."

"Yeah, I've heard that, too."

"Well, you saw the sorta kids they send here. Everybody's so good looking. I think that's partly because watching a good-looking kid get killed is more ... I don't know, more exciting, I guess. More *thrilling*. And then ..."

Her voice trailed off. Jack thought he understood the reason, but asked anyway.

"What is it?"

Kayce gave him a long look, then said: "Some of the kids who get sent here ... well, some of them were abused first."

Jack's voice was as soft as thistledown. "You're kidding."

"I'm not. That's another reason this freakin' game only involves kids. Some good-looking kid gets snatched off the street and gets ... well, I don't need to paint a picture. But then the kid gets sent here. After all, who're they gonna tell? Once they're here, there's no evidence, no witnesses. Kid just disappears forever. Some pervert back home not only gets his jollies, but contributes new blood to the game."

Jack felt chills—actually felt his blood turning to ice—as he listened.

Wondering if—while he'd been unconscious—maybe—

Kayce read the look on his face and said: "It doesn't happen to *every* kid. But it happens often enough to know it's a factor."

Jack shuddered, suddenly overcome with disgust. And revulsion. He'd never actually felt his skin crawl—had always thought it was just an expression—but as he thought about what Kayce had just said ... his skin literally began to crawl.

Like thousands of tiny worms had begun wriggling just beneath the surface.

He shuddered again, then looked at Artem—the twelve-year-old who looked ten—wondering if—

No ...

He tried to mask his worry, but Kayce guessed what he was thinking.

"We've talked about it," she said quietly, nodding at the younger boy. "And Artem's lucky ... well, you know what I mean."

"Thank God," Jack muttered as Artem nodded gloomily. Jack wondered if the boy actually understood the horror he'd been spared—

He seems so innocent sometimes ...

—then shook off the appalling images and turned back to Kayce. "Um, if this stupid game is about which kids last the longest ..."

He tipped his head toward Artem.

Kayce looked at the boy, who shrugged.

"It's okay," Artem said. "You can say it. I think I know it anyway."

Kayce looked at him like a doting older sister. "Artem's a special case. They've never sent anyone that small or young before."

"So why—"

"We're not sure. But my best guess is, no one ever thought he'd last very long: certainly not as long as he has. He probably came to provide a special opportunity. Like, how much are you willing to bet that an allosaur gets him? Or a dilophosaur, or a velociraptor, or maybe even another kid? Or maybe they had a pool where everyone simply tried to guess how long he'd last. An hour? Two? Three at the most?"

She shrugged.

"Who knows? That kind of stuff's impossible to predict, so a guy willing to risk a lot of money could win a buttload of cash by making the right guess."

She held up a fist to Artem, who bumped it enthusiastically.

"But we sure screwed 'em on that one, didn't we, Champ?"

"We sure did."

"I've got another question," Jack said.

"Jeez," Kayce said, feigning irritation. "What is it with you? Most kids just whine, whimper, and wail when they get here. But you ask questions like you're writing a research paper."

Jack ignored her and waved a hand. "All of us being here. Isn't anyone worried that we might change the future?"

Kayce and Artem looked at one another and then burst out laughing.

"What?" Jack asked.

"Everyone always thinks that," Artem said. "But there's not a chance."

"But of *course* there is—"

"Believe me," the boy went on. "There's no way a buncha kids are gonna have any impact on what happens over the next 150 million years. Seriously."

He shrugged.

"For one thing, seventy-five million years from now a big-ass asteroid's going to hit the Earth and practically wipe out the planet. It's gonna scrub it clean. So any changes we *do* make are going to be erased anyway."

"Still—"

"Listen to him," Kayce advised. "He looks like a goober, but he understands this stuff."

"Back home, people debate it all the time," Artem continued, giving Kayce a sour look. "There's even some story about a guy who travels back in time, steps on some tiny, insignificant plant, then returns home to discover that one little misstep completely changed the future."

He shook his head dismissively.

"But really? It's like peeing in a swimming pool. It might sound disgusting—"

Kayce: "It *is* disgusting!"

"—but it doesn't make a lick of difference to the pool. If it did, you can bet I'd be doing everything I could to mess things up for those jerks back home. You know, the asswipes who sent us here."

Yeah, Jack thought grimly. *And I'd be right beside you ...*

The three talked idly as the day lengthened, the sun set, and dark, impenetrable gloom settled over the forest. Talking like any three normal kids getting to know one another. It turned out that Kayce—like Jack—had an interest in sports, especially track and field, and before being snatched off the street had been training to run a marathon. Artem, on the other hand, had a passion for science fiction (which explained why he knew so much about time travel) and enjoyed working with his hands. Kayce revealed that Artem also had an excellent voice.

"He sings to me sometimes," she said as the boy blushed. "But only when we're alone."

"Can't sing around the other kids," Artem explained with a scowl. "They just make fun of me."

The boy was especially talkative at first—

Now that it's just me'n Kayce, he's willing to open up a little, Jack thought.

—but eventually slowed down and withdrew back into himself.

Been through a lot the past coupla days, Jack guessed. *He's gotta be pretty tired.*

Artem had declared his intention to spend the night in a tree. But as darkness claimed the woods and the chilling shrieks, bellows, and cries of diurnal animals gave way to the soft hoots, flits, chitters, and moans of their nocturnal cousins, the boy dozed off beside Jack.

Actually resting his head on Jack's shoulder.

Jack hesitated, then reached an arm around the boy's shoulders to keep him from toppling over.

"You've made a huge change in that kid," Kayce said quietly, not wanting to wake the younger boy.

"I've only known him for two days."

"So you don't see it. But I know what he was like before and believe me, there's a big difference."

"How so?"

"Well, he's the youngest kid they've ever sent here." She shrugged. "The youngest one we *know* about, anyway. And he looks even younger than he is. So the other kids pick on him a lot."

"Yeah, he kinda told me about that."

Kayce nodded. "I don't think they all intend to be mean. Most of the kids are just frightened, and they take out their fear and frustration on him because he's such an easy target. But you treat him as an equal; almost like a superior. And, you know—especially because you're another boy—he's drawn to that."

"He's a good kid," Jack said simply. "He's already saved my butt a couple of times. But even if he hadn't, he's good company."

"Yeah, well, I appreciate what you've done for him." She flicked a hand at the boy, who seemed to be lost in a restless, troubled sleep.

Maybe having nightmares ...

"He's become family to me," Kayce went on, still gazing at the kid and sharing what Jack thought was an especially sensitive vulnerability. "Really, we're all that either of us have."

And then, in an especially quiet voice: "So I know how incredibly selfish this sounds but, well, I'm glad you're here."

Jack didn't know how to respond, and both teens became quiet.

And in time drifted into nothingness.

14 Prehistoric Surgeon

It was the moan that woke him.

Jack had been dozing, not quite asleep, but not fully awake either. He opened his eyes, experienced a moment of confusion as his senses came online, then looked to his side. Artem was curled on the ground beside him, but the boy's restless sleep had worsened. Even as Jack watched, the boy twitched, and then moaned.

He's sick, Jack thought.

He reached over to touch the boy's arm, surprised to find it slick with sweat.

Crap, something's wrong ...

He remembered Kayce describing people being poisoned to give them expiration dates and caught his breath, then shook off the thought.

He's been here for months ... if he'd been poisoned it would have taken effect a long time ago.

Now fully awake, he glanced around to be sure there were no obvious threats, spotted Kayce sleeping lightly against the rocks a few feet away, then rolled onto his knees. Artem groaned again, his body twitching uncomfortably, and Jack reached out a hand to steady him. He touched Artem's cheek with the back of his free hand and instantly recoiled.

Jeez, the kid's burning up!

He rocked back on his heels, suddenly worried. He watched the boy for another moment, then turned and crawled over to Kayce.

"Hey," he whispered. He hesitated, then reached out and touched her lightly on the shoulder. "Hey …"

The girl came instantly awake, reeling back from his touch like he'd poked her with a hot wire. Her hands clenched into fists and for a second Jack thought she might hit him.

"Hey, it's just me," Jack whispered urgently. "It's okay, it's just me."

She seemed to be glaring at him in the darkness, and Jack flashed back to Travis, and Josh, wondering if she thought that perhaps Jack had similarly vile intentions.

"Something's wrong with Artem," he said, quickly redirecting her focus. "I think he's sick."

The words had the desired effect. Completely ignoring Jack, Kayce rolled onto her knees and crept toward the moaning boy. She smoothed the kid's hair like a worried mother and then placed the back of her hand against his forehead.

"Damn," she whispered.

She touched the boy's cheeks, tested his forehead again, and then felt the boy's wrist for his pulse.

"His heart's racing," she reported.

"What does that mean?" Jack asked: he'd crept up beside her. "Do you know what's wrong?"

"I'm afraid so," she said grimly.

She reached down and gently shook Artem's shoulder.

"Artem," she whispered. "*Artem* ... hey, wake up, buddy."

The boy moaned and tried to roll away, but she pulled him back toward her.

"*Artem!* C'mon, wake up, bud!"

The boy groaned, and then his eyes fluttered open. He looked up, though he didn't seem focused upon anything.

"Hey, champ ... are you still with me?"

The boy mumbled incoherently, and even in the darkness Jack could see the kid's face was sheened with sweat.

"Hey, buddy, it's me: Kayce," she whispered tenderly. "Can you hear me?"

"Kayce?" The voice was weak, confused, and troubled.

"Yeah. What's wrong, bud? Can you tell me?"

"Don't ... sick."

"Yeah, I know, champ. Did you get scratched by a thorn?"

Artem mumbled again, but then said, "I'm sorry!"

"Why didn't you tell me, kiddo?"

Another mumble. And after a couple of seconds: "—so scared ..."

"Hey, it's okay, champ. You're gonna be fine! You just rest now: me'n Jack are gonna take care of you, okay?"

Artem whispered something unintelligible, then mumbled, " 'Kay."

Kayce rocked back on her heels as the boy closed his eyes, then rose to her feet. She gestured for Jack to follow as she stepped away.

"A thorn?" Jack whispered when he'd joined her. "From the chatterwoods?"

"Must be," she answered, and for the first time Jack detected what seemed to be a tremble of fear in her voice. "And it's gotta be more than a scratch. As sick as he is, one must have broken off beneath the skin. Damn!"

"Is there anything we can do?"

"Not a lot. But there's one thing we *have* to do, and it's something we've gotta do right now."

"What's that?"

"We've got to find it. And then we've got to cut the damn thing out."

After her initial uncertainty, Kayce quickly regained her poise. And Jack was once again impressed with her resolve and leadership, beginning to understand how she'd managed to survive so long in such a savage, deadly world.

She instructed Jack to begin gathering firewood—

"We need the light to see," she explained.

—while she collected kindling and then—with the help of a butane lighter—

Probably took it from a hunter, Jack guessed.

—quickly had a small fire crackling beside the rocks. Jack carefully fed larger and larger sticks into the snapping flames and soon had the fire burning brightly enough to illuminate the primitive campsite.

"Keep an eye out," Kayce warned. "Firelight attracts animals. And that's a problem we don't need right now."

Jack lifted a stout branch like a club. "I'll be ready." And after a quick look at the trees: "What else do you need me to do?"

"Um, I hate to say this, but ... well, this is going to hurt, like, really bad. You might need to hold him still for me."

Jack muttered something unprintable beneath his breath. The circumstances—the prehistoric world, the dinosaurs, the poisonous thorns, the whole freakin' "game"—suddenly seemed beyond the scope of polite, ordinary language. But he nodded.

"Anything you need."

"Okay." She drew in a deep breath. "Let's find that thorn."

Kneeling beside the sick boy, she began running her hands up and down his arms, and hands, and legs, and back, and belly. After nearly a minute, she removed his left shoe, and sock, and began rubbing the sole of his foot, feeling for anything unusual.

"Hmmmm. Don't feel anything." She used her nose to point at the shoe. "Run your fingers along the inside, see if you can feel anything. But be careful! You might get stuck by a sliver, and I don't want you both down on me ..."

"Don't worry."

He took the shoe and gingerly began probing the insole for anything sharp. Kayce, meanwhile, removed Artem's right shoe and began rubbing the sole of the foot.

"Anything?" Jack asked.

"Nada. You?"

"Nothing."

"Check the other shoe for me."

Jack picked up the shoe and almost instantly felt something scratch his fingers. He carefully withdrew his hand and inspected it in the firelight.

"Find something?"

"Yeah ..." He peered carefully at his fingers where he'd been scratched and was relieved to see that the skin was marked but unbroken.

"Did it get you?"

"Yeah, but it didn't break the skin. I think I'm okay."

"Let me see."

Kayce took his hand, held it close to her face, and after a quick but critical examination, nodded. "Okay, that's gotta be it. You're lucky. Where was it?"

"On the right side, so"—he leaned over and touched the side of Artem's right foot—"it's gotta be right about there."

"Came in from the side, huh?" Kayce squinted, moving her head from side to side to peer at the boy's foot from different angles, then nodded. "Okay, I think I've got it. It's broken off, of course. But these little suckers still pack a helluva punch."

She pulled the dragon-slaying knife from her belt—it was the sort of tool you didn't refer to as a knife as much as a

KNIFE!—and Jack actually saw the cutting edge flash in the glow of the fire.

"Jeez, where'd you get that?"

"Off a hunter. Well, what was left of him." And then, as if reporting nothing more remarkable than a passing butterfly: "It was covered in guts. I cleaned it the best I could, but you can still see the blood stains."

Holy hell, Jack thought grimly.

She considered the sasquatch-sized blade for a moment, looked from it to Artem and then back to the knife again, then slowly slid it back into its sheath.

"What?" Jack asked.

"Nothing. Just think this is a job that requires a more subtle approach."

She fumbled with the waistband of her jeans, and after a moment withdrew a nasty-looking needle she'd pushed into the fabric. It looked like the sort of thing a veterinarian might use to sew sutures into a moose.

"Holy hell," Jack whispered. "You're like Rambo."

"Who?"

"Just an old movie character. Where in the hell did you get that?"

"One of the other kids had it," she said dismissively. "I don't remember why."

She moved around, positioning herself so that she could lean over Artem's foot without blocking light from the fire.

"Throw a little more wood on that fire, will you?" she asked without looking up. "I need more light."

"Sure thing."

"Then step over here so you can hold him when he starts kicking."

Jack did as he was told, then watched as Kayce rubbed a finger gingerly over Artem's foot. Still without looking up, she handed the needle to Jack.

"Stick the blunt end in a stick or something, then hold the point over the flames to sterilize it. Just for a second, then be careful not to touch it."

Jack once again did as he was asked, then held the needle-end of the stick toward Kayce. She was still examining Artem's foot, pinpointing the thorn. After a moment she reached up, tested the blunt end of the needle, found it cool enough to touch, and plucked it from the stick.

She scrunched her nose, then suddenly handed the needle back to Jack.

"Hold this for me. Be careful not to touch anything besides the blunt end."

" 'Kay."

She reached into a pocket, produced a pair of glasses, and parked them on the end of her nose. And then before Jack could comment, snapped, "Shut up!"

"What?" Jack asked. "They look good. Seriously."

Kayce scowled, but took back the needle and leaned over Artem's foot. She didn't move for several seconds, but then lifted the needle, brandished it over the suspected thorn tip, and plunged the point into the boy's tender flesh.

Artem cried out and kicked like a mule. The needle flicked from Kayce's hand and spun into the darkness.

"Damn!" Then, as Jack tried to calm the sick boy: "Come on, help me find it!"

Jack crawled over to join her and together—shoulder to shoulder—they began searching for the needle.

"Big as that sucker is, it ought to jump right out at us," Jack muttered after several minutes.

Kayce swore beneath her breath. "Man, if we don't find it ..."

Jack could just picture her using the sauropod-sticking knife to dig out the poisonous thorn, and began searching even more intently. And after several seconds said, "Hang on a second."

Moving carefully to avoid disturbing the ground any more than necessary, he returned to the fire, selected a thick limb that was burning vigorously on one, and carried it back.

"Hold this right here," he instructed. Then, as Kayce held the flame a few inches over the search area, he turned his head sideways and lowered it until one ear was just brushing the dirt. From ground level, he scanned the dirt—

"Move the flame back and forth a little," he coached.

Kayce moved the flame and Jack almost instantly spotted a flash of metal. He reached out and carefully plucked the needle from the soft earth.

"Oh, thank God," Kayce said. And then, with a tone of complete sincerity. "You might have just saved the kid's life. Again."

They re-sterilized the needle and then—with Jack holding Artem's leg as firmly as he could—Kayce once again dug after the poisonous thorn.

Artem cried out and tried to kick, but as much as it pained him, Jack held on even more tightly. Kayce continued digging, driving the needle in so deeply that blood was soon running freely from the wound.

"Damn," she muttered. "I can't see."

She reached up, mopped her brow with the back of her sleeve, took a deep breath, and once again pushed the needle deep into Artem's foot.

The boy jerked violently, nearly tearing himself from Jack's grasp.

"I can't see," Kayce cried. "Give me something to sop up the blood!"

Jack ripped a bandana from his back pocket, shoved it at Kayce, then instantly clamped his hand back on Artem's calf. Kayce sponged blood from the boy's foot and for a split second had a clear view of the wound.

"Okay, gotcha," she hissed. And then jabbed the needle into Artem's instep.

Artem cried out—he was now sobbing uncontrollably, though Jack wasn't certain he was actually conscious—and was thrashing back and forth, struggling to escape the agony of Kayce's needle. A bead of moisture ran down Jack's cheek, and he realized that he too was sweating, partly from the heat of the nearby fire, but mostly from the strain and anxiety. It broke his heart to see his young friend in such pain, but nevertheless held the boy's leg as tightly as he could, determined to hold it still until Kayce found the trouble-making thorn.

Kayce, meanwhile, was relentless. She drove the dreaded needle in again and again. And just as Jack was beginning to wonder if she'd ever find the thing, she rocked back on her heels.

"Okay," she said in a voice so weary Jack could actually hear the exhaustion. "You can let him go."

Jack released the boy's leg.

Kayce held out the needle. "There it is," she said.

Jack peered at the needle in the flickering firelight. Stuck to the point was a tiny, almost imperceptible sliver of something black.

"That's it?"

"Pretty sure. It doesn't look like much, but it's got the punch of a hungry allosaur."

Jack peered at the tiny fleck in wonder, then—careful to keep any sound of criticism in his tone—asked, "Are you sure you got it all?"

"I'm not sure at all. But I think so. At least, there's nothing more I can do now. It's too dark and there's too much blood to see. All we can do is take care of him and see if he gets any better."

"Will he?" Jack glanced at his young friend, who'd curled into a ball, still sobbing softly, though Jack thought he was too sick to actually be conscious. "Get better, I mean?"

"I think so. I mean, people usually snap out of it once the thorn's gone, but we'll have to watch him. And we need to get him some water. But we ought to know by morning if he's, you know, gonna make it."

Jack and Kayce sat side by side with their backs against the rocks, trying to rest. Artem had drifted back into a fitful, restless sleep. He twitched and jerked from time to time—

But he's no longer moaning, Jack thought, thankful for small favors.

"We need to get him some water," Kayce repeated after several minutes.

"How're we gonna do that?"

"I know where there's a canteen. And I know where to find water. I can get there and be back in—oh—thirty or forty minutes."

"In the dark?"

"It's not my first choice," she admitted. "But I've done it before."

She flicked a hand at Artem.

"Besides, the poor kid needs the water; he won't last without it." She shook her head. "I could kick the little jerk's ass for not telling me."

The girl's words were harsh, but there was deep concern in her tone.

"Um, I hate to see you go by yourself," Jack said softly. "But I don't know what else to suggest."

"You'll be okay watching him?"

Jack looked back evenly. "Do you really have to ask?"

She looked back and after a long moment shook her head. "No ... no, you've proven yourself."

"What about the fire? Want me to keep it going?"

"I'm ... not sure," she said in a rare moment of hesitation. "The kid's in shock and I know it's important to keep him warm. But like I said, firelight attracts animals. In a situation like this, I don't know if the benefit outweighs the risk."

"I'm still the new guy," Jack said, "so I don't know what's best. But it's actually a pretty warm night. Maybe even warm enough that he doesn't need the fire. And ... well, if he seems chilled I can cover him with my own clothes."

"That might be okay." And then: "Let's do that."

They carried Artem closer to the rocks, which were still radiating heat from the fire, then stamped out the flames. Kayce gave Artem a quick kiss on the forehead, gave Jack a friendly punch to the arm, then vanished into the trees.

Jack sat beside the ill boy, holding a club-like stick across his knees. He peered into the darkness listening, and listening, and imagining things ... believing that every creak, crackle, and crunch in the trees was a ravenous dinosaur creeping up on him—

He shook his head clear of the gloomy images, then reached down to feel Artem's forehead.

Is it my imagination, or has his temperature gone down?

He felt the boy's cheeks, and forearm, and then touched his forehead again. He wasn't certain, but thought the boy felt a little less warm, a little less clammy.

Hmmmm.

A tree creaked in the near distance, but not in a way that signaled danger. Jack nevertheless peered in its direction, thinking about Kayce.

Man, that girl ... those freaks back home really screwed up when they picked her for this.

He'd known kids like her before. The captain of his football team, for one: a kid able to stay calm and cool and steady, even when the team was in trouble and everyone else was freaking out and falling apart. Able to motivate and inspire and lead and—most impressive of all—pull a best from people they didn't even know they had.

Even the coaches ...

A kid in Jack's math class had a similar gift, able to change the temperature of a room just by walking in. Able to make people feel good just by being near them. Able to make people want to be better themselves.

I'm gonna be like that, he decided. *No matter what else happens, I'm gonna be that kid here.*

He leaned back against the rocks and closed his eyes as he listened to the sounds of the night. For several minutes he simply listened, but then began trying to isolate and focus upon the calls of individual creatures, attempting to identify them. There was a deep, resonant buzz in the background—

Gotta be prehistoric crickets.

—and there were intermittent hoots—

Are there owls here?

—drifting down from the tree tops. And—listening carefully—he picked out soft flits from higher in the sky—

Like some sorta bats, maybe? Hunting night birds?

—that he only picked up when he really concentrated. And—

Yeah, the leaves in the tops of the trees are swishing ... rustling in a breeze I can't even feel down here.

A thought hit him and he cocked his head, concentrating, but—

Don't hear anything that sounds big. Or dangerous.

He continued listening, but—

Yeah, I know there are big animals out there, but ... I don't really hear anything.

Something shrieked in the distance—

Okay, something's in a pretty mad mood ... but it's far enough away that it's probably not gonna bother us.

He listened some more, but was unable to hear any of the deep-toned bellows, roars, grunts, and moans of the really, *really* big animals. He wasn't certain if the big creatures took the night off ... or if perhaps they were just stealthier in the darkness.

Huh.

Closing his eyes made him sleepy, and he stretched and beat his arms around his chest, knowing he and Artem were both vulnerable and that he needed to stay awake.

And with a wan grin:

'Sides, if Kayce comes back and finds me asleep when I'm supposed to be watching Artem, she'll kick my butt!

The thought of Kayce kicking his butt opened his eyes, but it wasn't until a twig cracked in the woods—a sound that he realized wasn't the natural creak of a shifting tree—that he snapped to full wakefulness. He tightened his grip on the club and peered into the darkness.

I'm already between whatever-it-is and Artem, he thought, listening for another sound. *But if things get crazy—*

He glanced quickly behind him.

—if things get bad, I'll drag him into that crack in the rocks and hope it's deep enough for the both of us.

He heard another crackle—the crunch of dry leaves beneath something's foot—and thought he saw a branch move in the gloom. His fingers tightened around his club—

A shadow emerged from the darkness.

Kayce!

With an enormous sigh of relief he rose to his feet and crept to meet her.

"How is he?" Kayce asked immediately, looking past Jack toward Artem.

"He's breathing easier and he's stopped moaning. And—I'm not positive—but I think his fever's gone. At least, he doesn't feel quite so hot anymore."

"Oh, thank God for that!"

"What about you?" Jack asked. "You okay? Have any trouble?"

She shrugged, still looking toward Artem. "It was dicey, but nothing I couldn't handle."

"Yeah, I bet."

"Let's take a look at the kid."

Together they knelt beside the sick boy. Kayce ran her fingers through his hair, then tested his cheeks and forehead with the back of her hand.

"You're right," Kayce said to Jack, but in a light sing-songy tone meant for Artem. "He might be coming out of it."

She pulled a sock from a back pocket and lifted a plastic canteen from her belt. She moistened the sock with water and began sponging the boy's face.

"Poor kid," she whispered, though Jack wasn't certain if she was talking to him or to Artem.

She again moistened the cotton cloth and squeezed it over the boy's lips, trying to give him a little water.

"Is there anything I can do?" Jack asked.

Kayce shook her head. "No, you've done plenty already. All we can do now is give him a little time. And hope he's strong enough to recover."

Jack watched for another minute, then had to pat away a yawn. He tried to be discreet, but Kayce saw it.

"Why don't you get some sleep?" she asked.

"No, I'm okay," Jack insisted. "I want to help."

"You've had a tough couple of days," Kayce said. "A lot worse than what most kids go through, and you're pretty wasted. You're not gonna be any good to me or to Artem if you're dead on your feet."

Despite himself, Jack had to fight off another massive yawn. "You sure?"

"Absolutely." She pointed. "Kick back against those rocks and catch some Zs."

"What about you?"

"I got plenty of sleep earlier. Before ... well, you know. And I'm too wound up now anyway. I couldn't sleep if I wanted to."

Jack hesitated, and she pointed firmly.

"Go," she ordered. "Before I crack you with that stick of yours."

Jack grinned. "Yes, ma'am. But ... don't be afraid to wake me up if you need anything."

"Don't worry," she said. "You're number one on my speed dial."

15 Bad News

He was dreaming about football.

About all the guys—his friends—running, hitting, tackling, throwing, catching, and even scoring touchdowns.

And there was a girl.

At first, it was Brinley, a girl he'd had a secret crush on since the seventh grade. But then Brinley morphed into someone else.

Kayce?

Yeah ... there was her baseball cap and ponytail. It didn't seem unusual at all that she was there on the football field, as if she was part of the gang and always had been ...

A savage roar shook the forest, and Jack was in such a deep sleep it wasn't until the animal bellowed again that he jerked into wakefulness.

He sat upright and instantly began groping for his club.

The sun was already up, Kayce standing a few feet away, looking into the forest. She heard Jack moving and turned for a quick look, then returned her attention to the trees.

Shaking off the last traces of sleep, Jack struggled to his feet and joined her. The unseen dinosaur—

Definitely something big.

—growled irritably. Tree branches snapped, crackled, and popped as the animal thumped through the woods, but ... it didn't seem to be coming any closer.

But Kayce wasn't paying attention: she was looking in a different direction.

"What is it?" Jack asked.

"Trouble." And then: "Can't you feel it?"

Jack lifted his nose and looked around, but—

She took his hand and lifted it. "Look at your arms."

Jack looked and—

He saw the hairs on his arm standing on end, and ... he felt a gentle tingling in his skin.

The agitated dinosaur bellowed again, and birds and animals began shrieking from every corner of the forest. But Kayce wasn't paying attention to any of it.

The tingling sensation became worse: Jack could feel it now along his spine, and thighs, and the back of his neck. The leaves of the trees began to rustle, though there was no wind.

"What's going on," Jack asked, suddenly nervous.

"We're about to have company."

"Dinosaurs?"

"No, people. More people are coming."

Before Jack could respond, an eerie hum filled the air, audible even over the shrieks and howls of frightened animals. The air popped and crackled all around them, and

Jack heard an unsettling ... *sizzle* ... as if someone was frying bacon in an enormous skillet.

"Crap," Kayce muttered beneath her breath. She cast a quick look at Artem—

The boy was still sleeping, resting far easier now.

—then turned back to Jack.

"It's the Time Displacement Device," she explained. "Sending people through time isn't like beaming them down from the Starship *Enterprise*. They literally have to tear a hole through the fabric of time, and that causes a lot of problems. It scares hell out of the animals and sometimes even triggers earthquakes. Scary as hell."

Even as she spoke, Jack felt his skin begin to crawl, as if he were standing close to an enormous power generator. There was a flash over the forest, not unlike lightning, though the sky was free of clouds. Kayce's hair began to rise as it reacted to the static electricity in the air, moving in eerie dance-like moves—

Like snakes!

—and Jack realized that his own hair was standing on end. His stomach churned and the fillings in his teeth began to ache like he'd just bitten into a ball of frozen ice cream.

There was pressure against his ears that became uncomfortable, and then painful—he opened and closed his mouth, trying to get his ears to pop—and his eyes burned and throbbed as if they were about to burst from their sockets.

He gritted his teeth, aware that he wasn't the only one in pain. The entire forest was filled with terrified shrieks and howls. The sky flashed again, and again, and Jack could now see streaks of light tearing through the sky: bolts of lightning where no lightning could possibly be.

"Hold on!" Kayce warned, raising her voice over the crackling static and screeching animals.

"Wha—"

CRACK!

The explosion was so loud and unexpected—the sudden flash of light so bright and painful—that Jack stumbled and fell back on his butt. He'd automatically thrown a hand up to shield his eyes, but still felt like he'd been blinded.

Startled and disoriented, he looked left and right, but—

It took a moment, but then he realized the teeth-stinging buzz was gone. The sky was no longer flashing, the charge of electricity gone. Confused, agitated animals were still screeching and bellowing throughout the forest, which Jack suspected would continue for a while.

"Holy hell!" he stammered. "What was *that*!"

"That's how we know when someone's come through the wormhole. Same thing happened when you showed up: you were just unconscious at the time."

She glanced back at Artem, who'd slept through the whole thing.

"But ... damn. I was hoping we'd have a couple of days before they sent more people back."

"More ... people?"

"More kids. With Natalie and Megan gone, they've sent another batch of kids back to start a new game." And then: "Damn. This really messes things up."

"How so?" Jack asked. He struggled to his feet and dusted himself off: his brain was still swimming, like he'd just stepped from the world's wildest roller coaster.

"Well, I've gotta go get 'em. Don't want 'em just wandering around, but I don't know where to take 'em. Artem and I haven't really decided yet where we're gonna go." She glanced over at the boy. "And the kid's obviously not in any condition to move."

She reached up and rubbed her eyes with the heels of her hands.

"Well, damn." And then: "Okay, I've gotta go round up the troops. You gonna be okay with Artem?"

"Yeah, but ... anything in particular I need to do?"

Kayce shook her head. "No, just keep him safe. I'll leave you the canteen: give 'im something to drink if he wakes up."

"I can do that. How far have you got to go?"

She looked into the distance and scrunched her nose. "Couple miles, I guess. Oughtta be gone a couple hours, maybe ... unless we run into any problems along the way."

She shook her head in resignation, then walked back to Artem, checked his temperature, then kissed him on the forehead.

"Okay," she said. "I'm off."

"Take care of yourself."

"You, too." She flicked a hand at the sleeping boy. "Just remember that if anything happens to him, I'm gonna kick your ass."

"I bet you will."

"All the way up to your eyeballs," she promised.

Kayce trotted into the forest, and Jack thought she looked as natural in the prehistoric forest as an Olympic swimmer in a chlorinated pool. He watched her disappear, then glanced around the surrounding woods.

Can't get over all this, he thought, scrutinizing the immense, vine-covered trees. Most of the animals had finally settled down again, but the woods still sounded like feeding time at the zoo. A large dinosaur trumpeted in the distance—

Sounds like an elephant ...

—as smaller animals shrieked, screeched, and squawked as they went about their business. There was a soft squeak and Jack turned to see a small lizard creeping into the clearing. The color of sand, the lizard-thing was the size of an upright cat and walked on two legs.

Like a miniature allosaur.

The lizard-thing lifted its nose, and Jack could see its bulbous eyes darting up and down and back and forth. The creature sniffed at the air, and then took another step.

Farther into the clearing.

Right toward Artem.

With a start, Jack realized the animal was homing in on the boy's scent, hoping for a snack.

"Hey!" he shouted.

He picked up a rock and hurled it at the creature. The rock just missed, which startled but didn't discourage the animal. The lizard-thing cheeped in surprise, hopped a few feet to the side, and then once again set its bulbous eyes upon the sleeping boy.

Jack snatched up another rock, took aim, and flung it as hard as he could, striking the creature in the shoulder. The animal screeched—

Cheeee!

—and leaped three feet straight into the air before it turned and streaked back into the trees. Jack glared after it, then heard a weak voice.

"Nice shot ..."

Jack whirled around.

Artem was propped up on one elbow, watching him through red-rimmed eyes. Jack walked quickly over.

"Hey, bud! How're you feeling?"

"Like crap." The boy coughed and licked his lips. "What happened?"

"Kayce dug a thorn out of your foot. You were sick as a dog and had us pretty worried." And after a quick look at the boy's foot—

Still bloody, but at least it hasn't turned black ...

—he asked, "Are you thirsty?"

"Yeah, I'm dry as dust."

Jack reached for the canteen, cracked the lid, and held it to the boy's split lips. "Easy now ... don't drink too much too fast."

The boy took a couple of careful sips.

"Oh, wow," he said after a moment. "That tastes *so* good." And then: "Where's Kayce?"

"New batch of kids just got here. She went to round 'em up."

Artem's jaw dropped ... it literally dropped ... and his eyes bugged out. "What? *Seriously?* But—"

"I know," Jack said. "Kayce was as surprised as you are. But she went to get them. I'm supposed to watch out for you."

"Well, thanks, I guess."

"So, you're feeling better?"

"Compared to last night, yeah. Tons. But compared to normal, hell no."

"What's wrong?"

Artem scrunched his nose as he tried to put his feelings into words. "Weak, I guess."

"Huh. Can I get you anything?"

"A little more water?"

Jack helped him to drain a little more water from the plastic canteen.

"Are you hungry?"

"A little bit, I guess."

Jack sucked air in through his teeth. "Um, I'm not sure there's anything I can do about that. I could try scrounging up a few of those apple/pears, but I wouldn't even know where to begin looking." He shrugged. "And I don't want to leave you alone. Not until you get your strength back."

"Yeah, well, I'll be okay for a while. 'Til Kayce gets back, anyway."

"Okay. But if it'll help—"

There was a crackle of brush and Jack reached for his club, but the next instant Kayce burst from the trees, red faced and out of breath. She instantly looked for Artem, saw he was awake, and darted to his side.

"You little j-jerk!" she cried, grabbing the boy and holding him tight. Her voice cracked, and Jack saw tears streaming down her flushed cheeks. "Y-you scared the c-crap outta me!"

Artem mumbled something that Jack couldn't make out because the boy's face was buried in Kayce's shoulder.

"N-next time you have a problem, you tell me, damn it! You understand? You freakin' *tell* me!"

"I'm sorry," Artem croaked. He'd lifted his face clear and Jack saw that he and Kayce were both sobbing.

Jack looked away—looking for the new kids—then turned back. Kayce peered at Artem's injured foot, assessing its condition.

"Where're the new kids?" Jack asked quietly.

Kayce looked up for a moment, then used the back of her shirt sleeves to mop her eyes. Her face was still red and sheened with sweat, and she was chuffing for breath. Jack realized she'd been running.

Running hard and fast ...

She took a moment to catch her breath—and to collect herself—then looked from Jack to Artem and then back to Jack again.

"We're in trouble," she said. "They didn't send kids. They sent hunters."

"Hunters?" Jack asked, picking up on the plural.

"Three of them. With military gear, automatic rifles, and tracking devices." She nodded grimly. "And they're not here to adjust cameras or tag animals."

She glanced at the two boys to be sure they understood.

"They're here to hunt us down. To snuff us out. To get rid of us once and for all."

16 Allosaurus

Kayce gave Artem another quick up-and-down.

"I know you're sick," she said. "But they're going to be coming and we don't have a lot of time. Do you think you can walk?"

Artem nodded, but without conviction.

"Um," Jack said, "I'm the only one of us they can actually track, right? I mean, you two've cut the implants out of yourselves, right?"

"That's right."

Jack's blood was cold as ice, but he reached up to his shoulder, felt the lump beneath his skin, and said, "Then you've got to cut this one outta me."

"We might have to," Kayce agreed. "But we don't have time to do it now. I don't know who these guys are, but they're not like the hunters they've sent before."

"How so?" Jack asked.

"Hard to explain," Kayce said. "And I only watched them for a minute. But they seem more—I don't know—competent, I guess. More professional. The kind of guys who take their job seriously. And who won't quit until the three of us are bloody chunks of shredded dinosaur kibble."

There was something about the calm, matter-of-fact way Kayce talked that made the revelation all the more ominous. And all the more frightening.

Jack turned to Artem. "How are you at riding piggyback?"

"Huh?"

"You're a tough kid," Jack said. "But you're not at your best right now. And you're gonna have a heckuva limp. So if Kayce'll lead the way, I'll carry you piggyback. You know, just 'til you're feeling better."

"But I can walk!" Artem protested.

"I know you can. But it'll make *me* feel useful."

"He's right," Kayce agreed. "Until you're feeling stronger—and until we've gotten you something to eat—let Jack carry you."

"But—"

"Don't argue!" Kayce ordered, leveling a stern finger at him. "With those goons breathing down our necks, we don't wanna risk having you conk out on us." And then in a softer tone: "So let him carry you. Just until we're sure you're strong enough to solo."

Artem was still reluctant, but Jack helped him to his feet and onto a rock, and then Artem climbed onto Jack's back.

"Okay," Jack said, hoisting the boy a little higher and slipping his arms beneath the kid's legs. "You don't weigh a lot—"

"No, there's not a lot of me, but it's all loveable."

If Jack had been taking a drink of something, he would have snorted it out both sides of his nose. He started laughing so hard he had to put the boy back down for a moment to collect himself.

"Jeez, kid ... don't *do* that to me!"

Artem looked pleased at the reaction he'd caused—he was smiling weakly through his pale face—and even Kayce was grinning.

Jack wiped his eyes, then said, "All right, let's try that again, but without the jokes."

Artem crawled back onto Jack's back and Kayce asked, "Okay, everyone ready?"

Jack: "Yup."

Artem: "Ten-four."

Kayce: "What?"

Artem: "Ten-four. Roger. Affirmative. I'm trying to talk like a commando."

Kayce (with a scowl): "Let's make tracks."

Kayce led the way into the forest, striking off smartly, as if she had a destination in mind. Her pace was steady and deliberate, but slow enough that Jack realized she was being considerate of him with his bulky cargo.

"Where are we going?" Jack asked.

Kayce spoke over her shoulder without taking her eyes from the trees ahead. "Right now, we're just putting some distance between us and the goon squad."

Jack paused and hopped, boosting Artem a few inches higher on his back. "But if they can track us ..."

"We still have an advantage. For one thing, I know the best way through the forest." She gestured. "And I also happen to know there's a swamp ahead ... a swamp that's damn easy to get bogged down in if you don't know your way around."

She took a moment to look as a pack of small two-legged lizards scampered through the brush ahead. She made a sweeping motion with her arm.

"We're going to head straight for the swamp, and then circle around. If they're homing in on your implant, the guys with the guns will follow a straight line toward us. Simple geometry. They'll end up smack in the middle of the swamp while we're scampering around the far side, free and clear."

She nodded confidently.

"They'll be knee deep in mud and muck and slime and grime and six-inch, blood-sucking leeches before they even know they're lost. It'll be hours before they get back out and find their way around."

"Smart," Jack said, impressed with her strategy.

"Told you," Artem whispered in Jack's ear. "That's how—"

A distant earsplitting bellow shook the woods behind them, setting off a racket of terrified shrieks and screeches as startled animals reacted to some unseen danger. The next second there was a single gunshot—

Bam!

—followed by the rattle of automatic gunfire—

Rattarattaratta!

—and more gunshots—

Bababam! Bam!

—before the unseen battle went completely nuts.

Rattarattaratta!

Bam! Babambam! Bam!

Ratta—

All three teens had turned and were gawking in the direction of the gunfire, even though it was impossible to see anything through the trees.

Kayce: "Sounds like Tag-team Alpha just met the local wildlife."

Jack: "Think the dinosaurs ... *got* ... any of them?"

Kayce: "Probably not."

Jack: "Too bad. But I bet there's not a clean pair of underwear left between them."

Kayce smiled. "Yeah, and it still works in our favor. Your first encounter with a three-ton monster is pretty nerve-wracking, even when you're packing a machine gun. So now that they've had a taste of dinosaurs, they'll slow down. A lot. And they'll be a helluva lot more careful moving through the woods."

"Good," Jack said. He once again bounced Artem higher onto his back and readjusted his grip. "For the first time, I'm rooting for the dinosaurs."

Kayce started again through the trees, Jack following a few steps behind.

"You doin' okay, kiddo?" he asked Artem as he skirted a mound of fresh dinosaur dung: the juicy, steaming pile was already buzzing with bugs and flies. "Feeling any better?"

"So-so. Getting kinda hungry."

"Yeah, me too."

Jack adjusted his grip beneath the boy's legs, then whistled softly. When Kayce turned he lifted his head as a signal to stop.

"Kid's a little hungry," Jack reported when he'd caught up. "Any of those tasty apple/pears around?"

Kayce (glancing around): "Possibly—"

Jack: "Maybe a little roadkill?"

Kayce: "What?"

Jack: "You know, a little raw lizard?"

Kayce: "*Huh?*"

Jack: "Maybe a few grubs, or grasshoppers, or fat juicy worms—"

Artem: "Eeeew ..."

Kayce (finally catching on): "I think I could scare up some slimy dinosaur entrails."

Artem: "Okay, that's it ... I'm not hungry anymore."

Kayce grinned, and Jack congratulated himself for having eased the grimness of their collective mood. Kayce pointed through the trees. "Keep heading in that direction. I'm gonna peel off and try to scare up a few green fruits—that's what we call them—and catch up with you in a couple of minutes."

"Think splitting up's a good idea?" Jack asked, carefully measuring his tone to sound merely inquisitive and not critical.

"Not really," Kayce said. "And no offense, but you still don't know your way around, and your goofy passenger isn't yet well enough to be an effective tour guide. But the reality is that you—with your tracking implant—need to keep putting distance between you and the local gun club. So the only way we're gonna get anything to eat is if I go rogue for a while."

Jack nodded, accepting the explanation. He turned his head to speak to Artem.

"You okay with that, Chuckles?"

"Ten-four, good buddy."

"Okay," Jack told Kayce. "We'll keep going. Just remember that without a girl to slow us down, us guys'll probably be ten miles down the road by the time you come after us."

"Keep it up, funny boy," Kayce warned, "and I'll give you the fruit with the worms."

Jack grinned. He started through the trees, but then abruptly turned and whistled. As soon as Kayce looked he said, "See if you can't round up a buncha low-calorie grubs, will you?"

He hitched Artem back up on his back.

"Kid's getting heavy. I think he could stand to lose a few pounds."

"You're different," Artem said five or six minutes later.

"How so?" Jack asked.

"You didn't freak out nearly as much as people usually do when they get here. And even now you're going out of your way to make us laugh and feel better."

"Yeah, well, just trying to do what I can."

"I'm glad. It helps."

"Good."

"And ... Kayce likes it, too."

"How do you know?"

"Heck, she's been my best friend for like a year now. I know how she is, and I know how she acts around people. You wouldn't know the difference 'cause you haven't been around. But even with all the crap going on, she's not as ... I don't know, *uptight* ... as usual."

"Huh."

"Anyway"—Artem tightened his arms a little around Jack's neck, almost as if giving him a hug—"I'm sorry that you got dumped into this. I'm sorry they ruined your life. But I'm really glad you're here."

Jack wasn't certain how to respond. But he said: "Yeah, I can't say that I'm happy to be here. But ... all things considered, I'm sure glad you were here to save my butt—"

There was a sudden blood-curdling shriek from up ahead, followed by a tremendous roar. Brush and trees popped, cracked, and snapped like an explosion of fireworks as some animal blasted through the woods.

Coming straight for the two boys.

Jack whirled around, searching for a place to go or somewhere to hide—

"No!" Artem commanded, instantly taking charge. He pushed himself from Jack's grip and dropped to the ground. "Don't have time."

He pointed to an enormous, uprooted tree.

"Down there! Beneath the roots!"

Without waiting for a response, the boy hobbled toward the knot of twisted, gnarled roots with Jack hot on his heels. Artem dove beneath the roots and into the hole they'd torn from the ground. Being bigger, Jack struggled to get through the tangled wood, but was spurred by another fierce bellow.

He finally reached Artem, who was holding his fingers to his lips.

Shhhh!

Jack didn't have time to acknowledge the warning. There was a loud *crunch!*—the crack of a snapping tree—and a frantic, bird-like dinosaur came speeding down the trail. The animal was eight or nine feet tall, running on two legs like a huge, featherless ostrich, eyes bulging and yellow foam dripping from the corners of its mouth.

A deafening roar shook the forest, and a larger animal—

Allosaurus!

—blasted through the trees.

The ostrich/lizard screeched with fright as it neared the uprooted tree. It turned to avoid the roots, but the allosaur was suddenly upon it. With a thunderous roar—

Jack clamped his hands over his ears.

—the allosaur pounced upon the fleeing animal.

Jack watched in horror as the predator sank its teeth deep into the terrified animal's shoulder. Blood sprayed into the air, but with a squeal of agony the ostrich-thing turned—tearing itself free of the ravenous jaws—and once again darted for the trees.

The allosaur roared, then swung around in pursuit. As it turned, its powerful tail slammed the roots of the fallen tree and a shower of dirt and small rocks rained upon the two boys. A snapping root cracked Jack over the top of the head, making him yelp.

"*Yeowwww!*"

But the allosaur was too focused on the terrified ostrich-thing to notice. It lunged, slammed its head down, and snapped its terrible jaws around the smaller dinosaur's neck. Jack heard the sickening crunch of bones, and the unfortunate animal went limp.

The allosaur wrenched its head from side to side—violently snapping the dying creature's neck—then lifted its head and bellowed furiously.

Holy freakin'...

The allosaur looked back and forth as it stood over its kill—

Like it's checking to see if anyone saw what it just did!

—then lowered its head and sank its teeth deep into its prey. It shook its head, ripping an enormous chunk of warm flesh from the body. Jack watched in awe as the allosaur raised its head—red, dripping meat hanging from both sides of its jaws—and began to chew.

"Wow..."

Jack heard Artem whisper the word, but was unable to tear his own eyes away from the dinosaur. The allosaur pointed its nose at the sky as it chewed, allowing the red meat and hot dino juices to slide down its throat.

The allosaur finally swallowed the chunk of meat—

I can't believe it swallowed that whole thing!

—then leaned over and sniffed the steaming carcass, as if deciding which portion might be tastiest. The great jaws opened—

Artem suddenly sneezed.

Ker... cheweeee!

The allosaur's head snapped around and the slitted eyes focused on the uprooted tree. Jack shrank back in the hole as Artem struggled to stifle another sneeze. Jack's eyes were locked on the allosaur, but he heard Artem draw in his breath and felt the boy quiver as he tried to hold back—

Ker ... cheweeee!

The boy sneezed like sneezing was an Olympic sport and he was going for the gold.

The allosaur growled ominously, perhaps thinking that its kill was in danger from another predator.

Jack shrank even farther into the hole, pushing Artem back behind him. Artem was trembling—fighting desperately to stifle a third explosive sneeze—kicking his heels into the dirt to force himself farther away from the dinosaur.

The allosaur snarled, then took a step toward the upturned roots.

Thump!

And another one.

Thump!

Artem squirmed beneath the roots, trying to hold in the pent-up sneeze as much as to hide from the approaching dinosaur. Jack used his weight to push the boy back, forcing the kid behind his own body.

The allosaur quickened its pace.

Thump!

Thump!

Thump!

Artem abruptly lost his battle with the building sneeze—

Ker ... cheweeee!

—his shoes kicking into the air from the force of the blast. Jack winced but kept his eyes locked on the glowering allosaur, even as it lowered its head to the ground and bellowed—

Wooooooooooooar!

—the noise so loud and terrifying he nearly lost control of his bladder. He automatically turned his head and wrenched his eyes shut, but then jerked them open again.

The allosaur roared again—

Wooooooooooooar!

—then suddenly attacked the jumbled roots. Displaced dirt, rocks, and broken branches crashed down upon the boys as the dinosaur slammed into the rotting wood. The allosaur bit down on a thick root—shaking its head to rip it free—then bit down in another place. A splash of hot dinosaur slobber hit Jack in the face, and he smelled the animal's sour, stinking breath.

Felt gobs of foul, sticky dinosaur drool dripping from the terrible jaws.

Artem was screaming—right in Jack's ear—

"Aaaaaiiigh!"

—kicking and flailing as roots snapped and popped like gunshots beneath the allosaur's weight, the wood bending and breaking and battering the boys again and again. A snapping branch abruptly cracked Jack across the top of the head, and a burst of white light flashed behind his eyes. He swooned, teetering on the brink of consciousness, and might have blacked out—he was too dazed to know for sure—but then the allosaur bellowed—practically in his face—snapping him back to reality.

He could hear Artem sobbing in terror behind him. He looked up—

The allosaur's jaws opened wide, ready to snap down on a gnarled root—the only thing between Jack and the glistening yellow teeth—but at the last instant the animal stopped. And snapped to attention. It turned and looked off to the side.

Jack gasped in horror, and confusion, struggling to understand what was happening.

The dinosaur stood perfectly still—completely ignoring the boys beneath the tree—its head high as it stared into the trees. It growled in warning. And it was several beats before Jack realized the attack was over, or at least paused. He peered through the roots—desperate to see what was happening—then sucked in a deep breath.

Artem was still sobbing softly behind him. Jack looked back, then turned to wrap an arm around the boy's shoulders and pulled him close.

"You okay?" he whispered.

Artem nodded, then reached up and wiped his eyes with his shirt sleeves.

"You sure?" Jack asked.

"Y-yeah."

Jack squeezed the boy, then peered again through the gnarled roots toward the allosaur. The dinosaur was still growling—like a dog warning another animal away from its dinner bowl—as it peered into the woods.

Artem managed a sob at the same time as a soft sneeze—

Huhh-chewiiiiee!

—and Jack caught his breath, but this time—if it heard him—the dinosaur didn't react.

Artem sucked in a breath of air. "W-what's h-happening?"

"Not sure," Jack whispered back. He squeezed the boy's shoulder. "But we're okay for a minute, so hang in there."

Artem wiped his eyes again, then wiggled beneath Jack's weight, seeking a more comfortable position. Jack too moved his butt a little, taking advantage of the break to find a less awkward way to sit.

The allosaur made a sound like a bark, then took a step forward—away from the boys—lowered its head and bellowed. The roar was loud and terrifying, but not quite so startling as when it was mere inches away and directed at the boys.

There was another bellow, but ... from another animal.

Something's coming, Jack realized with a start. *It's either heard all the commotion or ... or ... or it can smell that dead ostrich-thing.*

And is coming for dinner ...

He almost forgot his own predicament as he watched. The dinosaur was laser-focused on the woods, able to hear or smell or even see the approaching animal. It took a quick step toward the trees—

Thump!

—then lowered its head and bellowed angrily.

Warning the other animal away.

It stomped back toward its kill, shaking the ground with every heavy step as it positioned itself between the bloody carcass and the approaching animal.

Jack finally tore his eyes away from the escalating drama to scan the twisted roots, searching for a way to escape. The trunk of the uprooted tree was behind him, lying flush with the ground. The roots were thickest there, which had protected the boys earlier but blocked any chance of escape in that direction.

The only way out is the same way we came in ... straight toward the dinosaur ...

Artem had finally calmed down some: he was still sniffling but no longer sobbing.

"You okay?" Jack whispered.

"Yeah. I t-think so." And after running a sleeve beneath his nose: "What're we gonna do?"

"Not sure, but ... something's coming. If we sit tight, the allosaur might leave to chase it away. With any luck it'll forget about us." He turned to the boy. "That okay with you?"

"Do we have another choice?"

Jack thought for a moment. "How 'bout this: you crawl out through the roots, sneak up behind the dinosaur, and give it a good hard kick in the butt. While you're doing that, I'll run screaming into the trees."

Artem pursed his lips as if actually considering the plan. "How 'bout *you* go out and kick it while *I* run screaming into the trees?"

"Ummmm. *Or* ... we can sit tight and hope it finds something more exciting to terrify."

"Okaaaay," Artem whispered glumly, as if disappointed. "You just *have* to take the fun out of everything!"

Despite the circumstances, Jack managed a grin. He knew he'd helped ease Artem's nerves, not to mention his own.

Jeez, he thought as he turned and peered toward the agitated dinosaur. *Monster big and mad enough to swallow us whole, and we're cracking jokes about it.*

He knew it was absurd, but also realized a person could only endure so much terror before becoming numb to it.

And then all the pent-up emotion gets channeled in a different direction.

He realized it had been nearly a minute now since the allosaur last moved—or roared or growled—and he began to wonder if the danger had passed. He thought that if—

There was a crack from the forest—the sound of rotting wood crunching beneath heavy feet—and Jack felt the ground tremble beneath him. The allosaur instantly dropped its head and bellowed another warning. And then again. It took a step toward the trees, shook its head angrily, and then bellowed yet again.

Even before the roars died away, the still-unseen challenger bellowed in reply. Jack felt his heart speeding up—heard Artem breathing fast and hard—knowing a savage confrontation was imminent. He watched the trees spellbound—

The allosaur roared in fury, and a moment later the trees shook and an allosaur with a gray, ashen face marched from the timber. Larger than the first allosaur, Gray Face roared boldly, trying to frighten the smaller animal away.

But the younger allosaur wasn't intimidated. And it wasn't about to give up its hard-won meal without a fight. It bellowed insolently, then sprang toward its larger adversary.

Gray Face roared loudly and turned into the charge. The two enormous predators collided with startling power and the next instant were a savage, bellowing flurry of flashing—slashing—teeth, claws, and jaws.

"Ay, yi, yi," Jack whispered, awestruck.

The dinosaurs fought furiously. As one attacked with its lethal claws, the other slashed sharp yellow teeth down its rival's flank. Within seconds, both animals were striped with rows of jagged, bloody gashes. Being bigger, Gray Face used its superior weight to shove and muscle its smaller adversary. And though the younger allosaur was lighter, it was also quicker, faster, and more agile.

Once, as Gray Face snapped at the smaller animal's neck, the younger dinosaur ducked, swung around, and bit deep into the other's shoulder. It instantly wrenched its head from side to side, tearing open a grisly wound.

Gray Face bellowed in rage and agony, then whirled around with such power it lifted the smaller animal off its feet, forcing it to release its hold. Without a pause, the larger dinosaur drove forward and dragged the teeth of its upper jaw down the other animal's hip, carving out deep, gruesome, parallel gashes that spurted streams of hot blood.

"Holy hell," Artem whispered, probably without realizing he was even speaking.

Jack just nodded. He knew the smaller dinosaur was outmatched. And outmuscled. But he was equally sure the young animal had no concept of this. And wasn't about to give up.

Gray Face suddenly lunged, but stumbled and went to its knees. The smaller dinosaur saw the opening and attacked, plowing into the larger animal like a locomotive. Both animals slammed to the ground and instantly became a tumbling, flailing, snapping, clawing frenzy of teeth, claws, blood, and gore.

The smaller dinosaur tried to stand, but was dragged back to the dirt and both animals rolled into the snarled roots of the upturned tree. Branches crunched and crackled and splintered into a thousand pieces beneath their weight. Dirt, rocks, and other debris rained upon the two boys, who scrunched tightly together, arms wrapped tightly around one another, fully expecting to be crushed any second.

One of the dinosaurs lurched to its feet—Jack couldn't tell which—but the other immediately smashed into it and both creatures once again crashed into the tangled roots, right above the boys. Artem screamed in terror, though his voice was barely audible over the roars and bellows of the battling allosaurs.

There was another sudden crunch and a pop, and a breaking limb slammed onto Jack's left knee. He screamed—

"*Aaaaaiiigh!*"

—the pain so excruciating he was certain the impact shattered his kneecap. He clutched the knee, fighting nausea so intense he lost track of Artem, and the dinosaurs, and everything but the blinding, excruciating, stomach-churning need to hurl.

He'd automatically clenched his eyes and rolled onto his side. And for several seconds knew nothing ... nothing but unbearable, overwhelming agony.

He wasn't sure how long it lasted, but it was a while.

A long while.

But then he moved his foot ... and realized his knee wasn't broken.

Realized Artem was no longer screaming in his ear.

And that he could no longer hear the dinosaurs.

He sucked in a great lungful of air. Fought back a dizzying wave of nausea.

Finally opened his eyes.

He could feel Artem behind him—could actually feel the kid's heart thumping.

It's going a mile a minute!

But ...

Where's the dinosaurs?

He couldn't see anything. Couldn't hear anything but the buzz of insects and the unrelated roars of distant animals. He hesitated, then craned his head to peer between the roots.

There's the bloody ostrich-thing ... or at least what's left of it.

He looked left, then right, then left again. And heard Artem's voice.

"A-are they ... g-g-*gone*?"

Jack looked back. "I'm ... not sure. But I don't see anything."

There was an eager squeal and Artem sucked in his breath, but then relaxed as a pair of tiny scavengers crept from the underbrush, headed for the remains of the ostrich-thing.

While the big predators are off ... well, doing whatever they're doing.

Jack rubbed his throbbing knee as he eyed the tiny dinosaurs, then scanned the woods for signs of danger. He didn't see anything, but several more small, chittering foragers suddenly scampered from the brush for a go at the bloody ostrich-thing.

Well, they *don't seem worried about anything.*

He rubbed his aching knee for another moment and felt his muscles relax, which felt unbelievably good after having been tight as knots for the past several minutes.

Man, there's never a quiet moment around here!

He closed his eyes and inhaled as the stress and tension and terror drained away like old dishwater.

Squeak!

He opened his eyes and instantly felt his muscles tighten again.

Artem sensed the change.

"What's wrong?" the boy whispered.

"I'm not sure," Jack whispered back. He pointed with his chin. "But look ... all the little guys have stopped eating. They're all staring into the trees."

"Crap," Artem cussed. He scrunched deeper into the hole. "Here we go again ..."

"No, wait," Jack said, peering intently through the roots. "Something's wrong."

"What are you talking about?"

"I don't ... I mean, I'm not, um, sure. But something's obviously coming. I can't hear anything, but something's got those things worried."

"Might not be anything big. Bigger than the little guys"—Artem gestured—"but not so big that it's knocking down every tree in the forest."

"You might be right, so ... let's just hang tight for a minute. See what's going on before we make a move."

"Okay."

For nearly a minute, nothing happened. A couple of the scavengers nibbled tentatively at the ostrich, but kept their eyes on the trees as they chewed. Jack realized after a moment that he was holding his breath, and he exhaled slowly.

Jeez, this is almost scarier than when I know what's coming—

The leaves rustled. Jack saw the brush move, but was unable to see what had caused it.

What the—

The brush moved again, and ...

It's ... a guy! A man! A man wearing camouflage! Sneaking around like some sort of nervous ninja!

The man was obviously one of the hunters Kayce had spotted, creeping through the trees and carrying some sort of rifle across his chest. His camouflaged uniform blended in so well with the prehistoric forest that when he stopped to peer through the trees, Jack actually lost sight of him.

Holy crap ... even his face *is painted.*

The man continued forward, only taking a step or two at a time before stopping to survey the woods. Without actually looking at the ground, he was mindful of where he placed his boots, careful not to step on anything that might snap, or crunch, and give him away.

Jack slowly turned his head so he could whisper into Artem's ear.

"Don't ... move ... a muscle."

"I know. I see him."

The hunter continued creeping slowly, and steadily, toward them, his rifle up and ready to fire.

But how'd he get here so fast? We were supposed to have a longer head start!

Jack tried to see past him—looking for the others—but the camouflaged hunter seemed to be alone.

Others get killed when they were attacked? Or are they going in different directions? Maybe trying to surround us?

Jack didn't think that splitting up was such a smart idea, especially in a place like this. But the hunters apparently believed differently.

The man came to the edge of the clearing and spotted the ragged remains of the bloody ostrich-thing. He stopped and studied the carcass, then raised his eyes and carefully scanned the trees.

Jack hadn't seen them leave, but realized all the little scavengers had vanished back into the brush. It seemed—

The man suddenly spoke.

Speaking so softly that Jack barely heard the words.

"... just a couple critters fighting over dinner. No sign of the kid."

Jack listened carefully, but didn't hear a reply. But then the man spoke again as he looked about.

"No, no sign of anybody ... just some big, half-eaten lizard."

He's talking into a microphone, Jack realized, spotting a thin wire curving around the man's cheek.

"So how close am I?"

There was a pause, and then: "Then something's wrong, 'cause there's no one here."

Another pause, and then the man raised his voice a notch, apparently irritated.

"Then maybe you ought to come and look for yourself! I tell you, there's no one here, but ... well, there's a helluva lot of blood splashed around. And a helluva lot of guts and gore strewn through the grass ... more than could have come from a single animal. Good chance one of the dinosaur's got him."

He tracked me here, Jack realized as his stomach dropped. *He hasn't got a tracking device, so someone else is guiding him.*

His shoulder began to itch where the tracking implant was embedded, suddenly wishing he could rip it from his body.

Knowing these guys used it to follow me?

Hoping to kill me?

He felt chills crawling up the back of his neck.

No wonder Kayce and Artem cut theirs out!

Goosebumps erupted up and down his arms as he realized how lucky he was that the guy wasn't carrying a tracking device.

If he was, I'd be dead already!

And just that fast he resolved that no matter how scary it was—no matter how painful it might be—he was going to have Kayce cut the thing out of him.

The camouflaged hunter swore under his breath, then snarled into his microphone.

"He's not *here*, I tell ya. And all the blood and guts and gore and little face-eating scavengers running around tell me the kid's *dead*!" Pause. "So how long's it been since he's moved? ... That long? See? He's not moving 'cause he's *dead*! He's *gone*, I tell ya!"

There was an awkward pause: Jack could see the man pulling faces as he listened to whomever was speaking to him. But after a pause:

"Roger that. I'll circle around, see if I can't pick up his trail again." Pause. "Yeah, yeah, whatever."

The man swore, then once again took his rifle in both hands and surveyed the clearing. He glanced toward the upturned tree and for a long, terrifying moment seemed to be studying the tangled roots. Jack's heart pounded as he wondered if the man had spotted them—or if he'd come for a closer look—but then the guy turned. He looked up as some animal bellowed in the distance, then crept past the remains of the slaughtered ostrich-thing and back into the trees.

Jack watched for as long as the man was visible, then remained still for another minute.

"Holy shit," Artem finally whispered in a voice so low Jack barely heard him. "I thought we were toast!"

"Me, too," Jack admitted. His eyes were still focused on the trees, his ears alert for the slightest suspicious sound, but he sensed the guy was gone. He reached up and wiped his sleeve across his brow. "Jeez, I thought nothing could be scarier than those freakin' dinosaurs, but ..."

"I know what'cha mean. Couple months ago some guy was chasing me'n Kayce and this kid named Tripp." The boy's voice became even softer. "We were waiting for a stegosaur to get off the trail. Tripp was right beside me, and all of a sudden his head exploded. Guy shot him and his head exploded: it literally *exploded*. Blew his brains right across my face."

Pause.

"I, well, I totally freaked out. I don't really remember, but Kayce said it took a while to snap me out of it. Said I sucked my thumb for a week."

"Judas Priest."

Several seconds passed, and then Artem asked, "What are we gonna do?"

"Don't wanna stay here," Jack said. "Not with that bloody carcass there. Who knows what animals are gonna come wandering by for a snack? Only thing is ..."

"What?"

"Well, the guys with the guns are obviously tracking me. We fooled 'em this time, but the second we start moving they'll know we're still alive and come running." He peered past the roots as a tree creaked in the woods, then said: "One thing's certain."

"What's that?"

"We've gotta cut this tracker thing outta me. And we've gotta do it as soon as we can."

17 More Cutting

The boys waited another couple of minutes, then wiggled and wriggled and slowly extricated themselves from beneath the tangled roots. Several small scavengers had once again crept from the woods to feed upon the fresh ostrich meat, and they quickly scattered amid a chorus of alarmed chirps and cheeps.

"Okay, in about another second those freakin' hunters are gonna know we're moving, so we don't have a lot of time," Jack said. "You feel well enough to hike?"

"I'm not a hundred percent," Artem admitted. "Probably couldn't beat you in a race to the river but"—he nodded firmly—"I'm well enough to get the hell outta here."

"Okay, then. You know where we're going?"

"Pretty sure."

"Okay. You lead the way."

Artem dusted off his clothes, took a quick look around, and then hitched up his pants and headed into the woods, opposite the direction taken by the hunter.

Jack peered carefully through the trees as he followed, wondering how the camouflaged hunters had avoided the swamp.

They must've split up, he reasoned. *Guy in charge might have been following a straight line the way Kayce predicted. But this guy, at least, might have circled around hoping to head us off or something.*

He shook his head at the injustice of it.

Trying to keep away from the frackin' dinosaurs is one thing. But now we've got people *hunting us? With* rifles? *Guys who can track our every move?*

Or at least mine?

He shuddered as he pictured having the tracking implant sliced out of his shoulder. He'd once been to the dentist to have a cavity filled. The dentist claimed the cavity wasn't deep and convinced Jack that perhaps it could be drilled without Novocain.

Jack had agreed—he thought that was better than going the rest of the day with his mouth numb—but the dentist miscalculated. As she drilled, she suddenly touched a raw nerve. And while Jack didn't exactly explode from the chair and out the nearest window, he'd come close. At the time, he was certain it was the worst, most excruciating pain he'd ever experienced.

But what's it gonna feel like having my shoulder carved up like a Thanksgiving turkey?

He shuddered again, but realized the alternative was having guys with rifles stalking him through the forest.

Following him.

Hunting him.

And just knowing they're out there? Tracking my every move? Jeez, knowing they could show up the second I close my eyes, I'll never dare go to sleep ...

An allosaur or a torvosaur or something equally terrifying bellowed in the woods.

Judas Priest, he thought miserably. *What's it gonna be next?*

By now, Jack had become so used to the noise of the forest that he barely noticed the chirps, cackles, and calls of busy animals, or even the snorts and moans of large sauropods (none of which he'd yet encountered). And unless they were close, he rarely even looked up at the roar of hunting predators.

But now he was listening more carefully, listening for anything that might betray the presence of an approaching animal.

Or a guy with a rifle.

And now that he and Artem were moving again, he knew that whomever had the tracking device definitely realized he *was* still alive.

And on the move.

And will be coming for me ...

He peered ahead at Artem. The boy was moving briskly, but with a noticeable limp.

"Hey," Jack called softly.

Artem turned his head without actually stopping or taking his eyes from the woods. "What?"

"How's your foot? Doing okay?"

"Yeah. Still hurts, but ... I'm okay. You all right?"

"Hanging in there." And then: "Still know where you're going?"

"Think so."

They continued hiking. It was impossible to know for sure, but Jack suspected they were moving faster than their pursuers.

We're not moving all that fast, but the guys behind us still have to be more careful. Have to keep checking their scanner, then searching for trails and avoiding obstacles ... all while watching out for dinosaurs.

The minutes passed, and in time they came to a steep, rocky hillside. Artem instantly started up the slope, Jack right behind him. But it was tough going: Jack's shoes slipped constantly in the soft dirt and he had to grab at the branches of prickly shrubs to pull himself uphill. But once they reached the top, he was rewarded with a fantastic view of the prehistoric forest.

"It's not a *perfect* spot," Artem admitted as he rested on a large rock. "But we've got places to hide up here, and we can watch for anyone coming. Maybe spot somebody trying to sneak up on us."

"And it doesn't look like there's been a lot of large animals up here."

"You're right," Artem said, checking for tracks in the dirt. He was puffing lightly, winded by the pace of their journey.

"Any idea where Kayce might be?" Jack asked.

"None. I mean, who knows where she might have gone while we were busy dodging dinosaurs?" He looked at Jack. "She's okay, though."

"How do you know?"

"I know Kayce, and I know that it takes more than a buncha big teeth to slow her down. She's okay."

Jack looked out over the forest. The woods below were filled with dinosaurs, obviously. But that wasn't why his veins still felt like they were filled with ice water.

There're people out there, too. Guys tracking my every move.

He couldn't shake the image of some kid's head ... exploding.

Like a melon!

He felt an itch in the middle of his back—right between his shoulder blades—as if some guy's rifle scope was pointed right there. He couldn't help casting a quick look over his shoulder, just to be sure no one was actually there. And he was certain that every creep, creak, and crack in the woods was a man with a gun.

Coming for me.

Coming to kill *me!*

His stomach churned like a bucket of frogs, but he once again pictured some kid's exploding—*exploding!*—and he suddenly turned to Artem. "You have a knife?"

Artem nodded casually. "Uh-huh."

"I want you to cut this implant outta my shoulder."

Artem's eyes widened in surprise. "W-what?"

"You heard me. I want you to cut this damn implant outta my shoulder. Like right now. Before those freaks with the guns track us down again."

Artem leaned away, shaking his head. "Um, ah, I don't think so ..."

"Look, I don't wanna do it either," Jack insisted. "Believe me. But we don't have a choice."

He flicked a hand out over the forest.

"As long as I'm packing this thing, those guys're gonna find me sure as hell. So we've gotta get rid of it."

"N-no ..."

"What's the problem?" Jack asked. "You had yours cut out. And you sliced out Kayce's."

"Yeah, but that was different."

"How so?"

"Um ... well, *Kayce* was there. You know, to talk me through it."

"Yeah, I get that. But Kayce isn't here, is she? And as long as I'm carrying this damn thing, we're both in danger." He tried a different tack. "Let me see your knife."

The boy reached into a pocket and fished out a small multiblade pocketknife, similar to what any well-prepared Boy Scout might carry.

It's not nearly as scary as that squid-sticker of Kayce's, Jack thought as he took it. He unfolded the blades and tested them with a finger. *But it's not very sharp ...*

As Artem watched, he searched the ground until he found a flat stone with a rough surface. Then he sat back on a rock, spit on the stone, and ran one of the knife blades over the surface a dozen times or so.

He tested the blade again, pleased to discover that it felt sharper.

Okay, then ...

He worked the blade for several more minutes, honing the steel until the point was needle sharp and the cutting edge fine as a razor.

Or at least as sharp as I'm gonna get it.

His heart was pounding and his stomach bubbling, but he unbuttoned his shirt and removed it.

"Okay," he said, handing Artem the knife. He sat on a large rock. "Let's do this ... before I chicken out."

"I—I can't," Artem whispered. His hands were shaking as he held up his hands to refuse the knife.

"Come on," Jack insisted. "We don't have time to argue. Those guys in camouflage might show up any minute. You don't do this and ten minutes from now we might both be dead."

Artem hesitated—his hands still shaking—but he reluctantly took the knife. Then stood and stepped behind Jack.

"Just like you did with Kayce," Jack said. He measured his tone to sound supportive, the way he imagined Kayce might. "And don't worry about me. I'll be fine."

Artem was breathing fast and hard, but finally realized that Jack was right. And as horrible as the task was, that it had to be done. He held the knife—

"Wait," the boy said suddenly. He stepped away, looked around, and picked up a stick about an inch thick. He broke it in half and gave it to Jack. "Bite down on this. It'll help."

Jack did as he was told, closing his eyes and clenching his fists.

Come on, he thought, tensing up like he was expecting a kick to the head. *Come on come on come on ...*

Artem once again stepped behind him, putting his left hand on Jack's shoulder to steady himself. Jack's heart was hammering harder than ever—

Artem fingered the lump on Jack's shoulder, hesitated, then suddenly plunged the blade into the skin. Jack sank his teeth deep into the stick, clenching his fists so tightly his fingernails dug into his palms. Tears poured from his eyes and ran down his cheeks. He remembered watching Kayce drilling into Artem's foot with her needle and knew Artem was doing the same thing to his shoulder, driving the steel blade deeper and deeper—

The point of the blade touched a nerve and lightning bolts of agony seared through Jack's shoulder like hot electricity. Despite the stick in his mouth he screamed, and jerked, and felt his stomach lurch ... knew he was on the verge of passing out.

But now that he was committed, Artem wasn't stopping. He plunged the knife deeper into Jack's flesh, twisted the blade, and then pushed down, using the blade as a lever—

Jack bit deep into Artem's stick as something popped.

And finally felt Artem remove the knife.

Jack slumped on the rock with his eyes closed, breathing so fast and hard he was almost panting. He tried to spit the stick from his mouth, but his teeth were embedded in the wood and he had to use his hands to pluck it from his mouth.

He sucked in a deep, lung-filling breath and then finally cracked an eye.

Artem was sitting on a log a few feet away. He'd dropped the bloody knife and was hunched over his knees, crying softly.

It took Jack a couple of minutes to collect himself, but then he twisted his head to try for a look at his mangled shoulder. He couldn't see anything but a mass of blood that made his brain swim. He clamped his shirt over the ragged wound to stop the bleeding, then closed his eyes—gulped down a shot of air—and struggled to his feet. His head was woozy and he nearly stumbled, but he tried again, managed a couple of steps, and then staggered over to Artem. He touched the boy's shoulder with his good hand.

"Hey," he said. "You okay?"

Artem nodded without looking up.

Jack picked up the knife, wiped the blood off on his pants, folded the blade back into the handle, and handed it back.

"Thanks," he said sincerely. And then: "Where is it?"

Artem looked up, wiped his eyes, then glanced around and pointed. "I think it's over there."

Jack walked through the grass, searched around for a moment, then picked up a silver disk about the size of a dime. He studied it in revulsion. For a moment he thought about planting it in a piece of raw meat on the chance some dinosaur might swallow it and lead the hunters on a wild goose chase ... but decided against it.

Don't know when or where I might find a chunk of meat, and in the meantime they'll still be following me.

He looked around, then threw the disk as far as he could off the cliff and into the jungle below. He was weak and shaky from his experience—and pretty unsteady on his feet—but he tottered back to Artem and helped the boy up.

"Let's go," he suggested. "Get as far away from that damn thing as we can before those hunters show up."

Artem nodded, though he was even shakier than Jack.

"Hey," Jack said. He waited until the boy looked up and met his eyes, then pulled him into a snug, brotherly hug. "Thanks, man. For everything."

And then, whispering in his friend's ear:

"You might have just saved both our lives."

The boys hiked glumly through the woods, rattled by their unsettling experience but still alert for wandering predators. Jack noticed that Artem was no longer limping—

Like he's suddenly got more serious things on his mind than a sore foot ...

—and realized how deeply the kid had been shaken.

Man, I thought I was the one being traumatized. But it was almost as bad for him ...

He felt a twinge of guilt, belatedly realizing the pressure he'd put on the poor kid, then blinked, reminding himself that he couldn't afford to become distracted.

Yeah, the second I quit paying attention, some monster's gonna explode from the brush and gobble me up—

"Dammit!"

Artem turned around. "Huh?"

"It's nothing," Jack said in disgust. "I'm just having a hard time keeping focused."

He waved a hand at the forest.

"It's all kinda getting to me, y'know?"

Artem nodded. "Yeah. Been there and done that. Like, twenty-four/seven."

"Do you ever get over it? Or get used to it?"

"No. Not yet anyway." And then: "You wanna take a break?"

Jack sucked air in through his teeth, then looked back over his bloody shoulder, as if he might spot some guy with a gun sneaking up behind them. His shoulder had stopped bleeding, and he was wearing his shirt again, even though it was stained heavily with blood.

"No. I mean, I feel like crap and I'm hungry as hell. But I won't feel good until we've put a little more distance between us and those freakin' thugs."

He turned back to Artem.

"Are you worried about Kayce?"

The boy shrugged. "I am ... but I'm not."

Jack nodded wanly. "Yeah, I get that."

"Kayce's good. Anything can happen out here, but Kayce has a way of getting through things."

"Uh-huh ... I know people like that."

"Anyway, let's keep going. And I'll keep an eye out for something to eat." He glanced back the way they'd come. "We should've carved a couple of steaks off that bird-thing the allosaur killed."

Jack faked a shudder. "I don't think I'm quite that hungry. Getting close, but I'm still not ready for dinosaur sushi."

"You'll change your mind," Artem promised, and Jack felt a chill as he realized the kid wasn't joking: he was stating a fact.

"How's your foot?"

Artem looked down. "It hurts. But only when I think about it—"

There was a soft whistle, like from a small bird or animal, and both boys looked up.

"Kayce," Artem whispered. He glanced around for a moment before the girl stepped from the brush ahead.

Without another word he rushed forward and wrapped her up in an enthusiastic bear hug.

"Hey, kiddo," she said affectionately, returning the hug. "You feeling better?"

"Yeah! Lots!"

"Well, good!" She glanced down at the kid's foot. "You sure gave us a scare."

"I know." And then: "How'd you find us?"

"Wasn't hard," she replied, tossing Jack an apple/pear. "You move through the woods like an Indian, but the new kid makes more noise than a high school marching band."

Jack grinned as he bit into the juicy fruit: he knew she was teasing, both for his benefit as well as Artem's.

She handed the younger boy a couple of fruits, then noticed Jack's bloody shirt.

"Oh, crap," she said, guessing what the boys had done. She walked over and lifted the collar of Jack's shirt for a closer look. "I can't believe you did that."

"Didn't have any choice," Jack said, munching on his apple. "Some hunter walked right up on us. Didn't spot us, obviously. But if he'd actually been the one holding the tracking device, he'd have nailed us."

He shook his head savagely.

"I didn't want to go through that again."

She peered at the torn flesh from several angles, then turned back to Artem. "You did this?"

"Didn't want to," the boy admitted. He'd crunched down his first apple and was just biting into the second. "Jack sorta made me."

"Huh." And then to Jack: "Make fist"—and after he'd done that—"now rotate your arm like you're throwing a ball."

Jack did as he was told, and then Kayce felt the temperature of his palms, and fingers. She finished by pressing on his fingernails and watching as the blood rushed back afterward.

"Well, as far as I can tell, you didn't suffer any permanent damage. That's good work."

She gave the crusting wound another careful inspection, then replaced the collar and thumped Jack on the back. "I have to admit that I'm impressed ... with both of you." And to Jack: "Hurt much?"

"About like having my spleen ripped out. But I feel ten tons lighter just knowing the thing's gone."

"Yup." She tipped her head toward Artem. "We both know how you feel."

The boys quickly filled her in on the rest of their adventure.

"The only thing I don't get," Jack concluded, "is how that lone hunter found us so quickly. I mean, I thought they'd be up to their necks in gooey swamp mud for a while."

"They should have been," Kayce agreed. "But they must have split up. I thought they'd stick together ... I mean, that would have been the smart thing to do. But they might have gone different directions to cut us off ... probably didn't know they were outguessing us."

"Doesn't really matter now," Jack said. "But he came within a whisker of nailing us."

"I know. Well, now that they can't track us, we should be able to stay away from them. I'm just guessing, but if they're like the others they'll have short expiration dates. All we have to do is keep away from them for another day or two and we'll be okay."

"So what now?"

Kayce glanced into the woods ahead, turned for a look behind, pondered for a moment, then seemed to make a decision.

"How 'bout this?" she asked, speaking to both Jack and Artem. "You two keep going. Get a little more distance between yourselves and the Deadly Duo—"

Artem: "Or the Terrible Threesome."

"Right. In the meantime, I'll circle back a little and try to get a feeling for where they are and what they're doing."

And with a meaningful look at Jack: "Even if they can no longer track you, it'd be nice to know exactly where they are. You know, just so we don't accidentally wander into them."

Jack nodded. "Sounds good to me, but ... well, I hate to sound critical, but are you okay wandering around alone?"

"Yeah. I'll be fine."

Jack didn't look convinced, and Artem nudged him with an elbow. "When Kayce's out on her own like that?"

"Yeah?"

"You're better off worrying about the animals."

Kayce quietly nodded her agreement.

18 Neckosaurs

After Kayce trotted back into the trees, Jack and Artem started again through the woods. They'd just settled into an easy, comfortable rhythm when Jack heard a series of deep-throated rumbles and grumbles. A moment earlier an unearthly groan filled the air like the growl of distant thunder.

Artem grinned at Jack, crooked a finger—

Follow me!

—and crept off the trail and into the brush. Jack followed curiously. After a few feet the trees began to thin and he caught a glimpse of daylight ahead. The next minute they came to the edge of a sweeping prairie, and Artem knelt beside a tall tree.

He pointed.

"Check it out."

Jack was already looking, his mouth open.

A herd of giant dinosaurs were grazing in the grass, mere feet from the edge of the trees. The animals were sauropods—

massive long-necked, long-tailed, four-legged dinosaurs—but were different from any he'd ever seen pictures of.

The animals were absolutely enormous—

They've gotta be more than a hundred feet long!

—but unlike brontosaurs or brachiosaurs or any of the other large dinosaurs he was familiar with, these animals had absurdly long necks ... so long they were nearly as long as their tail and body combined.

"Holy *f-frick*," Jack whispered in awe. "W-what ... what in the heck *are* they?"

"Don't really know," Artem whispered back. "Might be called mamenchisaurs, but we call 'em neckosaurs—"

"I can see why ..."

"—and I've always thought of them as vacuum cleaners."

"Huh?"

Artem pointed to an especially large animal. "Look at the way it's eating. You'd think they'd use those necks to rip off the tops of trees, but they don't really do that."

Jack instantly got it. The dinosaur's head was low to the ground, brushing back and forth over the grass like a fifty-foot vacuum attachment sweeping the floor.

He shook his head incredulously.

"Man, I've never seen anything like them."

"I know, right? I knew you'd want to take a look."

"Yeah, absolutely. Um, they're not, ah ... *dangerous* ... are they?"

"Depends on what you mean."

"How so?"

"Well, they're not gonna take a bite outta your butt, if that's what you're worried about. But if you happen to be in the way when they're in a hurry to get somewhere, they'll squash you flatter'n a pancake."

"Jeez, I—"

There was a crackle of brush and Artem and Jack whipped around, ready to run for their lives. But it was Kayce, bursting from the foliage with her face red and sweaty from running.

"Holy frackin' puke stains," she gasped, chuffing for breath. "What the hell are you *doing* over here? You're *supposed* to be heading for the hills."

"I just wanted to show Jack the neckosaurs ..."

Kayce glanced onto the plain, then shook her head in such a way that Jack knew she was thinking, *Boys!* She gulped down a lungful of air.

"We've ... got ... a problem," she said, spitting the words out between gasps.

"What is it?" Jack asked.

"The Rotten Wranglers have gotten back together again— all three of them—and"—*chuff!*—"they're coming this way. They're"—*wheeze!*— "only about ten minutes behind me."

Jack's stomach dropped, and he peered automatically into the trees, as if he might actually spot one of the armed, camouflaged commandos.

"H-holy h-hell," Artem whispered, rattled by the news. He was clearly frightened.

"I know," Kayce agreed. She arched her back to stretch her muscles, sucked in an enormous lungful of air, held it, and then let it whoosh back out again. Jack knew she must have been running flat out for several minutes.

"B-but how did they f-find us?"

"I don't know. But—wait"—and speaking to Artem—"what did you do with Jack's implant? After you cut it out of him?"

"Jack chucked it off the cliff."

Kayce scrunched her nose, then shook her head as she turned to Jack. "With your implant gone, they shouldn't be able to follow you. It doesn't make sense. Maybe they just headed for the last place they got a reading and stumbled onto your trail. Blind luck."

Jack thought the theory was possible, but unlikely.

"If that's the case," he said, "maybe we could just hide out somewhere. Somewhere close. And hope they hike on by."

"Could work," Kayce conceded. "But are you willing to bet your life on a 'maybe'?"

"Not really."

"Neither am I." She glanced around, weighing possibilities, then pointed across the flat. "Let's go that way. Stay just inside the trees and skirt the plain. Get on the far side of those neckosaurs and then cut back through the open to the forest on the other side."

She nodded confidently.

"We do that and we'll be able to tell if they just stumbled onto your trail, or if they're actually tracking you."

She looked from Jack to Artem and back to Jack again, looking for disagreement.

"Sounds good to me," Jack said.

"Me, too," Artem agreed.

She glared at Artem. "Tell me the truth now, kiddo. Do feel well enough to hike?"

"Absolutely."

"You feel okay? Your stomach, your foot?"

"Yes."

"Artem ..."

"*Yes!* Yes ... tell her, Jack! Tell her I can hike."

"He's good," Jack agreed. "Especially if we don't push him too hard."

"And what about you?" Kayce asked Jack. "You've been through a pretty nasty ordeal yourself. Think you can keep up?'

"I wouldn't want to suit up for a game of football, but yeah. I'm fine."

Kayce didn't look convinced, but she nodded.

"Okay, then. Let's make tracks."

They stuck to the trees as they hiked, just skirting the edge of the grassy plain. The neckosaurs made deep, sonorous rumbles as they grazed—

Like content, ninety-ton cows!

—which added a touch of gloom and melancholy to the glum atmosphere. And Jack quickly saw that the neckosaurs weren't the only behemoths on the plain. Through breaks in the trees he caught glimpses of animals whose front shoulders were taller than their hips, which lifted their necks high into the air.

Jack didn't know dinosaurs as well as many kids—he'd never been much of a dino-nut—but he'd seen enough pictures and movies to suspect the animals were brachiosaurs. There were also knots of animals that he *suspected* were stegosaurs, but definitely not the dacentrurus he'd seen the day before.

At least they don't have those goofy fat butts ...

And then he spotted a herd of creatures that—like dacentrurus—*looked* like stegosaurs—

Close enough to be cousins, anyway ...

—but were darker in color and weren't mixing with the stegosaurs. But the biggest difference were four-foot spikes that protruded sideways from their front shoulders. And the spine plates that rose from behind their diamond-shaped heads only reached their shoulders before morphing into parallel rows of sharp, armored spikes.

Ay-yi-yi, Jack thought, picturing a hungry predator trying to take a bite of one of the spiked animals.

Artem saw him eyeing the odd dinosaurs and whispered: "Some kid told us they're kentrosaurs. Wouldn't want to tangle with one, but they're actually pretty tasty."

"You've *eaten* one?"

"We once found a recent kill. And I used to have one of those shoulder spikes: I thought it might make a good weapon, but they're pretty heavy—"

"You two coming?" Kayce called softly from just ahead.

"Yeah, right behind you," Artem responded, picking up his pace.

Kayce waited until the boys caught up, then gave Jack a quick glance. "How's the shoulder?"

"Hurts. But I still feel better knowing the implant's gone."

She nodded knowingly—

Been there and done that!

—then turned to Artem. "And what about you? Still feeling okay? Not getting tired or anything—"

"Kayce!"

"Hey, you were one sick little kid last night, and you haven't had time to really recover. All this hiking can't be doing you any favors."

"Yeah, I know. Sorry. And yeah, there's nothing I'd like more than to take a long nap in the sun. But"—he jerked a thumb over his shoulder—"not while we've got rifle-packing putzes in the neighborhood."

Kayce frowned, then looked at Jack, as if trying to gauge his thoughts.

Jack shrugged. "He *looks* okay." But then to Artem: "But if we start pushing you too hard, let me know! I'll start packing you again."

"*How?* I just cut the crap outta your shoulder!"

"Yeah, well, I'll just pack you on the other side."

Artem looked doubtful, but nodded anyway. "If I get tired, I'll let you know."

Jack, mimicking Kayce's doubtful tone: "Artem ..."

"Yes! Yes, I promise!"

"Okay," Jack reported to Kayce. "I think we're good."

Kayce peered past Jack into the trees for a moment, and Jack asked, "Think they're still coming?"

"I don't know. I don't know how they could possibly see our tracks in all this ground cover, but"—she shook her head—"I've got this creepy feeling. Like a tickle on the back of my neck. Like we're being followed."

"Oh, crap," Artem whispered grimly.

"What?" Jack asked.

Artem gestured. "Those tickles on her neck. She's got like this radar or something. And she doesn't see ghosts. So when she starts getting creepy feelings you've gotta look out, 'cuz they usually mean something."

Jack felt a shiver though he wasn't cold, and he couldn't help taking a quick look back himself.

Kayce studied the trees for another moment—Jack could see the worry lines on her face—then finally seemed to relax, as if she'd come to a decision.

"Well," she said, "let's keep going. Let's get a little farther ahead and then cross to the other side. Then we'll watch to see if anyone follows us across."

By now, Jack had become completely accustomed to the sounds of the noisy forest. As absurd as it seemed, he barely noticed the constant shrieks, screeches, squawks, and squeals of small mammals, birds, and dinosaurs unless he actually took time to listen for them.

Can't believe it's possible to just get used to all this, he thought.

On the other hand, he'd once spent the weekend with a friend who lived near a set of train tracks. At first, Jack jumped every time a train passed, grabbing onto the nearest chair or table as the house shook and rattled. But he quickly adjusted to the noise and tremors and by the end of the weekend barely noticed anymore.

An allosaur or a torvosaur or something equally terrifying roared in the distance, and the herd of spiky kentrosaurs began honking and snorting in alarm.

Jack peered through the trees and onto the plain, thinking it was like a wild animal park ... the kind where tourists could drive around as exotic wild animals calmly went about their business.

Except that these animals are enormous! Just one of those neckosaurs has gotta weigh as much as an entire herd of modern elephants!

It was an incredible thought, and he couldn't help—

He abruptly realized that Kayce and Artem had stopped ahead, and was just able to keep from walking into them.

"What do you think?" Kayce asked, peering through the trees toward the plain. "It's not quite as far across right here. Ready to give it a try?"

"I'm game," Jack said, trying not to sound nervous. "Think we'll be safe?"

"From the animals?" Kayce shrugged. "Around dinosaurs, there's no such thing as 'safe.' If those neckosaurs or brachiosaurs or even those spiky kentrosaurs find some reason to stampede, we'll all be mashed to jelly."

She pointed to a knot of two-legged creatures near the far trees, animals that resembled half-grown allosaurs. The animals were eyeing the grazing stegosaurs and licking their chops.

"And any predators that spot us may or may not come for a look. But the grass is tall enough that if we stay low to the ground—if we get down and crawl—I don't think those jerks with the guns will see us, even if they're looking."

She reached over to swat a six-inch beetle that had just crawled onto Artem's shoulder.

"But we need to get to the other side to see if they're actually tracking us. It's the only way."

"That's true," Jack conceded.

"So let's get going. If they are tracking us somehow, they might be getting closer."

Jack gestured. "Lead on, boss."

The first thing Jack noticed as he crawled through the grass was the incredible amount of ... fertilizer ... spread over the ground. The stuff was everywhere, much of it old and dry and crumbling to dust, but much of it new, juicy, and buzzing with bugs and flies.

The three teenagers were crawling army-style through the yellow grass, traveling single file, weaving their way between herds of calm, grazing animals. At first, Jack tried crawling around the piles of musty, decomposing compost, but eventually gave up—

Stuff's everywhere!

—and simply concentrated on avoiding the moist, really fresh stuff.

There was a herd of kentrosaurs ahead. Kayce was angling toward them, though Jack knew she was on a direct line for the nearest trees and that the animals simply happened to be in the way.

He eyed the plump, spiked dinosaurs.

I wouldn't mind giving those spikosaurs a little more space, though ...

The teens were close enough to the kentrosaurs that he could hear them grunting as they munched on the yellow grass like fat contented pigs—

Four gunshots snapped sharply in the dry air—

Crack!

Crack!

Crack-ack!

—and all three teens instantly looked up and back as the rifle shots echoed through the forest.

Maybe a quarter mile away, Jack thought. *Still back in the trees.*

He waited another moment, then crawled quickly forward to catch up with Kayce.

"Not exactly where I expected them to be," he whispered.

"Me, either," Kayce agreed. "So I've gotta wonder if they're still together, or if they've split up again—"

One of the neckosaurs trumpeted, making a sound like an agitated elephant and was quickly joined by another, and another, and another until the entire herd had joined in, making racket like a hundred-car freight train with rusty wheels. The animals had turned away from the gunfire and were lumbering in the opposite direction. But the lumber quickly turned into a trot—and then into a gallop—and then into a full-out run. And the next instant the entire herd was thundering through the grass.

Directly toward the bewildered teens.

"Oh, *shit!*"

Kayce leaped up, reached down, and jerked Artem to his feet. She shoved him savagely toward the trees, shouted, "*Run!*" then looked to be sure Jack was coming too.

Jack didn't need to be told what to do. He could hear the thunder of heavy pounding feet. Could see the clouds of dust roiling up from the ground. Could feel the earth shaking from the weight of the stampeding dinosaurs.

The brachiosaurs, stegosaurs, kentrosaurs and others were all large bulky animals. But they weren't stupid. And they knew they didn't stand a chance in the path of the startled neckosaurs. As if they were all wired into the same central command, every animal on the plain was suddenly running for its life.

Straight toward Jack, Artem, and Kayce.

"Run!" Kayce shouted back over her shoulder.

"Yeah, no kidding!" Jack shouted back. He was already running flat out—running as hard as he could—trying to keep his balance on the shaking ground.

Up ahead, Artem was rushing through the grass, though he'd picked up his limp again, and was unable to sprint nearly as fast as a twelve-year-old should be able. Kayce was right on the kid's tail, shouting—

"*Come on, kid, go! Go, go, go!*"

—prodding him to run even faster.

There was a loud, agitated snort, and Jack shot a look to his left. The spiked kentrosaurs were thundering toward him in a cloud of churning dust, the sharp shoulder spikes seemingly ten feet long.

Crap oh crap oh crap ...

He lowered his head and pumped his arms as he ran even faster, but a panicked animal abruptly charged into his path. Jack turned to angle behind the spiked dinosaur—

A chuffing kentrosaur stormed into the spot Jack was heading for and he slammed on the brakes, coming to a complete stop. A huffing animal pounded past behind him—

Jack felt the impact of the heavy feet, heard the wind as the animal's lungs heaved in and out.

—another cutting him off from the front. He whipped his head left and right, now entirely cut off from his friends, unable to see Kayce or Artem through the stampeding animals and the boiling clouds of choking, unbreathable dust.

He coughed, struggling to see, then darted ahead as a thundering animal rushed toward him. He staggered through the grass, trying to clear his lungs, then looked up to see a frothing kentrosaur barreling toward him. The four-foot shoulder spike was coming right for his face—

"*Ay-yi—*"

Jack dropped flat, just as the deadly spike flashed overhead—just missing him—the kentrosaur's feet hammering the earth mere inches from his head. He choked on the dust—could barely breathe with all the dirt and grit and dry dung in the air—but knew he had to get up.

Knew he'd be run over and killed if he spent another second on the ground.

He struggled to his feet—ducked as another kentrosaur thundered past—then turned for the trees.

Gotta ... gotta ... gotta get outta here ...

He stumbled toward the woods, coughing and unable to fill his lungs. There was a rift in the ground ahead: a shallow gully or dry stream bed or something. He staggered toward it, collapsing to the bottom just as the first brachiosaurs arrived.

One of the animals trumpeted, blasting the air with an explosion of noise. The ground shook and rocked beneath the massive animals' feet, the dust so thick it was impossible to breathe, impossible to see.

Jack curled up against the side of the rift, knowing it was a useless gesture. Flat heavy feet were slamming the earth all around him, pulverizing the dry ground and crushing everything in their path.

The last of the brachiosaurs finally thundered past, but almost before Jack could draw a breath the enormous neckosaurs arrived: trumpeting, bugling, and blasting the air; hammering the ground and jarring Jack into the air again and again and again.

He struggled to flatten himself against the side of the rift, knowing it would only take a single misplaced foot to crush him beyond recognition. He was coughing, and choking, dizzy from the lack of air. He was so lost in fear, and misery, it didn't register when the last of the dinosaurs pounded past and the shaking ground and sound of thunder finally began to diminish.

He instinctively curled into a ball against the side of the berm.

One of his arms—and then the other—stretched away as something pulled at him. He jerked himself free and once again tried to flatten himself against the dirt.

"Jack, it's me! C'mon ... we've gotta get outta here!"

He heard the words, but they didn't register. His head was swimming, his stomach churning, his limbs shaking, his blood icy with fear. But then he was being dragged through the dirt.

"Ah ... ah ..."

The words didn't quite form. His brain still wasn't quite working—still starved for oxygen—and he instinctively tried to pull his hands free.

There was suddenly a hand on his shoulder, another gently patting his face.

"Jack! Jack, c'mon, now! We've gotta get outta here ..."

A single eyelid finally fluttered open.

A blast of sunlight stung his eye, but he recognized Kayce—Kayce and Artem—hovering over him.

"Wha—wha"—he coughed so violently that his lungs stung, then tried again—"what happened?"

"Gotta get outta here," Kayce repeated.

Jack's brain was only operating at about thirty percent, but this time he didn't resist as his friends pulled him to his feet.

"C'mon, now," Kayce urged. "Let's get into the trees."

Jack felt his arms being draped around Kayce's and Artem's shoulders as the two helped him to stagger along.

"Wha—what happened?" Jack asked again, his brain finally sparking a little better.

"We thought we'd lost you," Artem said as they neared the woods. The boy sneezed, and then sneezed again, a result of all the dust in the dry air. "Didn't think we'd find anything more than a splash of wet red goo in the dirt."

"Ho—ho—hope you weren't ... too ... disappointed ..."

19 The Worst News

By the time they reached the trees, Jack had sucked in enough of the dusty air that he was able to stagger along a bit easier. His muzzy brain cells were once again sparking a little and he glanced around, surprised to see the herd of neckosaurs feeding calmly in the grass a few hundred yards away.

"They didn't go far," Artem said, guessing what Jack was thinking.

"Here," Kayce said. She helped Jack onto a fallen log inside the cover of trees, then held her plastic canteen to his lips. "Don't gulp this ... just swish a little around in your mouth."

Jack did as he was told, rinsing the dust and dirt and dry pulverized dinosaur dung from his mouth before spitting it back out again.

"Okay," Kayce instructed. "Now, take a couple of small sips. But like eaaaaaaasy."

Jack once again did as he was told, the semi-fresh air making him woozy ... like he was emerging from the Novocain-induced fog that followed a bad root canal.

"Holy h-hell," he stammered. "I thought I was dead meat."

"You very nearly were," Kayce said. And in a tender tone: "And Artem's right ... we didn't think there'd be anything left to find."

Jack shook his head. His knees were knocking and his fingers still trembling: lingering effects of the terror of his close call.

"Think you can walk?"

Jack put his hands on his knees to keep them from shaking, not wanting his friends to see how rattled he was. "Yeah ... yeah, I think so. Won't beat you in a race to the nearest Starbucks, but—"

"Kayce?"

Kayce looked up: Artem was peering through the trees toward the plain, motioning with his hand. Kayce patted Jack on the knee, then went to see what the younger boy was looking at.

"Damn," she whispered.

"What is it?" Jack asked. He tried to stand, wanting to take a look himself, but a flash of dizziness buckled his knees and he quickly sat down again.

Kayce gave him a quick glance, then looked back at the plain.

"Hunters," she said. "All three of them."

Artem: "And coming right for us."

Artem shook his head in disbelief.

"But *how*?" he asked. "How're they tracking us?"

"I don't know," Kayce whispered back.

"Did they see us crawling through the grass? Or do they have another way to find us?"

"I don't know ..."

"It was their gunfire that started the stampede," the boy went on. "Was that just coincidence—were they shooting at some predator—or were they *trying* to get us trampled?"

"I don't *know*," Kayce repeated, a little more sharply this time. She peered through the trees for another moment, then turned to Jack. "I hope you're ready to hike," she said. "Cause we've only got a couple of minutes before they get here."

Jack had to force himself to his feet, knowing he had no choice. But after a few minutes of breathing fresher air, he was feeling a little better.

And a lot stronger.

And within a few minutes was stumbling at about half-speed through the woods.

Kayce was leading the way, but she'd insisted that Jack come next, with Artem bringing up the rear.

"Just until we're certain you've recovered," she explained. "Don't want to turn around and find you've collapsed half a mile behind us."

But after several minutes—now feeling about sixty percent normal—

Not ready to tangle with a testy allosaur, but trending in that direction ...

—he dropped back to hike alongside Artem.

"How're you doing?" he asked the younger boy. "Hanging in there?"

"Oh, yeah."

"I mean, dude! You were knocking on heaven's door last night. No one would blame you—"

"I know that song," Artem said, cutting in with the snap of his fingers. " 'Knocking on Heaven's Door.' Bob Dylan, right?"

"How do you know Bob Dylan? He was like *way* before your time."

"Yours too, doofus. And, aah, my folks like oldies ... and besides, Guns N' Roses play a nice cover. How do *you* know him?"

"I've got—had—a guitar, and playing Dylan is pretty much a rule for any serious player—"

"You play guitar? That's awesome!"

"Well, I *used* to. Anyway, you really were teetering right on the edge for a while. So you've still gotta be feeling it a little, right?"

Artem glanced ahead to see if Kayce was listening, then lowered his voice. "I'd pay a hundred dollars for a chance to lie down and sleep for a couple hours, but"—he shrugged—"well, you know." And then, after stepping around a pool of runny green dinosaur excrement—

Jeez, what's that *thing been eating?*

—he asked: "What about you? Little while ago I was carving you up like a slab of roast dinosaur. And then you came within a whisker of being trampled to jelly."

"I've been better. But"—he gestured toward Kayce and spoke in a whisper—"I don't want her to know that."

"I hear you, brother."

Jack pushed Artem ahead, retaking what he'd come to consider "his" place at the end of the line. Though he still wasn't feeling completely better—

Like 7 now, out of 10 ...

—he wasn't going to complain.

Especially since Artem's gotta be in worse shape than I am!

He glanced at Kayce.

No idea what she might be going through, but I know she'd have to be on the verge of death before admitting to being anything less than a hundred percent.

He remembered an old movie—a comedy—in which an inept knight had his arms cut off in battle but insisted, "They're only flesh wounds!"

Yeah, that's Kayce right there.

When the girl finally stopped for a moment, Jack walked up beside her.

"What'cha think?" he asked. "Are we getting away?"

"I don't know, but ... probably not. At least, we're able to hike where we want, as fast as we want. They've got to take their time, have to be a little more careful." She blew out her breath. "Look, I hate to split up again. But I want to go back again, make sure they're really on our trail."

"Things didn't work out so well the last time we did that."

"I know. But we've got to know what's going on."

"What if they're able to track you?"

She shook her head. "They've never been able to before. Well, not since Artem cut that damn implant out of me."

"So you think they're still homing in on me somehow?"

"I don't see how. But something screwy's going on. And we're not gonna be able to relax until we know what it is."

Jack and Artem exchanged glances.

"So, you wanna us to keep going this direction?" Artem asked.

"More or less, yeah. I mean, you don't need to be anal about it, but a straight line will get you farther faster."

"But—"

"Don't worry ... I'll find you again."

"How?" Jack asked.

"She's a kind of jungle woman," Artem stage-whispered. "She could track us over solid rock, in the dark, and with her eyes closed."

Kayce grinned and ruffled the kid's hair. "So, I'll just circle back a little, see if I can't figure out what's going on. See if they're still coming and—you know—how close they are."

She looked at Jack.

"You good with that?"

"I don't like it. But you seem to know what you're doing, so I'm not gonna argue."

"See that?" Artem asked Kayce cheerfully. "He's learning."

Kayce peeled off and vanished into the trees, and Artem led Jack deeper into the forest. The boys had only gone a short distance before Artem turned and darted sideways into the trees.

"Hey!" Jack called after him. "What the hell—"

"Hold on a second," Artem called back over his shoulder.

Jack peered after the boy, then scanned the woods, checking for danger. But a few seconds later Artem marched back from the trees with an armful of apple/pears.

"Just spotted these," he said, handing three to Jack.

"You're my new hero," Jack said. He polished an apple on his shirt and then sank his teeth into the soft fruit. The juice gushed into his mouth and he closed his eyes, savoring the fruity sweetness. "Oh, man, these are *so* good!"

"I know, right?" Artem was snogging down an apple of his own, ignoring the juice dripping down the front of his shirt. Still munching, he nodded back to the trail. "Let's keep going. We can eat while we hike."

The fruit rejuvenated Jack like a stiff shot of adrenalin.

Stuff's better than triple-caffeinated coffee, he thought as he chomped into his second apple. *Things'd be great snacks during halftime at football games.*

He was just polishing off the last apple when there was a whistle and Kayce came trotting up from behind.

"How do you do that?" Jack asked, wiping his mouth with his sleeve.

"Do what?"

"Ghost through the trees. I never hear you coming."

"And you never will," she said with a hint of warning.

Artem: "That's why you never want to get on her bad side."

Kayce: "It's no great trick. Artem can be just as quiet ... when he *wants* to be."

Artem, with a grin: "That's true."

Kayce: "Anyway, you'll figure it out soon enough. If you want to live."

Jack nodded, then tipped his head back down the trail: "So, what'd you learn?"

Kayce became instantly serious. She took a quick glance over her shoulder, then used her nose to point into the woods ahead.

"Let's walk while we talk."

She waited until they were once again marching through the trees, then said: "We're in deep shit."

"How so?" Jack asked.

"They're definitely tracking us. I got close enough to hear them talking, and to see them working some kind of homing device."

"But it didn't pick *you* up, obviously," Jack noted.

"And it's probably not tracking Artem, either."

"Which means it's me."

Kayce shook her head. "Artem, I know this is a stupid question, but when you cut out that implant, are you *sure* you got it?"

"Kayce—"

"Yeah, yeah, I know. It was a stupid question, but I had to ask."

"So what could it be then?" Jack asked nervously. He didn't like the direction the conversation was heading.

"I'm not sure," Kayce said in a tone that suggested she was thinking out loud. "But maybe it's no coincidence that you showed up all alone like you did."

"Why's that?"

"I'm only speculating, but maybe they sent you back as a trap. They knew we'd pick you up, and so they might have wanted to be *sure* they could keep track of you. You know, cuz if they find *you*, they find *us*."

"But we cut out the implant!" Jack protested.

"I've been thinking about that," Kayce continued. "They might have guessed that we would. And might have even counted on it."

"What does *that* mean?"

"I'm still only guessing, but what if they gave you a *second* implant? You know, thinking we'd be too stupid to think of that."

"But where would it be?" Jack asked.

"I'm not sure. But as soon as we get a little farther ahead, let's check your clothes. Make sure you're not packing any surprises."

Jack felt cold—like his veins were full of ice water. He hiked along in silence for nearly a minute, then said: "I'm sorry, guys. I really didn't know."

"No way you could have," Kayce said. "You had no idea what was going on."

"Yeah. But it's just creepy knowing I was ... used." And after another moment: "Worse than that, knowing they were using me to get to you."

"Welcome to our world," Artem said grimly.

Kayce led them briskly through the forest. In time they reached the base of a steep, rocky cliff, and without a second thought Kayce and Artem began climbing. Using small bumps and fissures as hand and footholds, they were nearly a third of the way up the rocks before Kayce noticed that Jack wasn't following.

She looked down. "You coming?"

"Um, yeah. Right behind you."

They've done this before, Jack thought, jamming his hands into tiny fissures and gripping the rocks with his fingertips. Gritting his teeth, he began to climb. There were enough cracks, crags, clefts, and crannies that he was able to make his way.

Okay, it's not the climbing wall at the rec center. But ... it's not that bad ...

They climbed for nearly ten minutes. And as soon as they reached the top, Kayce turned and hiked along the edge of the cliff for several more minutes before she finally stopped.

"Okay, their tracker will bring them in this direction, but the cliff's too steep for anyone to climb right here," she explained. "It'll take them a while to find the way up, so we have a few minutes."

She looked at Jack.

"So let's check out those clothes."

Jack removed his shirt, shoes, and socks, and while Kayce and Artem checked each item for anything that didn't belong, Jack carefully patted down his jeans. It only took a few minutes for everyone to feel confident there was nothing hidden in his clothing.

"Yeah, that would have been a little too easy," Kayce said, giving Jack a worried look.

"So where else could it be?"

Kayce thought for a moment, furrowing her eyebrows so deeply they merged together—then blew out her breath.

"All right, consider this: they knew that we might cut out your implant. You know, if we became desperate enough. So what if they implanted a *second* device ... maybe placing it somewhere we wouldn't think to look?"

"Like where?" Jack asked, becoming nervous.

"If I knew, we wouldn't have to look, would we?" She thought for another moment, then turned to Artem. "Okay, look: I'm going to sit here and watch for company. And while

I'm doing that, I want you to take Jack back in the trees and look for a second implant."

She gave him a stern glare.

"And I want you to look *everywhere*."

"Okay."

"And Artem ... I mean *everywhere*!"

"Yeah, yeah, I get it," Artem muttered in a way that suggested he was as nervous as Jack. And then to Jack: "C'mon, dude ... let's get it over with."

Jack and Artem walked into the brush, and Jack quickly stripped down to his boxers. Then—while Jack ran his hands up and down his arms, legs, and feet—Artem dug nail-bitten fingers into his back and neck and shoulders and hips.

Probing.

Poking.

Pushing.

Probing some more.

But ... nothing.

Artem cleared his throat uncomfortably. "Um, that just leaves ..."

"Yeah, yeah, you don't need to paint a frickin' picture," Jack griped. "But let me do it."

"Um, Kayce said—"

"Yeah, yeah, I know what Kayce said. But let me hang on to my one last shred of dignity."

Artem seemed doubtful, but nodded. "Okay."

Jack waited a moment, then said: "Dude, turn away. You don't have to watch."

Artem huffed and turned his back, and Jack got to work. And found it almost immediately.

A small, insignificant scratch with a barely perceptible lump just beneath.

High on his inner thigh.

Like, *really* high.

Just about as high as it could be without—

He felt a chill of revulsion, and was surprised to realize it wasn't because of the presence of the second implant. But because he remembered what Kayce said about perverts. And knew that whomever had planted the second device had obviously—

"You find something?" Artem asked over his shoulder.

"Um, yeah. I did."

Artem turned for a look, and Jack spun quickly away to pull up his boxers.

"Where is it?"

"Not where I'd like it, that's for sure." Jack pulled on his jeans, zipped up the fly, and then patted his inner thigh. "It's right about here."

Artem's eyes widened. "Holy—"

"I know, tell me 'bout it."

Artem shook his head. "I was thinking we weren't actually gonna find anything. I mean, not ... well, nowhere like that." And after a pause: "What are we gonna do?"

"I don't know. But ... I guess we'd better tell Kayce."

20 Ay-yi-yi

Kayce took the news calmly, and without surprise. Her cool, straightforward manner eased Jack's dread—if only just a little—and increased his respect for her.

"Well, it's got to come out," she said matter-of-factly. "We'll never get any rest until it has."

"But ... how're we gonna do that?" Jack asked. He shuddered, remembering the agony of the last time.

And the nerves in a guy's shoulders are nothing compared to the ones ... well, there.

Kayce pursed her lips as she thought about it. "Couple problems. You already know the obvious one, but there's a major artery down there too. It's called the feminine or femoral or something. I don't know how close it comes to the implant: I'll have to take a look to know—"

Fat chance of that, Jack thought miserably.

"—but if we even *nick* the thing, you're dead. Seriously. You'll bleed out in like four minutes—maybe less—and there's not a damn thing we'll be able to do about it. You'll be dead"—she snapped her fingers—"like that."

"Judas Priest ..."

She nodded, and then looked at Artem. "You carved out the last one. And you cut out mine. Think you're up for the job?"

Artem's eyes were already as wide as pumpkins, and he was shaking like he'd just climbed from an ice-cold pool. Jack could picture those shaking hands holding a razor-sharp knife close to his—

Forget the damn artery! One wrong move and I'll be singing soprano ... permanently!

"I, um ... I don't know," the boy finally said.

He held out his hands, which were quivering like fresh gelatin.

"I mean, *look*!"

"You could use my knife," Kayce offered. "It's sharper than yours and would be easier to cut with—"

Artem was shaking his head before she finished. "If I make a mistake ..."

Kayce nodded kindly and placed a hand on the boy's shoulder, letting him know that she understood. And that she wasn't critical of his feelings.

She turned and looked at Jack.

"What about you, cowboy? Think you can do it yourself?"

Jack exhaled loudly.

It was hard enough letting Artem carve up my shoulder ... felt like that knife was red hot and three-feet long. No way I could go digging around myself ...

"I don't think so."

"Well, then ... that just leaves me."

"Uh, yeah, I don't think so—"

"Oh, grow up," she ordered, waving a hand. "Both of you. All the crap we're gotta put up with and you're worried about your *modesty*—"

An odd expression abruptly crossed her face as if something had just occurred to her.

"Oh," she said slowly. "You're not shy ... you're *embarrassed*, right?" And then in a near whisper: "Is it *teeny*?"

Jack bristled. He set his jaw and clenched his fists. "No, it's not teeny! It's—"

He spotted the gleam in Kayce's eyes—the corners of her mouth were turned up in a barely noticeable grin—and knew she'd punked him. He blew out his breath and tried to relax as Kayce punched him playfully in the shoulder.

"Okay, *there's* that cowboy spirit! So ... are we ready to do this?"

Jack and Artem both nodded sheepishly, then Jack turned to Artem and in a stage whisper said: "Okay, now I know how she's managed to live this long." And then: "And—I might as well admit it—I'm officially more terrified of her than I am of the dinosaurs."

Kayce nodded. "Damn straight."

Kayce took her knife—as well as Artem's—with a sharpening stone to the edge of the cliff to keep an eye out for company as she worked.

"You two build me a small fire back in the trees," she instructed before leaving. "Just big enough to sterilize the knife blades."

Then she'd jabbed a stern finger at Artem.

"And if I see any smoke, kiddo, I'll kick your ass."

"Yes, ma'am," the boy said in a tone that may or may not have contained a note of sarcasm.

"Can't believe I've gotta go through this again," Jack muttered a few minutes later. He fed several sticks into the fire he and Artem had started.

"Yeah, well, Kayce's better at it than I am," Artem said. He snapped a dry stick and poked the pieces into the flames. "Maybe it won't hurt as bad this time."

Jack gave him a sour look. "You don't really believe that, do you?"

Artem shrugged, and then shook his head. "No. Not really." And then: "It's gonna hurt like hell."

Kayce came back after a bit and held the newly sharpened knife blades over the flames, then handed the instruments to Artem.

"Hold these for me, but be sure not to touch the blades." And then to Jack: "Come over here."

She led the way to two large rocks set about three feet apart.

"Okay, cowboy ... take off your pants. And then pull your, you know ... underwear ... off to the side."

She pointed at the ground.

"Then I want you to lie down here, with your feet on the outside of these rocks. That'll keep your legs spread and keep you from kicking me. You know, if it hurts."

"If?"

"Okay, *when*. Either way, let's get to it."

Jack looked back evenly, but didn't move. It took Kayce a moment to figure it out, but then she said: "Seriously? Everything we're about to do and you're worried about me *peeking*? Holy harpin' hooters from Hell!"

She gave him a sour look, but then turned primly away as Jack nervously removed his jeans.

I can't ... believe ... we're doing this.

He sat on his butt, then pulled aside his boxers to expose his thigh. "Okay. I think I'm ready."

His heart was hammering in his chest, his blood cold as ice, his breathing hard and fast. He realized that he wasn't actually scared.

I'm freaked outta my mind!

Kayce turned and inspected the layout and, despite himself, Jack felt a flicker of gratitude for her calm, confident, businesslike manner.

She looked him in the eyes.

"I'm sorry about this," she said in a tone of complete sincerity. "But you know we don't have any choice."

"Yeah. I know."

She took the knives from Artem and placed them on a large leaf she'd plucked from a nearby shrub—careful not to let the blades touch anything—then said to Artem: "Go over to the ledge and keep an eye out. Let me know if you see anyone."

"You sure?"

"Yeah. We don't any surprises while we're working."

Artem turned to go, then came back and knelt beside Jack. "You'll be okay," he promised, patting Jack's good shoulder.

"I know." But then: "Hey, find me stick, will you? To bite on?"

"Oh, yeah. Good idea."

The boy hunted around for a moment, found a stick the size of a ballpark frank, and handed it over. "This work?"

"Perfect. Thanks."

"You bet." And then: "Good luck."

"I checked out my own thighs a minute ago," Kayce said to Jack as Artem trotted into the trees. "And I think I've got that artery located." She ran a finger over the nick on Jack's thigh. "It's close, but the guys who planted this thing didn't want to nick it either and gave us a little room to work. I think we're gonna miss it."

She shrugged.

"Unless, you know, I get nervous or giggle or sneeze or something."

"Great ..."

"Uh-huh."

She reached into a pocket for her glasses and parked them on the end of her nose. Her eyes narrowed as she became more serious, studying Jack's leg. Jack's heart was still hammering—his stomach bubbling like it was full of tadpoles—but her demeanor made him feel—

Well, not confident, exactly. But a little better.

She finally met Jack's eyes.

"Okay, cowboy ... bite down on that stick and let's make magic. If things get bad, clench your fists and bite down hard. But other than that, try to keep as still as you can."

Jack nodded. His eyes were watering though his mouth was dry as sand.

"Ready?"

He nodded again.

"Okay. Here we go ..."

She picked up her wicked, freshly sharpened Kommando Killer, thought for a moment, then switched it for Artem's smaller, more manageable blade. She nodded to herself, then leaned over and placed a hand on Jack's bare leg in the middle of the thigh.

Jack flinched at the unexpected touch, then screwed his eyes shut, clenched his fists, and bit down as hard as he could on the dry stick. For several long, agonizing seconds, nothing happened. He was just about to crack an eye to see what was happening when Kayce sliced the knife across his skin.

Jack jerked, involuntarily arching his back. The knife burned like fire—like white-hot lava splashing over his thigh—but he forced himself to hold as still as he could. He was biting Artem's stick so hard he thought he might bite through it; his fists were clenched so tightly his fingernails drew blood as they dug into his palms.

Kayce sliced even deeper. Artem's knife felt as big as an axe and hot as glowing coals, and Jack bit down even harder, struggling to hold still. Inside he was screaming—shrieking—biting so savagely he expected Artem's stick to snap in half.

Kayce pushed on her knife—

Jack jerked like he'd been electrocuted.

—and something popped.

And just that fast it was over.

The knife slipped out and Jack relaxed, quivering like a bowl of jelly, tears streaming down both cheeks, his leg burning like it was covered in hot tar. He was in such shock that it wasn't until Kayce patted his knee that he opened his eyes.

"You okay?"

"Yorphhha—" He spat out the stick and sucked in an enormous chestful of air. The trees spun in circles above him, everything blurry from the tears. "Y-yeah."

"You did good," Kayce said with more compassion, and tenderness, than he knew she possessed. "Real good."

She gently placed a wad of cloth on the wound, then took Jack's hand and placed it on top of the makeshift dressing.

"Hold that right there to help stop the bleeding. Then, you know, just rest and relax for a couple of minutes before we get you dressed."

Jack's muscles were twisted in knots, tight as steel bands. Tears streamed from his eyes, no longer from pain but from the enormous stress—and anxiety—suddenly bleeding away.

I'm not crying, he thought to himself. *It's just tension ...*

He eased himself onto one elbow, took a quick peek beneath the dressing, then dropped onto his back again.

Judas Priest ...

Kayce was quickly back again, kneeling beside him and taking his hand. "I'm just gonna take a quick look, make sure you're not bleeding too much."

She lifted the dressing for a second, then replaced it. "Okay, good ... I think you're gonna make it. We missed that freakin' artery anyway."

"Y-yeah. Good. T-thanks."

"You ready to get dressed again?"

"Y-yeah. I-I think so."

"Can you do it yourself? Or would you like a little help?"

Jack's pride told him to do it himself, but he was still shaking uncontrollably. "I, uh ... I guess I could use a little help."

With the utmost care—and tenderness—Kayce helped him to stand, gently helped him into his jeans, and then led him to a rock to sit.

"Keep pressure on that dressing," she instructed. "Just keep your hand on it, keep pushing."

"Yes, ma'am."

Kayce grinned. "Hey, your sense of humor's coming back! That's a good sign."

"Ay-yi-yi," Jack said, croaking out the words like a bullfrog with a smoking problem. "I hope that's the last one. If it's not, I think I'll let the damn hunters shoot me 'stead of going through that again."

"Don't blame you. You wanna see it?"

"No. Huh-uh." He shook his head firmly. But: "What're you gonna do with it?"

"Oh, I've got an idea I wanna try—"

There was a rustle of brush, and Artem bounced into the clearing. The boy's face was creased with worry, but he lit up when he spotted Jack sitting up on the rock.

"Hey, you made it!" In a move that caught Jack completely by surprise, the boy gave him a quick hug, then turned to Kayce like a green marine reporting to a four-star general. "Bad news. We've got a couple of dirtbags in camouflage poking around the bottom of the cliff, and it's only a matter of time 'til they find the way up. We have a little time, but they're gonna get here."

"Yeah, I knew it was too good to last."

"And there's another problem."

"Today's the day for it. What is it?"

"Like I said, there's only two of them."

"Damn ..."

"But t-that's a good thing, r-right?" Jack asked. His voice was still unsteady. "What's the p-problem?"

"The problem is that we don't know where the third guy is."

"Dinosaurs m-might have gotten 'im—"

"Which would be great. But we don't know that's what happened, so we've gotta assume that he's still out there. You know, *somewhere*. And until we know for sure, we need to worry about him."

She frowned at Jack.

"In the meantime, you need to take it easy. I mean, you got carved up twice in one day! Good crap! You're in no shape for any heavy-duty hiking. Not 'til that wound's good and scabbed over, anyway."

"What other choice do I have?"

"Well, I've been thinking about it. There's a hole in the rocks not far away—Artem knows where to find it—and the two of you could hide out there for a bit. It's nothing special, but it'll keep you safe ... long enough to catch your breath, anyway. And while you're hiding out"—she flashed the implant she'd cut from Jack's thigh—"I'll take this thing and lead our shadows off in the other direction."

Her eyes sparked.

"And maybe find them a nice surprise or two along the way."

"Hey," Artem cut in, suddenly. "You've been doing all the work lately. Why don't you hang out with Jack, and I'll drop rocks on the goon squad from the top of the cliff. And then, you know, lead them straight to the biggest, meanest, hungriest torvosaur in the forest."

He nodded confidently.

"I can do it ... seriously."

Kayce smiled warmly. "I know you can. But you're not back to a 100% percent either. I mean, I know you want to help—and I appreciate it—but let's get the two of you back up to speed before you go commando."

Artem looked crushed, but Jack punched him playfully.

"Listen to her," he urged. "You and I can get into the action later. Besides"—he snapped a finger at Kayce—"with her out there?"

"Yeah?"

"I actually feel sorry for those guys with the guns."

Jack felt a twinge of nervousness as Kayce left. And it was nearly a minute before he realized why.

Every time she leaves, Artem and I get into trouble ... have some terrifying close call. And there's no reason to think this time is gonna be any different.

Even so, he knew they didn't have any other choice. His recent ... *procedure* ... had left him weak, and woozy, and sick to his stomach. He desperately needed time to recover.

And so does Artem, he thought, glancing at his young friend. *The kid's trying to act tough, but he's still one sick little hombre.*

He glanced around as the weight of the situation hit him.

Two messed up kids. Both of us too sick to hike, too weak to run ... and being hunted by guys with rifles. And all the while trying to steer clear of thirty-foot dinosaurs with eight-inch teeth.

He sighed.

Just another sunny day in the neighborhood ...

21 Megalosaurs

Artem paused after several minutes, looking suddenly worried.

"You lost?" Jack asked. The forest was so thick it was impossible to see landmarks, and the trails all seemed to weave aimlessly through the trees.

"No, I know where we're going. But ..."

"What?"

The boy licked his lips, then pointed to the ground ahead. Jack looked, spotting a three-toed track in the hard-packed dirt. The tracks were huge—seventeen or eighteen inches long, obviously the prints of a large predator—and fresh, though travelling opposite the boys' direction. They'd obviously passed it somewhere in the forest.

"Know what it is?" Jack asked.

"Hard to tell without seeing it. Could be an allosaur or a torvosaur or any one of their cousins. The tracks all kinda look alike, and I don't pay enough attention to know one from another."

"But we've passed it, right? It's going the other way?"

Artem nodded. "Yeah, it must have taken another trail, but it's still close."

"How do you know?"

Artem gave him a long look. "Can't you feel it?"

"Feel what?"

"Close your eyes," the boy suggested. "Just try to experience the forest for a moment."

It seemed like a strange request—

Like some mystical voodoo crap!

—but Jack sighed and closed his eyes. He felt a little bit stupid—

Kid better not be pulling my leg ...

—but then realized the hairs on the back of his neck were prickling. And without knowing why, he sensed a nearby ... presence ... in the forest. The presence of something big.

Something close.

Something dangerous.

He felt it as certainly as he felt the warmth of the sun slanting down through the thick canopy of leaves.

"Gee-muh-nee," he whispered. He opened his eyes and began rubbing down goose bumps that had suddenly erupted up and down his arms; he scanned the trees for danger. "I see what you mean." And then asked again: "Know what it is?"

Artem shook his head. "It's hard to say. But it doesn't really matter, does it? I mean, thirty-feet long with six-inch claws and eight-inch teeth? Who cares what the damn thing's called? It gets its teeth in you and tomorrow morning you're still just another gooey lump in a pile of steaming dinosaur crap."

"Gee-muh-nee," Jack repeated. "So what—"

"There's more than one set of tracks," Artem said, pointing to the trail. "So they might be megalosaurs."

"Megalosaurs?"

"They're the first species of dinosaur to ever be named. And we're not sure that's what they actually are—some kid named Todd told us they were, but he was a jerk who didn't know his ass from his elbow—but they like hunting together, so ..."

"Together?"

"In small packs, yeah. Like three or four, sometimes. And if there's a male and a female trying to feed their young, they usually hunt as a pair."

"Ay, yi—"

"Shhhh!" Artem hissed, holding up a hand.

Jack had learned not to question his young friend. And this time he knew what was happening. Animals were still screeching and roaring in the distance. But the woods closer in suddenly seemed eerily quiet.

Way, way *too quiet.*

Artem looked up, ready to explain, but Jack waved him off.

"I can hear it," he whispered. "They're close, aren't they?"

Artem nodded grimly. "They've probably picked up our scent. Which means they're hunting us—"

"That's just our luck."

Artem gave him an odd look. "You haven't figured it out yet, have you?"

"What's that?"

Artem waved a hand. "There's no luck involved in any of this. There's no good luck and there's no bad luck. It's just the way things are here." And then, before Jack could respond: "Let's keep going, but *quietly*. If we make any noise, it—they— might decide to attack."

"How much farther do we have to go?"

Artem scratched his chin, thinking as he peered ahead. "Ten minutes. Fifteen, maybe."

"Then let's not waste any more time."

They struck off through the trees, and though it wasn't extremely noticeable, Jack realized the boy was pressing on with more determination than ever.

He's worried, he thought, keeping a close eye on the trail behind them. *But then, so am I. And we've got every right to be.*

The trail was easy enough to follow, and Jack had to fight the urge to run.

But dinosaurs are probably like dogs, he reasoned. *You run from one and it's sure as heck gonna chase you.*

He kept his head on a swivel—constantly looking left and right and up and down—peering behind every tree and beneath every clump of brush for the slightest sign of danger. The presence of hunting predators had frightened most of the nearby wildlife into silence, though more distant animals maintained a constant, steady din, making it difficult to hear if anything was creeping up on them.

There was a squeak—and then another and another—and several small dinosaurs suddenly tore from the trees, racing past the boys through the brush. The creatures didn't as much as glance at Jack or Artem as they passed.

Artem jumped in surprise, then gave Jack a worried look.

Jack met his eyes. "Is that ..."

Artem nodded grimly. "Whatever's following us? They're scaring the crap out of everything in the forest."

Artem picked up his pace. And Jack wasn't certain—there was too much noise in the background—but thought he could now hear occasional cracks and snaps from the trees behind him.

They're getting closer ...

Artem obviously heard them too. Without a word the boy began hiking even faster. His limp was back, giving him a staggering, almost comical gait. And after a moment he called back, "Almost there!"

Jack pushed himself to keep up. A stick or branch popped in the trees behind them and Jack was about to tell Artem to run when the boy abruptly turned, left the trail, and shot directly into a thick wall of vines and leaves. Jack shot after him and the next instant spotted several jumbled boulders through the foliage.

Artem glanced back—just to be sure Jack was still with him—then gave up all pretense and bolted for the rocks. Jack set his teeth and sprinted after him. He wanted to look back, but heard a deep reptilian snarl and knew he was out of time. He lowered his head, pumped his legs, and reached the rocks a split second behind Artem.

Artem dove headfirst into a hollow beneath the first big boulder, his arms and legs whirling furiously as he scrambled for safety. Jack hit the ground behind him but had to flatten himself and scuttle sideways to make it beneath the rock.

There was a crash from the timber, a savage roar, and an enormous dinosaur blasted from the trees. Jack caught a quick glance—

Oh, shit!

—and tried to roll deeper beneath the boulder, but a jagged point of stone snagged his belt, anchoring him in place. He thrashed at the rock, trying to free himself, but couldn't get loose.

Artem suddenly grabbed his belt and tugged for all he was worth, fighting to pull him beneath the boulder. As the boy pulled, Jack's jeans tightened against his inner thigh, which was still tender where Kayce had sliced out the hidden implant. For a split second it felt like Kayce's knife was once again slicing into him and he screamed—

"*Aaaaaiiigh!*"

—in pain as much as terror. The ground shook beneath him as a heavy foot slammed down, bouncing him into the air and cracking his head against the rock. His brain swam, but he fought through the pain and twisted as hard as he could. Something gave—either the rock broke or his jeans ripped—and he was suddenly free. He rolled beneath the rock, Artem still pulling on his belt, his jeans still agonizingly tight against his injured thigh.

The next instant the dinosaur was there. It bellowed as it shoved its nose into the gap beneath the rock.

Jack was still scrambling to get out the way, his arms and legs clawing at the dirt and rocks. The dinosaur roared—its jaws mere inches away—and the rows of yellow teeth cracked together.

Artem screamed, but Jack wasn't paying attention, too intent on escaping the dinosaur to think of anything else. He scrabbled as deep beneath the rock as he could get, then jerked his knees up to his chest to get them as far from the dinosaur as possible.

He hadn't gotten a good look at the animal. But with nowhere to go, he finally looked back. All he could see were the black flaring nostrils and the sharp yellow teeth as they snapped at the rocks and dirt. Then he spotted enormous clawed feet behind the snout and—when the animal twisted its head to peer beneath the boulder—a black slitted eye.

Even then, he had no idea if the dinosaur was an allosaur, a torvosaur, or something else.

Holy freakin' buckets! Jack thought, trying to wedge himself even farther beneath the rocks. His heart was pounding so hard his temples began to throb. His face felt wet, and when he reached a hand to his hair it came away slick with blood.

Oh, yeah, he thought, a faraway part of his brain reminding him that he'd struck his head.

The dinosaur bellowed—the open jaws *right there!*—filling the cramped hollow with hot, sour dinosaur breath. Jack jerked his head away from the nerve-rattling noise, but then looked back, checking to be sure he was far enough from the yellow teeth to keep from being snagged.

The ground shook, more clawed feet appeared, and Jack realized there were now two dinosaurs outside the rocks. The second animal stuffed its nose into the hollow and Jack tried to force himself even more tightly against the rocks, but was already mashed against the boulder as far as he could go.

The two dinosaurs were fighting one another for a chance at the boys, and one abruptly snapped at the other as it wrestled for a better angle.

Artem had stopped screaming, but was wheezing noisily, his mouth just behind Jack's ear. Worried that the kid was on the verge of hyperventilating, Jack tried to calm him down.

"W-we're okay," he stammered, trying to keep the shakes out of his own voice. "I d-don't think they can g-get in here."

The boy didn't reply, but Jack sensed that he might have nodded.

The dinosaur on the left bellowed furiously and Jack cringed, struggling not to panic.

It's trying to frighten us ... trying to scare us into running.

The second animal tried to shoulder its rival out of the way, the first animal pushed back, and both animals began snapping at one another, momentarily ignoring the terrified boys. It took Jack a beat to realize what was happening, but then he took advantage of the respite to shift around beneath the rock, seeking a safer position.

He twisted his head to look back at Artem. "You okay? H-hanging in there?"

The boy nodded, his dusty cheeks streaked with tears. "Y-y-yeah."

"Just t-try to stay t-tough," Jack stammered, struggling to sound more confident than he actually felt. "We'll b-be okay."

He glanced outside. The two dinosaurs had quit fighting, and the scuffle seemed to have calmed them down. They were still standing just outside the rocks, but were no longer battling to get inside.

Jack blew out his breath, knowing he and Artem had just dodged a bullet—

One of the dinosaurs abruptly lowered its nose to the ground just outside the rocks. Twin spouts of dust erupted from the dirt when the animal exhaled, and then the great snout turned toward the hollow. The black, fleshy nostrils flared as the dinosaur snuffled through the dirt. Jack didn't know, but thought the dinosaur was uncertain about them, not sure the boys were still there.

The dinosaur growled softly—

Almost sounds like it's purring ...

—and the second dinosaur joined it, sniffing at the rocks and trying to peer into the hollow. Jack kept perfectly still, then glanced at Artem: the boy held a finger to his lips, already knowing to be still, and quiet.

One of the dinosaurs snorted, snapping Jack's attention back to the animals. But ... the urgency seemed to have passed. The enormous predators were still there—both of them close enough to touch—but they no longer seemed to have anything more than a passing curiosity toward the two boys.

Jack watched the dinosaurs for several long seconds, wondering why they'd lost interest. And then, incredibly, one of the animals straightened and thumped away, disappearing around the rocks.

Holy buckets, Jack thought incredulously. *I can't believe they're giving up.*

He turned to look at Artem—the boy's red-streaked eyes were big as doorknobs—who shook his head as if saying: *I don't get it, either.*

The boy reached to brush something from his back as Jack once again turned to check on the dinosaurs. Only one of the animals was still in sight, but Jack couldn't see anything more than its feet and couldn't tell what it was doing. He began breathing a little easier, though Artem was fidgeting restlessly behind him, as if trying to relieve a hard-to-reach itch.

The dinosaur snuffled the ground.

Don't know what it's doing, but if we're quiet it might just wander off in another minute—

He glanced around the hollow.

—and then we can get the hell out of here.

Artem was still squirming nervously, and Jack began to worry that the dinosaur might hear him. And possibly decide to have another go at them.

He turned again to check on the boy—

Artem abruptly screamed—

"*Aaaaaiiigh!*"

—and began flailing about the cramped space. His arms and legs thrashed wildly—like he was being electrocuted—his eyes wide as saucers. He screamed again—

"*Aaaaaiiigh!*"

—and Jack caught a glimpse of an eight-inch centipede racing over the kid's shoulder.

Holy shit!

He twisted instantly around, dodging the kid's flailing hands and feet, and swiped at the terrifying bug, even as another appeared and sped around Artem's ankle and inside his jeans and up his leg.

Artem screamed in horror—

"*Aaaaaiiigh!*"

—and slapped at his pants, trying to mash the bug to mush. A third centipede zipped around the boy's waist and Jack slapped it away. He looked—

One of the dinosaurs shoved its nose beneath the rock and bellowed, so unexpectedly that Jack jumped, once again cracking his head against the sharp rocks, and instantly felt blood running down his temple.

He whipped his head around, saw that his legs were dangerously close to the snarling jaws—

Holy crap!

—and jerked them up to his chest, just as the second dinosaur returned and snapped its teeth, barely missing his shoes.

Artem screamed, practically in Jack's ear, and one of his flailing fists clipped the back of Jack's head. Jack winced, and for a moment was so overwhelmed that he nearly snapped.

Dinosaurs!

Centipedes!

Artem's ear-piercing screams ...

A flying hand slapped Jack across the face, snapping him back to reality. He shot a look at the dinosaurs—they were both bellowing, snapping, clawing at the dirt as they fought to get inside—then turned back to Artem. Ignoring the noise of the roaring dinosaurs, he swept a hand across the boy's shirt, flicking away two more of the repulsive arthropods, then brushed one off his own leg. He grabbed Artem's nearest arm and jerked the boy around so he could brush off the back of his shirt—

EEEEEEEEEEEE!

A shrill, piercing, nerve-shattering shriek filled the air, blasting Jack's ears like flights of rusty nails. So loud and painful that it stung the fillings in his teeth and made him want to scream. He clamped his hands over his ears and screwed his eyes shut. Artem screamed even louder—still kicking and flapping—trying to shut out the noise while fighting off hordes of centipedes.

The dinosaurs roared with fury. They were just outside the hollow, but no longer fighting to get inside.

EEEEEEEEEEEE!

Jack kept his hands clamped over his ears—cringing in pain—but forced his eyes open again. He gawked at the dinosaurs—ducked one of Artem's flying elbows—then turned back to the dinosaurs. The earsplitting noise was relentless, blasting his ears, driving pain like red-hot needles deep into his bones, wrenching every nerve in his body like they were being ripped from his spine.

It was doing the same to the dinosaurs.

Jack couldn't see anything more than the animals' splayed, three-toed feet. But the animals were slowly retreating from the shrill, incapacitating noise. They bellowed in agony, made a few false starts in the direction of the shrieking howl, but then backed slowly away. And after nearly a minute vanished back into the trees.

The excruciating shriek stopped instantly, and the sudden silence seemed almost jarring.

Artem didn't care.

The instant the noise stopped he shot from the rocks and began dancing around. He stamped his feet and slapped his clothes as he fought off the repulsive multi-legged bugs.

"*Artem!*"

Worried that the dinosaurs were still nearby, Jack darted after the boy, ready to drag him back beneath the centipede-infested rocks. But the animals were gone and he spent several seconds helping to clear away the bugs. He brushed the back of Artem's shirt, and jeans, then had to swipe at a centipede speeding up the leg of his own jeans.

His ears were still ringing from the awful shriek, and he could barely hear the normal howls and screeches of the forest. But after a moment he realized that he and Artem were no longer alone.

With a hand poised to swat away a particularly nasty-looking centipede, he lifted his eyes.

And reeled back in surprise.

Standing just outside the trees was a man.

A man dressed in camouflage.

Holding a rifle.

And looking straight at him.

21 Hunter One

Jack gawked for several seconds, then reached out and grabbed Artem by the arm and pulled him close. The boy was sobbing—still swatting at bugs crawling through his clothes—but as soon as he looked up and spotted the hunter, he became still, and quiet. A centipede streaked unnoticed over his shoulder.

The camouflaged man stared back without expression. There was a sharp reptilian snort from the woods and he glanced briefly into the trees, dismissed the sound as unimportant, and returned his attention to the two boys.

Jack was looking at the man's face, but realized the guy was holding *two* guns: a rifle in one hand and a fat pistol-looking thing in the other. As he watched, the man returned the pistol to a holster on his belt and Jack realized:

It's not a gun! It's some sort of noise maker. He used it to chase off the dinosaurs!

He kept perfectly still, almost as if thinking the man might not see them if they didn't move. He felt Artem shaking, felt the boy easing behind him for protection.

Jack put out an arm—just to make certain he knew exactly where the boy was—as he stared at the camouflaged man.

Same guy we saw before, he thought, though he wasn't really certain.

With the noisemaker back in its holster, the man took his rifle in both hands and held it diagonally across his chest. He stared at the boys evenly.

"Who're you?" Jack suddenly blurted, unable to stand the suspense.

"You two are hard to follow," the man said in a gravelly voice, not answering the question.

"How'd you find us? We got rid of your implants."

The man pointed at the ground with the barrel of his rifle. "You still leave tracks."

"You don't have to do this," Jack whispered, knowing the man would know what "this" referred to. He knew the rifle wasn't for shooting dinosaurs. And he couldn't help remembering Artem's description of some kid being shot.

And the kid's head exploding ...

"It's the only reason I'm here," the man said flatly. "But I wanted to track you. Looked forward to the challenge. And now that I've found you, I'll track down your snarky friend."

Jack's blood turned cold at the callousness of the man's tone.

Yeah, I'm gonna shoot the two of you. Then I'll shoot the girl. And then maybe take a few pictures of the scenery.

Jack couldn't help glancing around, looking for a way to run, or to get away.

The man noticed and pointed the rifle at his belly.

"Don't try it," he warned. "You won't get two steps."

"What're you going to do?"

The man shrugged, then adjusted the grip on his rifle. He lifted—

Jack saw something fly through the air—a small rock or a clod of dirt—and into the brush at the man's side, crackling as it fell through the branches. The man turned to look—it would have been impossible not to—and the instant his eyes flicked away there was a blur of motion.

Kayce!

The girl burst from the brush, brandishing a thick stick like a baseball bat. The man heard her and turned, raising his rifle, but didn't have a chance. Kayce planted her feet, twisted her hips, and swung with all her might.

The club cracked across the guy's shoulder with a sickening *crunch!* He gasped in pain and surprise, then tried to swing around—trying to raise the gun with his other arm—but Kayce was already swinging again. Her club slammed into the rifle, smashing the man's fingers.

"*Aiiiii—*"

But Kayce was too filled with rage to stop. With the fury of a mother bear protecting a helpless cub, she swung a third time, this time aiming for the guy's knee. There was a sickening *crack*, and the man dropped like rock. The guy howled, writhing on the ground and clutching his crushed fingers, his injured leg bent at an impossible angle.

"*Ahhhh—*"

The man gasped for breath, then opened his eyes, glowering in fury. He spotted Kayce and spewed a string of foul, vile, pain-inspired curses.

But if Kayce was affected, she didn't let on. She calmly grabbed the guy's rifle and without taking her eyes off the writhing, swearing man, held it toward the boys.

"Hold this," she ordered.

Jack was still gaping in shock, but Artem darted forward and took the rifle.

"Be careful where you point it," Kayce warned.

"I know."

Carefully avoiding the man's fists and boots, she snatched the noisemaker from its holster, tossed it to the ground behind her—

"Never seen one of *those* before ..."

—then took a pistol—a real pistol this time—from a second holster. The wounded man also had a combat knife—nearly as wicked-looking as Kayce's—and she yanked it from his belt and tossed it aside. She made a quick check to be sure the man wasn't armed with anything else, then collected the noisemaker, pistol, and knife and finally looked away from the man to peer at Jack and Artem.

"You two okay—"

The hunter kicked out with his good leg, striking Kayce in the ankle. She stumbled—dropping the newly acquired weapons in a clatter—but Jack lunged forward and grabbed her in time to keep her from falling.

She glared at the scowling man, then carefully picked up the weapons and led the boys a few feet away to where they were out of reach.

"Damn asshole," she muttered. And then: "You two okay?"

"Yeah, we're fine," Artem answered. "Scared shitless, but ... you know."

She reached out with the blade of the man's knife and flicked a centipede from the kid's shoulder. "Okay, well, let's get outta here. All that noise, those other goons'll be heading this way."

Jack's jaw dropped. "But—"

"But what?"

He flicked a hand at the man cursing and writhing on the ground. "What about him?"

"What *about* him?"

"Are we ... just gonna leave him?"

"You wanna take him with us?"

"No, but ... uh—"

"Look," Kayce snapped, a little more harshly than Jack was expecting. "Another second and he was gonna put a bullet in your brain. And then Artem's. And then he was gonna do the same to me. You get that, right?"

"Well, yeah ..."

"So what's the problem?"

"I ... uh ... look, we can't just *leave* him!"

"Damn right we can!"

"But—"

"Look," Kayce said, losing patience. "Go ahead and babysit him if you want. But understand this: you get one inch too close and he'll rip your throat out ... with his bare hands if he has to."

Jack felt torn. He *knew* the man had come to kill them. Had been with seconds of doing so. And that he still would if he somehow got the chance.

But the thought of just leaving him to die ...

Artem reached up and tugged on his sleeve.

"I know how you feel," the boy said in a voice barely loud enough to hear. "But Kayce's right. We can't do anything for him. And we shouldn't. It's hard, I know, but ... you've gotta get past it."

Jack's stomach turned, and twisted, but Artem's gentle, understanding tone convinced him.

He looked at Kayce and nodded.

"Let's get out of here."

The man began cursing even more foully than before, shouting at Kayce and calling her names nastier, and uglier, and more horribly vile than anything Jack had ever heard.

Jack swung around and pointed an angry finger.

"*Hey!*" he shouted. "Knock it off! Now! Or I'll break your other leg!"

The warning didn't do any good. The man continued swearing, and cursing, using language so horrid, and dreadful, that it hit Jack like a slap to the face. Jack glanced at Artem, but the boy seemed totally unaffected.

As if the words were no more offensive than what he'd hear in a Disney movie!

There was a crackle of brush, and Jack turned to see several small dinosaurs standing just outside the trees. They were scavengers, obviously, and hungry: drawn by the smell of blood and the prospect of an easy meal, they were bobbing with excitement.

The wounded man saw them too, and was instantly struck by the full gravity of his predicament. He quit cursing and began to beg.

"No, don't leave me!" he pleaded. "*Please!* Please don't leave me! Don't leave me like this!"

Kayce ignored him, tipping her head toward the woods. "We probably don't have much time. Let's get out of here."

She started for the trees, Artem right behind her.

Jack took a final look back before following. The injured man was thrashing violently on the ground, kicking desperately with his one good leg at the hungry scavengers as they crept closer.

"No!" the man shrieked in terror. "Get *out* of here!" And then to the departing teenagers: "Don't leave me! Please, please, don't—*don't leave me*! Aaaaaiiigh!"

Jack turned away as one of the scavengers dodged the man's kicking leg and hopped onto his belly.

The man screamed.

"*Aaaaaiiigh!*"

22 Ambush

Artem was still twitching and wiggling as if he still had a few centipedes crawling around inside his shirt. Jack didn't believe that was actually the case—

Kid'd be screaming bloody murder!

—but something was certainly bothering him. Jack waited until they'd put some distance between themselves and the doomed hunter—

His freakin' friends've gotta be coming ...

—then finally called out: "Hey, Kayce. Hold up a second."

As soon as she turned, he stepped up to Artem and lifted the boy's shirt.

Artem jerked away in surprise. "Hey—"

"Hold on a second," Jack repeated. He lifted the boy's shirt so that he could see his back, then turned him around so that Kayce could see. "Centipede bites."

Kayce leaned in for a better look, then gave Artem an exasperated shake.

"Holy hell, man! Why didn't you *say* something?"

"Had more important things to worry about," the boy replied sheepishly. He scratched at his sides and belly like a kid with a bad rash.

Like a kid who's been rolling in poison ivy.

But Kayce wasn't having it. "First you don't tell me about the thorn, and now this? Frickin' kid! What's the *matter* with you?" And then in a softer tone: "I thought you trusted me."

"I do," the boy said. His voice wavered and Jack knew he was on the verge of bursting into tears. "I just ... I-I don't know ..."

Kayce blew out her breath, then pulled the boy in for a hug. That was too much for Artem and he turned his face into her shoulder and began to sob.

Kayce held him for a moment—gently patting his back and whispering in his ear—then glanced at Jack. "Thanks for picking up on that."

"No problem. Are they dangerous?"

"The bites? I don't think so. I mean, we've all been bitten, but never like this; never more than once or twice at a time. That's not a big deal, but if he's absorbed a lot of venom ... well, I just don't know."

She pushed away from the boy and lifted his shirt for another look, trying to imagine what the rest of his body looked like.

"Well, I know they itch like hell, so let's make a little mud. Kinda gross"—she bobbed her head from side to side as if to say, *But what'cha gonna do?*—"but hey, that's life in the outback, huh?"

While Jack watched curiously, she knelt and scooped a small mound of fine dirt together. She plucked a few tiny rocks from the pile, then stood and dusted the knees of her jeans.

"So you know what to do, right?" she asked Artem.

The boy nodded, but with a definite lack of enthusiasm. "Yes ..."

"Okay. I'll walk back down the trail a little way, see if anyone's following us, and be back in a couple of minutes."

She clapped the boy supportively on the shoulder, then jogged back down the trail.

Jack watched as she vanished into the trees, then peered curiously at Artem. "What's going on?"

The boy sighed, then pointed at the pile of dirt. "You've gotta pee on that."

"*What?*" Jack wasn't certain that his jaw dropped all the way to his knees, but it certainly felt like it. "You're joking, right?"

"Yeah, I wish. But haven't you heard that? Something about urine eases the pain of jellyfish stings, and bee stings, and—well—centipede bites." He pointed again. "So you pee on that, and then we'll rub the mud on these bites. It'll keep 'em from hurting so much. And from itching like crazy."

Jack had heard—and seen and endured—a lot during the past two days. But even after all the crazy, stupid, unbelievable things he'd been through, this suddenly seemed too much.

"I'm sorry," he said, shaking his head. "I'm not sure I can do that."

Artem looked at him for a moment, then reached for his own zipper. "Fine. I'll do it myself, but ... I kinda thought we were better friends than that." And then in a stage whisper: "I'd do it for you ..."

Jack quickly reached out and stopped him.

"Wait," he said. "You're serious about this?"

"Serious as a heart attack." And then: "That's why I didn't say anything. I mean, I don't care how bad these things itch, but who wants to rub pee all over himself?"

Jack pulled a face, hesitated, then gave in. He shook his head.

Jeez ...

"Okay. I'll do it."

"Thanks. I, uh, wasn't sure I could actually do it myself. I mean, I haven't had a lot to drink and I'm pretty dry."

"Yeah, I'll bet." He looked from Artem to the pile of dirt and then back to Artem. "Um ... you're not gonna watch, are you?"

The boy threw up his hands like an exasperated teacher with a student unable to add two and two. "Oh for crying out loud! After everything we've been through already? And *now* you wanna be modest?"

He turned his back and folded his arms with an indignant huff.

Jack rolled his eyes, then peered again at the pile of dirt.

Jeez, of all the dumb, stupid things I've ever had to do for a friend ...

When Kayce returned several minutes later, Jack was just smearing the last of the mud over the last of the centipede bites. She glanced at Jack, took a quick look at Artem's mud-slathered skin, and nodded her approval.

"Very well done." And to Artem: "Feel any better?"

"Lots."

And then to Jack (with a look that Jack thought *might* have hidden just a trace of smirk): "Nice work."

"I'm sure. But please don't tell me this is something I have to look forward to every day."

"Oh, heck no," Kayce assured him.

"Thank heavens for that!"

"Maybe two or three times a week, max ..."

"*What?*"

"And then, 'course, we'll do it for you, too—"

"Hey—"

"Oh, lighten up," she scolded. "Don't have such a negative attitude."

"No? Why not?"

" 'Cuz you just had to stick your fingers in a little pee. Most of the time when you get bitten around here?"

"Yeah?"

"You get bitten in half."

"So what about our shadows?" Jack asked. "Any sign?"

Kayce sighed. "No. Not yet. But they're coming."

"How do you know?"

"Just do." She looked at Jack and cocked her head. "Are you doing any better? After, you know, leaving that guy to the dinosaurs?"

"No. Not really. I mean, you're right, of course: we just did what we had to do. But it's still a lot to handle."

"Yeah, well, I appreciate the fact that you didn't wig out on me. Didn't get all self-righteous or holier-than-thou." She swatted at a bug buzzing around her ear. "Thing is, the rules are different here. Back home, we never could have done that."

"But then, back home we never would have *had* to."

"Right. That's it exactly."

"So, have you decided where you're leading us?" Jack asked as they started again down the trail. He was careful to keep his tone curious, and not critical. "Or are we winging it?"

"Little of both."

"Care to explain?"

She glanced up to her left, frowned at a flash on a nearby hillside—

Like sunlight reflecting off a piece of glass, Jack thought.

—then spoke over her shoulder. "I know the direction I wanna go. Just haven't figured out exactly what we're gonna do when we get there."

Jack shot another glance at the hillside—

There's that flash again. Like an old bottle or piece of metal reflecting the sun but ... that's not possible!

—then looked back as some animal crashed through the timber a short distance away. By the sound of the cracking limbs and branches, Jack knew it was something large.

But it's going the other way ... might not even know we're here and if it does, it isn't interested ...

He looked away, still amazed to be dismissing the presence of big animals as nonchalantly as Kayce and Artem—

There was a high-pitched whine, followed by a heavy thud, and flakes of bark flew from the trunk of a tree just ahead.

Crack!

The teens flinched in surprise, but then more bark exploded through the air and a clipped branch dropped to the ground.

Crack-ack!

"Down!" Kayce shouted. "They're shooting at us!"

Jack dropped, landing partially on top of Artem, but managed to roll away just as more bullets whistled overhead. Whoever was shooting was far enough away the bullets were crashing into the trees a half second before the crack of the gunshots arrived.

Jack flattened himself against the ground and army-crawled toward Kayce.

Good crap, he thought. He peered through the grass as he crawled and once again saw the sun glint off a rifle scope or a pair of binoculars or something. *Like we don't have* enough *to deal with?*

Kayce was obviously rattled.

"Wasn't expecting that," she said as Jack eased up beside her. "They did that on purpose. One of 'em got behind us and pushed us into the sights of his idiot buddy waiting on the hill."

"No kidding." Jack tried to remain flat on the ground, lifting his head just enough for a glance up through the brush. Almost instantly there was a sharp snap—he actually *felt* the bullet zip past his head—and a spurt of dirt erupted from the ground a few inches to the side.

Holy hell, he thought, dropping flat again—

A flurry of brush and leaves and twigs abruptly rained down from the trees, followed by a sinister *rattarattarata!*

"He's shooting automatic!" Kayce shouted. "Stay down, but let's get outta here!"

She began scrambling away on all fours, tearing straight for a thick stand of trees. More bullets slammed into the ground and brush and trees, but the shooter could no longer see his targets and was simply spraying the woods, hoping for a lucky hit.

Kayce turned and angled toward a line of drooping pines. Jack had let Artem pass—once again placing the boy between himself and Kayce—but stuck close to the kid's shoes. Kayce stopped when she reached the pines, took a careful look around, then gestured for the boys to come alongside.

"That was close," Kayce said. And then to Jack: "Never seen these clowns do anything that clever before."

"No?"

She shook her head. "They usually just crash around in the brush, thinking their guns make them invincible. 'Course, the people they recruit for this usually aren't the smartest guys in the neighborhood."

"I've got a feeling they've changed strategies," Artem whispered.

Kayce nodded grimly.

"I was hoping that last guy might have been the smart one," she admitted. "But I dunno. These guys are either really smart or really lucky."

"From what I've seen so far," Jack said, "I don't think luck's got anything to do with it."

"Shoot," Kayce said, looking back and forth as if searching for options. "I was hoping things wouldn't get this far, but I think we're gonna have to change strategies ourselves. We're gonna have to get serious ... take some chances."

Artem's eyes widened and he whispered, "No ..."

Jack wasn't sure, but thought the blood suddenly drained from the boy's face.

"Do you have another idea?" Kayce asked.

"No ..."

"What about weapons?" Jack asked. "Artem told me that you have some guns—"

Kayce was already shaking her head. "Too dangerous. There's more to shooting a gun than pulling the trigger, and we don't have time to figure it all out. Besides, Artem already told you that not all the ammunition works, right?"

"Yeah ..."

"So how'd you like to get into a firefight with one of these dough-heads, only to have your gun jam? Or come face-to-face with a pissed-off allosaur and suddenly run out of bullets? I'd like to be able to shoot back, too. But that's just not gonna happen."

"Okay, I see your point." And then: "So what's your idea?"

"The torvosaur nests."

Jack frowned. "The torvosaur ... *nests*?"

Kayce nodded. "It's a sort of nesting ground for torvosaurs. And because of the nests, and the eggs, and the newly hatched babies, the adults are even meaner and more aggressive there than when you run into them wandering through the woods."

Jack's jaw dropped and this time he *did* see the blood drain from Artem's face. "And you want to go there *intentionally*?"

"I don't see another option. It's risky, sure. But if we can get these creeps to follow us in—and then keep outta sight and, you know, keep from being spotted ourselves—the torvosaurs might take care of them."

She shrugged, as if suggesting the plan were no more dangerous than heading to the corner convenience store for a bag of chips.

"Piece 'a cake."

"Seriously," **Kayce said**. "I think this is our best chance to lose these guys. And yeah, it'll be risky—"

"But everything we do in this frickin' place is risky," Artem said softly. "You can't step behind a tree to take a leak without wondering if something's gonna snatch you outta your shoes. But ..."

"But deliberately hiking into a place so dangerous ..." Jack held up his hands to show that he wasn't disagreeing, but simply pointing out the dangers. "I mean, you guys both know a helluva lot more about this than I do, so I'm with you, whatever you decide. I just, you know ..."

"I get it," Kayce said. "And I appreciate your support."

She glanced up at the sun, judging how much daylight they had to work with. She finally glanced back and forth between the two boys.

"But the way I see it, we can either keep wandering around and hoping for the best, or we can go commando—"

"Commando?"

"You know ... be proactive and try to lose these goobers once and for all."

She gave each of the boys a meaningful look.

"Look, this is a big deal. It's not gonna be easy—we'll be taking a pretty big risk—so we can't do it unless all three of us agree."

"Holy cow," Artem said to Jack. "I've known her for almost a year ... and this is the *only* time she's ever asked for a vote."

"Yeah," Kayce retorted. "But in my defense, most of the time everyone else is too stupid to *have* a vote."

She shook her head.

"But this is different. We really will be putting a lot on the line and, well, the two of you are pretty smart. I want your input."

"Is it just me?" Jack asked Artem in a stage whisper. "Or are we gonna have a group hug?"

Kayce threw up her hands. "Okay, that's it. I take it all back—"

"Hey, hey," Jack said. "Just kidding. And, really, I appreciate your asking my opinion. But like I keep saying, I can't give you an honest answer. I don't *like* the idea of tramping through torvosaur country. But I don't really know what I'm getting into. And I don't have any better ideas, so I'll go along with whatever you two decide."

Kayce gave him a long look, then turned to Artem. "Well, it's up to you then, kiddo. You get the deciding vote."

Artem's eyes flickered, and Jack understood the pressure the kid was feeling. The boy looked at Kayce with unabashed fear.

"You really t-think going in's our best s-shot?" he asked nervously.

"I really do, bud. At least if there's another option, I don't see it."

The boy nodded. He glanced at Jack and then turned back to Kayce and nodded again. "Okay, then. Let's do it. Let's get these shitkickers off our ass."

23 Torvosaur Country

Jack was nervous, but it only took a quick look to see that Artem was absolutely terrified.

'Cause he's seen it before and knows *what we're getting into ...*

He quickened his pace until he was just behind the boy, then said, "Hey ..."

Artem gave him a quick look before again sweeping his eyes around the forest. "Yeah?"

"You okay?"

Artem gave him another glance. "Yes and no."

"What's *that* mean?"

The boy rubbed his elbow. "I'm feeling better, if that's what you're asking. Like, maybe, 80% or something. But if you're asking if I'm scared, then hell yeah."

"That's what I was afraid of. Wanna tell me about it?"

The boy stepped over a rotting limb that would have crunched like a pile of dry corn flakes if he'd put his weight on it. "You'll see for yourself soon enough. Kayce's right, though. I mean, you know what torvosaurs are like. You've got to be crazy to go anywhere near them. But we've gotta do *something* to get away from those bozos with bazookas."

"How bad's it gonna be?"

"*Real* bad."

Kayce was several steps ahead of the boys, but she had the ears of an owl and had been listening to the conversation. She stopped, waited for the boys to catch up, and said: "It's gonna be tricky. And scary as hell. But we can do it. More importantly, we *have* to do it. It's our best chance for getting rid of our shadows. Probably our *only* chance."

Jack peered into the trees. "How far away is it?"

"An hour maybe?" Kayce glanced at Artem for confirmation. "Hour and a half?"

"Then let's get going."

Jack barely noticed the cries and bellows filling the prehistoric forest anymore. But now that he was laser-focused on the thought of torvosaurs—and what awaited them in the dinosaur nesting ground—he was shutting out the rest of the world completely.

Once, as they were hiking, Kayce abruptly stopped and gestured urgently for the boys to crouch in the brush. Jack had no sooner dropped to his knees than some dinosaur crashed through the timber just ahead.

Holy crap! he thought as his heart pounded. *Didn't even hear that one coming!*

Jack wasn't certain if the animal was chasing something—or if it was *being* chased—or if it had some other reason for its mad dash through the trees. But after several seconds the noise diminished and the dinosaur was gone.

Kayce waited another couple of seconds, then rose, peered into the brush, and motioned for the boys to follow.

Ay, yi, yi, Jack thought. *Close one!*

And for the umpteenth time realized how important it was to stay alert.

And to pay attention!

Following Artem's lead, he began scanning the woods in all directions—up, down, left, right—searching for ... for ...

Hell, for whatever might be out there!

And as they drew closer to the ill-omened torvosaur haunts, he began to notice a change. The air seemed warmer. And thicker. Making it harder to breathe. And he sensed a suffocating ... *heaviness* ... in the forest. As if the woods were pressing in on him.

At first, he thought it was his imagination. But then he noticed something else. The woods were still noisy, of course ... still filled with wild shrieks and howls and cries. But he realized that fewer and fewer of them were the sounds of large animals.

Like the big guys know this is forbidden territory.

And are staying away ...

He'd no sooner had the thought than Kayce stopped dead in the trail. She peered deep into the trees, glanced around, then motioned for the boys to join her.

"We're close," she whispered. And to Jack: "It's not like there's a line on the ground, or a sign saying 'Welcome to Torvosaur Country.' But every step we take ... well, every step takes us closer to the belly of the beast."

"The 'belly of the beast'?"

"It's just an expression, give me a break. Anyway, until we're on our way out again, every step we take is more dangerous than the last."

Jack took a deep breath, then exchanged nervous looks with Artem before turning back to Kayce. "So what's your plan?"

Kayce considered for a moment—deciding how to put her thoughts into words—then said: "What if we hike straight in for another, oh, ten or fifteen minutes. And then start circling around. With any luck, we can get to the other side without having to go right through the middle."

She nodded toward the trail behind them.

"With any luck, those last two hunters won't realize where we've taken them until it's too late."

"Um, we tried that back at the swamp," Jack pointed out. "And it didn't work out so good."

"I know. But if we're lucky, this time they'll stumble into some torvosaur before they realize what's going on. And—hopefully—it'll be the biggest, meanest damn animal in the forest."

"Sounds good to me," Jack said as Artem nodded. But: "What are the chances *we'll* run into something like that?"

"Pretty good," Kayce admitted. "Probably better than even. The torvosaurs are here, obviously, and there are a lot of them. But they're not used to seeing other animals in here—not big ones anyway—so they won't be looking for us."

Artem: "But ..."

Kayce: "But they're fiercely protective of their territory. And their nests."

Jack: "So if they get wind of us ..."

Kayce, with a grim nod: "Yeah. If they get wind of us, they won't give up until we're nothing but strips of bloody red meat hanging from the brush."

Jack: "Oh-*kaaaay*. Sounds like fun."

And Artem: "What are we waiting for?"

Kayce smiled, knowing the boys were just trying to lighten the mood and make the best of a thorny situation. "I guess I don't have to remind you lunks to be quiet, right? And to watch your step? Dinosaurs make a lot of noise, but *you* step on a dry stick and the animals will know the difference. Every torvosaur in the county'll come running."

Jack: "Gotcha."

Artem, with a mock salute: "Yes, *ma'am*!"

Kayce gave the boy a mock punch to the arm, then—instead of speaking—crooked a finger to say, *Follow me.*

She hesitated a split second, then headed again down the trail. And Jack instantly noticed a difference. Kayce always travelled with a cautious but steady gait. But instead of walking normally, planting her heels first—

Heel-toe, heel-toe, heel-toe ...

—she now touched the toe of her shoes to the ground first—gently, carefully—before placing her full weight on the foot.

And she only took two or three steps at a time before pausing to scan the forest, tipping her head frequently to listen for danger. Artem was doing the same, and Jack quickly followed their example.

Toe-heel, toe-heel, toe-heel ...

But:

Can't believe we're really doing this, he thought. His stomach had dropped to the bottom of his belly and suddenly seemed full of acid.

He took a deep breath to calm himself, breathing in through his nose—

Whoa!

He realized with a start that the forest had taken on a foul, rancid smell. The pleasant, comfortable scent of must, decay, and fresh fertilizer he'd become used to—

Like what you might smell in a greenhouse ... or on a farm after a fine summer rain.

—was now overpowered by the stench of rotting garbage and sour meat.

And death ...

He realized that Kayce was right. That there wasn't a definitive line marking the torvosaurs' territory. But there was no question they were now clearly on the inside, and the smell of the monstrous carnivores permeated the woods like a thick, rancid fog.

He rubbed his arms, trying to smooth down the goose bumps that suddenly began lumping his skin—

There was a loud *crack!*—the sound of a log crunching nearby—and Kayce crouched beside a leafy shrub. The boys followed her example, and Kayce held up a hand that Jack took to mean, *Stay calm!*

There was another soft *crunch*, followed by the rustle of brush.

Something's walking around up there, Jack thought, trying to slow his breathing. *Something big, but ... it's just wandering around. Just nosing through the brush and not actually chasing anything.*

The unseen dinosaur—

It's gotta be a torvosaur! Jack thought, picturing the huge, menacing animals.

—continued crunching about—

Maybe just checking on its nest or nudging one of the kids back to the house.

—and after a moment Kayce looked back at the boys. She made a curving motion with her hand—

Let's start circling around.

—and Jack and Artem both nodded. She peered once more toward the sound of the puttering torvosaur, then rose and began angling silently in a different direction. Jack followed Artem, spending as much time watching for dry twigs and leaves on the trail as for dinosaurs among the trees. He hadn't really noticed before, but now realized the ground was covered with tracks.

Huge, fresh tracks ... and lots of them!

So many, in fact, that they were imprinted over one another so that only the freshest prints were easily identifiable.

Jeez, Kayce and Artem weren't kidding ... this is, like, Torvosaur Central.

There was a rustle in the trees to the left, and Jack peered toward it. He didn't see anything, and neither Kayce nor Artem seemed to have heard it. He wavered a moment, then remembered Artem saying that Kayce would rather deal with a hundred false alarms than suffer a single nasty surprise.

He snapped his fingers softly, making a sound no louder than a fingernail tapping against a tooth. But Kayce and Artem both heard him and stopped in their tracks. Jack waited until Kayce looked, then tapped his ear and pointed to the left. Kayce looked, just as the brush rustled again.

Whew! Jack thought, relieved that he hadn't been imagining things.

Kayce glanced back and mouthed the word *Thanks!* She made a chopping motion with one hand, indicating a direction that passed between the two known dinosaurs.

Jack nodded—as did Artem—though his heart was pounding.

Ay, yi, yi, he thought anxiously. *We're cutting this pretty close ...*

He glanced around, almost praying that he'd spot another way to go.

But the only other option is to go back the way we came ... where we might walk right into the goons with the guns.

He inhaled deeply and concentrated on creeping along as quietly as Kayce and Artem.

Toe-heel, toe-heel—step over a dry leaf—toe-heel, toe-heel.

There was an excited chirp from the right, followed by several more. Kayce listened for a moment, then glanced back and lifted a hand, holding her forefinger and thumb about an inch apart, indicating something small. Then she turned the fingers upside down and began "walking" them quickly back and forth.

Artem nodded, and Jack caught on a second later.

Ah! She's saying there's a bunch of little ones running around over there!

He nodded his understanding. Kayce held a finger up to her lips—

Shhhh!

—obviously knowing the boys were smart enough to be quiet, but nevertheless needing to be absolutely sure.

This isn't the time for taking chances. And it isn't the time for making mistakes.

They crept on, listening for any sign that the dinosaurs on either side had detected them. Jack was so focused upon the trail and the trees that it was several seconds before he noticed Artem twitching nervously.

What the—

The boy was shaking his head as if clearing it of prehistoric cobwebs, twisting and scrunching and wrinkling his face. Jack thought that perhaps another batch of centipedes had staged an attack—

But then it hit him like a snowball to the head.

He's going to sneeze!

Without taking time to think, Jack rushed forward and in one swift motion grabbed the boy, spun him around, and mashed his face into his own shoulder. Artem struggled briefly and then tensed, froze, and then sneezed violently into Jack's shirt.

Kayce spun around, her eyes wide in alarm.

The sneeze was muffled, but still loud enough to be heard. Jack and Kayce scanned the trees anxiously as Artem rubbed his eyes and wiped his nose. Jack turned his head slowly, listening for the slightest indication that a curious torvosaur was coming to investigate. There was a growl from the right—

Jack, Kayce, and Artem turned as one to look.

—followed by a surprised *cheep! ... Cheep! Cheep!*

There came another growl, along with the sound of softly crunching brush.

Just Mama Torvosaur chasing Baby Bob back to the nest, Jack thought with relief.

He glanced at Artem—

The boy's eyes were red, his cheeks puffed out as he held his breath.

—and then Kayce, whose eyes were wide and anxious. She met his gaze and rolled her eyes as if saying, *Close one!*

Jack nodded as she looked at Artem and in a barely audible whisper asked, "You okay?"

The boy nodded.

Kayce looked at Jack, shook her head, then pointed down the path. After a final glance in the direction of the mother torvosaur and her energetic babies, she once again began creeping down the trail.

Holy cow, Jack thought as he followed. *If I don't get eaten by a dinosaur in the next hour, I might just die from a heart attack!*

By now, his nose had become accustomed to the stench of rotting garbage. But he inhaled slowly and realized the sour tang was now stronger than ever.

We've not only invaded torvosaur territory, we're right smack in the middle of it. And still going ...

He looked around, noticing that the deeper they plunged into the torvosaurs' nesting grounds, the more the woods thinned.

All but the largest trees—and most of the brush—have been tramped down by the big animals.

And he realized that the thinning forest made things even more dangerous. It made the teenagers easier to see, and gave them fewer and less-effective places to hide.

If something spots us, it'll have us before we even have a chance to run.

Not only that, but the ground became more and more littered with old chewed and splintered bones, piles of excrement, and shards of broken eggshells.

Up ahead, Kayce paused and pointed to the side. Jack looked and saw an abandoned nest. It was a shallow depression in the dirt, maybe six feet across, lined with mud and grass and littered with the remnants of hatched eggs.

Jack had to fight back chills as he studied it. Just knowing this had once been a torvosaur's home—and that he was standing right beside it—made his stomach churn.

There was a smattering of crunches and crackles from the left, followed by a chorus of excited, high-pitched squeals. Jack didn't need Kayce or Artem to explain what was happening.

Buncha little dinosaurs over there, he thought, peering hard through the trees. *And mom or dad just brought home dinner.*

He pictured the scene, imagining the tiny dinosaurs fighting over whatever had just been dropped into the nest. And then—

Holy crap, he thought, glancing again in the direction of the mini feeding frenzy. *I wonder if the thing was dead ... or if the babies are being taught to hunt.*

And kill ...

He rubbed down the goosebumps that were suddenly erupting up and down his arms.

Judas Priest ...

Kayce continued creeping along, her head swiveling left and right between the two groups of dinosaurs. They were no longer following an actual trail, but there was no need. The brush had been so crushed and flattened by generations of large animals it was possible to travel in any direction without being blocked by anything but the largest trees.

And the farther they hiked, the more animals they heard. Listening closely, Jack realized he could hear the squawks and squeaks of small torvosaurs in every direction.

There was a flash of movement and all three teens dropped to their knees. The next instant a large animal—clearly a torvosaur—thumped through the trees twenty or thirty yards away. It was angling toward them—Jack saw Kayce set her legs, preparing to run—but then altered course, thumping off to the right.

Kayce turned her head to follow it, and Jack was startled by the size of her eyes.

She's as scared as I am, he thought with a start, realizing that he'd never seen her any way other than calm and unruffled. *We must really be in deep crap!*

Kayce swept her eyes around the forest, then looked back at the boys. She pointed—

A roar like booming thunder shook the woods behind them. There was a shout—a *human* shout—followed by bursts of automatic gunfire.

Rattarattaratta!

Rattarattaratta!

There was another roar—from a different direction—and a bellow from still another animal. And then another. And another. As if the entire drove of nesting torvosaurs simultaneously realized their home was under attack, and the woods were suddenly filled with furious roars and bellows. Trees cracked, snapped, and popped as enormous animals barreled through the woods, rushing to defend their nests.

Jack was looking back and forth, overwhelmed by the noise and confusion, too much going on to—

Kayce abruptly whirled around and yelled, "*Get down!*"

She dropped flat on her face and Artem instantly did the same. It took Jack an extra beat to catch on, but then he too dropped to the ground and wrapped his arms over his head. He screwed his eyes shut, just catching a glimpse of an outraged dinosaur pounding toward him, its head down and its jaws open, bellowing mightily as it thundered through the trees. Jack knew he was lying in plain sight: all three of them were. All the dinosaur had to do was look down—

But the animal was laser-focused on something in the distance and it thundered past unaware, just a few feet to Jack's right. The next instant a second massive animal pounded by on his left, jarring the ground like an earthquake as it stormed past.

The bellowing continued, as did the shouting, and shooting. The sounds of a pitched, savage, all-out battle. Kayce abruptly leaped to her feet and yelled.

"Come on! Let's get *out* of here!"

Neither Jack nor Artem needed to be told twice. The boys bounced to their feet and dashed after Kayce as she tore through the woods. The girl was taking a straight line through the trees, but turned to avoid a large rock and then stopped so abruptly that Artem careened into her. Jack was trailing Artem so closely he didn't have time to stop and barreled into him and all three teenagers crashed to the ground.

For a moment the three were an impossible tangle of thrashing, flailing, flapping arms and legs, each of them yelling and screaming incoherently. But then Jack managed to roll off the pile. Artem quickly disentangled himself and hopped to his feet, leaving Kayce floundering and trying to catch her breath.

Jack pushed himself to his hands and feet—

An excited squeak stopped him.

He looked up, straight into the face of a baby dinosaur.

What the—

He was lying at the edge of a circular depression, six feet across. The shallow pit was filled with chewed, gnawed, and splintered bones, as well as broken eggshells and fresh, green excrement.

And squirming, squeaking, chicken-sized baby torvosaurs.

One of the tiny animals was right in front of him—*looking right at him!*—squeaking excitedly.

A second small torvosaur tottered across the nest, quickly joined by another and another, six of them altogether. The baby dinosaurs chirped and squealed with excitement, as if thinking Jack was bringing them breakfast.

One of the babies scrabbled up the side of the nest, squeaked hungrily, and promptly fell back into the nest, taking three of its siblings with it like toppling bowling pins.

Kayce had eased to her feet and was backing cautiously away from the nest.

"We've gotta get away from here," she hissed. "*Now!* Don't make any sudden moves, but let's *go!*"

Jack nodded without speaking. With his eyes locked on the tiny dinosaurs, he carefully pushed himself to his knees, and then to his feet. And finally began backing away.

The hungry animals were clearly anticipating a meal, and they didn't want their visitors to leave. They began squeaking and squealing more vigorously than ever, begging for a snack.

One calf—more determined than the others—tumbled over the top of the nest and tottered toward Jack. Before he had time to react, the baby lunged forward and nipped at his leg.

"*Yee-ayyyy!*"

Jack tried to pull away. But though the animal had merely scratched his leg, its teeth became snagged in his jeans. And when he stepped away, he dragged the animal off its feet.

As its siblings squealed, the tiny torvosaur squawked in alarm. It flapped its puny arms and tried to shake its teeth loose. And then—unable to free itself—it began to scream.

Weeeeeeeee!

Jack reeled back in surprise. The infant's scream was high-pitched, drawn-out, and blood-chilling. And was answered almost instantly by a roar of rage from the direction of the nearby firefight.

"*Jack!*" Kayce hissed anxiously. Come *on!*"

"*Dude!*" Artem added unnecessarily.

Holy hell, Jack thought. He shook his leg, but the little torvosaur was thoroughly snared.

There was a mighty bellow, and in a moment of perfect clarity Jack knew what was happening. Over all the noise and chaos and confusion of the pitched hunter/torvosaur battle, one particular torvosaur—the mother of the tooth-snagged baby—heard the terrified cry.

Instantly recognized the sound and knew it was her kid.

And that it was in danger.

And was now storming back to the rescue.

Ohhhh jeeez!

Jack tried again to shake the little dinosaur loose—the animal was actually swinging by its teeth through the air—then dropped to his butt in the dirt. He grabbed the thrashing, squawking animal with both hands, but was unable to hold the squirming animal still and try to free it at the same time.

Judas Priest—

Artem suddenly dropped to his knees beside him

"Hold the damn thing still!" the boy ordered.

Without waiting for a response, Artem gently took the infant dinosaur's head with one hand and Jack's jeans with the other—

"Yee-*yowwww*!"

The boy jerked away as the dinosaur's needle-sharp teeth dug into his thumb. He glared at the animal as he shook the pain from his hand—

For a split second, Jack thought the thumb-bit boy might toss the animal into the trees.

—then gritted his teeth and once again went to work on Jack's jeans, whispering as he worked.

"Freakin', frackin', frumpin'—"

"Hurry," Jack pleaded: the mother dinosaur roared again as it crashed closer, mere seconds away.

"Don't. Rush. Me."

"Sorry, but"—there was an explosion from the woods and Jack looked, knowing the outraged dinosaur had run over a tree which must have burst like a stick of dynamite—"we're outta time!"

Artem leaned over, bared his teeth, and pulled the infant free. He pushed the animal toward its nest, then grabbed Jack and with surprising strength hauled the older boy to his feet.

"Now, come *on*!"

The mother dinosaur bellowed again from the trees, and Jack felt the ground shake, heard the cracks and pops of exploding tree branches as the animal rushed to save its offspring.

Man!

Leaping to his feet, Jack pushed Artem ahead and raced from the nest.

"Ohmigawd," Kayce spat as the boys joined her. She turned to run, just as an earsplitting roar shook the forest. All three teens whirled around as an enormous torvosaur burst from the trees. Even from a distance Jack could see the rage in the dinosaur's eyes and knew the animal meant business.

The torvosaur quickly scanned the woods, then quickly thumped to the wandering cub and nudged it gently back toward the nest. For that brief moment, the dinosaur seemed calm.

Almost gentle.

But Jack didn't have to be an expert to know she was holding her anger in check. And that she was about to show her full, unabashed fury.

Kayce began stepping backwards—moving as slowly as possible to keep from attracting the dinosaur's attention—and spoke out the side of her mouth.

"Split up," she hissed. "And *run!*"

Both Jack and Artem had the same idea. They began backing toward the trees, slowly at first, then more quickly. Spreading out and increasing the distance between themselves.

Jack's eyes were locked on the torvosaur. The mother nudged her wayward cub back into the nest, then nuzzled each of the youngsters as if assuring herself that everyone was unharmed and accounted for.

And then—finally convinced that her brood was safe—the dinosaur lifted her head and scanned the trees with rage in her eyes.

Oh, shit!

Without waiting, Jack turned and raced toward the nearest stand of trees, forcing his injured leg to keep up.

The torvosaur bellowed with such rage and fury that Jack was certain it wilted the leaves of nearby trees. His recently injured thigh burned like it was being flamed with a blow torch, but he forced himself to run even harder. Tree branches cracked and popped and snapped, and it was several beats before he realized the dinosaur wasn't actually pursuing him, but was instead chasing Kayce or Artem.

Rather than feeling relieved, his stomach sank, knowing one of his friends was in danger.

Crap oh crap oh crap ...

He spun around the roots of a gnarled tree and almost fell into a second nest of young squealing torvosaurs. He stopped, dropped, and lay flat on the ground. The nest was just ten feet away, six small torvosaurs tottering around.

He slowly began crawling backward—

A horrified scream suddenly cut through the confusion. Jack knew instantly it was an unknown voice: that it wasn't Kayce or Artem.

It's ... it's a guy! It's one of those damn hunters!

He'd no sooner had the thought than he heard a thump and a crackle of snapping branches. He stared hard and after a moment spotted an animal crunching through the trees. There was another blood-curdling scream—

Holy shit! It's got the guy in its teeth!

The animal thumped closer, and now Jack could clearly see a camouflaged hunter dangling from the torvorsaur's mouth. The dinosaur's lips were curled back, its teeth clamped onto one of the man's legs. The hunter was hanging crudely, awkwardly, flapping and flailing and screaming in horror and desperation, but unable to free himself from the powerful jaws.

Jack watched in horror.

What's it doing? Why hasn't it killed him?

Or eaten him?

Every dinosaur he'd seen so far had only been interested in one thing, and that was blood, gore, and dinner.

But this thing—

The small torvosaurs in the nest began chittering with excitement as the dinosaur—

Their mother, obviously!

—thudded closer.

The hunter howled in agony, then bent up at the waist to pound on the dinosaur's nose.

The torvosaur thumped close to the nest and dropped the man to the ground. The guy screamed—

"Aaaaahhh!"

—and then howled in agony when he hit the ground.

"*Ayyyyyy!*"

But the torvosaur didn't give him a second look. It stepped carefully into the nest—careful not to step on any of the chittering youngsters—and began nosing each of the tiny creatures.

Jack didn't know if dinosaurs could count, but the torvosaur seemed to be assuring itself that each of its cubs was safe, and present. Jack looked back at the camouflaged hunter. The man's right leg—the one the torvosaur had been gripping with its teeth—was bloody and twisted at an impossible angle, clearly broken. The man writhed awkwardly and then—unable to stand—began crawling away from the nest, toward a meager clump of scrub, the only cover in sight.

C'mon, Jack thought as he watched. *Keep going, keep going, keep—*

A second adult torvosaur came trotting from the trees. Smaller than the female, it stepped into the clearing and swept its head around, instantly taking in the nest, the baby dinosaurs, the mother, and the moaning, terrified hunter crawling pathetically for safety.

Oh-oh, Jack thought, sensing this had to be the first animal's mate, the cubs' father. *Daddy's home ...*

The male torvosaur rumbled ominously, then stepped toward the crawling hunter.

No, no, nooooo! Jack thought in horror. *Don't—*

The torvosaur stepped right up to the moaning man and lowered its head—

No, no, nooooo!

—but didn't snap him up. It studied the hunter curiously, then sniffed the man's head, and back, and bad leg, as if wondering what the strange creature was. Jack was certain the animal would snatch the man up, biting and crunching and—

The animal stepped in front of the injured man, preventing him from escaping. It lowered its nose and again sniffed the guy's head.

"No, no, oh gawd, no ..." the hunter mumbled wretchedly.

The dinosaur sniffed again, then gently nudged the man with its nose.

What the hell? Jack wondered. *What's it* doing?

The wounded man changed course, trying to wriggle around the dinosaur's thick, splayed toes. But the animal stepped back and nudged him again, a little more forcefully this time, turning him back toward the nest.

What the—

The dinosaur prodded the terrified man again. The female torvosaur—still in the nest—growled and stepped aside, no longer standing between the excited, squeaking youngsters and the injured, groaning hunter.

It hit Jack like a punch to the gut.

No, no, no! They're teaching them to hunt! They want the babies to hunt the guy!

Jack's stomach bubbled, and hot bile rose into his throat so sharply he thought he would throw up.

The hunter was still moaning—

"*No, no, let me go ...*"

—still trying to crawl past the male torvosaur. The dinosaur prodded him again, then dropped its nose, flicked its head, and flipped the man three or four feet closer to the nest. The guy landed on his ruined leg and screamed in agony.

"*Aaaaaiiieeee!*"

No, no, noooo ... Jack thought miserably. The horror of the situation was magnified by the absolute certainty there was nothing he could do.

Nothing!

The female watched her tiny offspring trying to scrabble up the side of the nest. The small animals could clearly see the man—could hear his pathetic cries of desperation—and could smell the hot, fresh blood leaking from his broken leg. But they kept slipping as they tried to scrabble up the side of the nest.

The mother watched for another moment, then dropped her nose behind the nearest cub's tail and lifted. The young dinosaur's legs pumped comically, but then it flopped out of the nest. It tipped onto its nose, but quickly righted itself, squawked excitedly, and wobbled toward the terrified hunter.

As Jack watched in dread, the female lifted a second baby from the nest, and then another. The first cub reached the man and like a dog after a bone clamped its sharp, tiny teeth deep into the guy's bad leg.

The man screamed, rolled onto his back, and tried to use his good leg to kick the dinosaur away. The animal squeaked, then lunged again for the bloody leg. It was quickly joined by a sibling, and then two more. As the adult torvosaurs looked on, the infants swarmed the kicking, screaming, flailing man.

Jack watched in horror. But when one of the small animals leaped onto the man's chest and began snapping at his face, he had to look away.

The man screamed—

"Aaaaaiii—uhg ... gug ..."

—but the screech died to a series of gurgles, and after a long, horrible minute fell away all together.

Jack looked up briefly, saw the excited baby torvosaurs enthusiastically ripping strips of red, juicy meat from the carcass and gobbling them down.

He fought off a wave of nausea and then began backing away, back into the brush.

24　Last Stand

As soon as he was a safe distance from the nest, Jack quit crawling and listened. He could no longer hear the baby torvosaurs—

Probably too busy eating ...

—but there were occasional grunts and growls that he assumed came from the proud, watchful parents.

He turned his head—struggling to choke down the hot bile in his throat—and tried to gauge the measure of the forest. There were intermittent squeaks from the occupants of other nests, along with the sporadic snarls of larger animals. But the battle between hunters and dinosaurs had ended, and at least one more of the camouflaged killers was ... gone. And he could no longer hear the big female that had gone after Kayce or Artem.

He sucked air through his teeth, hoping his friends had escaped. He couldn't help feeling miserable—feeling guilty, even—that the animal hadn't come after *him*.

Nothing I could have done, though, he thought wistfully, trying to shake off the nagging sense that he'd somehow let his friends down. *Heck, for a couple of seconds, I thought it was after me!*

He scratched an insect bite on his elbow—

Freakin' bugs!

—and surveyed the woods, wondering what to do. He'd no sooner decide on a way to go than something would snort, or growl, or snarl from that exact direction.

Not a lot of choices here. I'm smack in the middle of Town Torvosaur, and I'm gonna run into animals whichever way I go.

He rubbed his eyes as he tried to think, then finally glanced to his left.

Well, as far as I can remember, that's the direction Kayce was leading us. And—if she got away—that's probably the way she'll go. Artem, too. So ... that's my best bet.

He sighed, took a final look around—

Nothing sneaking up behind me ...

—and headed into the trees. Following Kayce's and Artem's examples, he kept his eyes peeled, looking up and down and left and right, not forgetting to check the woods behind him. After less than a minute he heard squeaking ahead, realized he was closing in on another nest, and altered course to give it as wide a berth as possible. But he hadn't taken more than a dozen steps before he heard more noise—

Not babies, this time, but ... something big.

—and had to backtrack before striking off in a different direction.

Place is like a maze, he thought dourly as he stepped past a pile of dung so fresh it was still steaming. *Except that if I make a wrong move here, I get eaten.*

He remembered the image of the hunter being swarmed by infant torvosaurs being taught to hunt—and kill—and realized there were worse things than simply being bitten in half.

He shook his head clear, determined to focus on the trees, and the trail, and the animals.

Like a prehistoric ninja, he thought, surprised he was able to find some humor in the situation.

He kept moving. There were enough nests and wandering animals that he had to change course several times. And twice he had to drop flat to the ground when some traveling dinosaur thumped close.

He wasn't certain how long it went on.

Twenty minutes?

Twenty-five?

Thirty?

He didn't know. But the vegetation eventually became thicker. And denser. And the hard-packed ground once again began resolving into distinct paths and trails amid clumps and clusters of leafy brush.

Okay, then. I might finally be getting out of here!

He crept on, beginning to feel a little less anxious, though not yet ready to relax. He moved slowly, and quietly, putting more and more distance between himself and the creepy torvosaur nests. He kept a careful eye over his shoulders—

making certain nothing had picked up his scent—and once again began angling in the direction he thought Kayce had been heading—

There was a sneeze in the trees ahead and he froze in midstep.

That wasn't an animal! he thought excitedly. *That was human!*

He remembered Artem sneezing earlier and felt a surge of elation ... not just because he'd found his friend, but because he knew that Artem—at least—was still safe.

He instantly began creeping toward the sound of the sneeze. He thought about calling out, or whistling.

But some torvosaur's as likely to hear me as Artem ... and come running.

Even so, he couldn't help sneaking along a little faster, anxious to rejoin his friend.

Just to be sure he's really safe—

There suddenly came another sound—the sound of someone hawking a loogie and spitting it out—and Jack froze in his tracks.

That *wasn't Artem!*

Suddenly wary, he hunched low in the brush, took a careful look around, then began creeping forward as carefully as he could. And after a moment heard a sound.

The sound of a voice.

A *man's* voice.

And ... he's whispering. Talking to someone ...

Jack hesitated. His first thought was to turn around. To get as far away from the man as possible.

But his two friends are both dead, so ... who's he talking to?

Kayce?

Artem?

Someone else?

A fourth guy?

The very thought of sneaking up on the guy—

A guy sent here to kill me!

—made his skin crawl. But he had to know what was happening.

Especially if Kayce or Artem is up there.

He hesitated another moment, cast a quick glance over his shoulder, then started again down the trail, darting from tree to tree to remain hidden. The man was still speaking quietly, though Jack couldn't make out the words. He paused and listened for a moment—

I don't hear anyone else, though. ... The guy's either talking to himself, or he's carrying on a one-sided conversation.

Earlier in the day—when he was cowering beneath the roots of the fallen tree with Artem—he saw one of the hunters talking on his radio and was only able to hear one side of the conversation. But—

This doesn't sound like that. This guy's not pausing for replies and, anyway ... the other two guys are both dead.

Baffled by what was happening, he eased around the boughs of a fragrant, drooping pine, and finally saw something move. He froze, watching carefully, trying to figure out what he was looking at.

It's just one guy, he finally decided, *dressed in camouflage. So ... who's he talking to?*

He dropped to his belly and began army-crawling through the brush. He was close enough now to hear what the hunter was saying, though the guy wasn't making any sense.

"Stupid, freakin' kids anyway. Never thought any of this was a good idea ..."

Jack crawled closer.

Keeping his eyes and ears sharp for signs of danger or ambush.

"... and the second I find your damn friends, there's gonna be *hell* to pay. Yes, sir, I can promise you that. They're gonna need a whole new word to describe *pain* ..."

Jack eased up behind a prickly bush, carefully reached out a hand, and pulled aside a leafy branch.

The hunter was sitting on a log, awkwardly wrapping a gauze bandage around his left forearm. The man's camouflaged uniform was torn and bloody, his head wrapped in blood-soaked gauze.

Guy got away from the torvosaurs, Jack thought in amazement. *But just by the skin of his teeth, from the looks of it ...*

There was a military-sorta rifle at the man's side, leaning against the log within easy reach.

Okay, then ... so who's he talking to?

Jack swept his eyes around. At first there wasn't anything to see. For a moment, Jack thought maybe the man's mind had snapped, and that he'd begun talking to himself. But then a bush twitched. He craned his neck and spotted a pair of small shoes.

Artem!

Jack hesitated, and then—moving as carefully as a mouse that knew the family cat was nearby—crept a little closer. Straining for a better look. And finally had a clear view of his young friend. The kid was lying on the ground, his arms and legs wrapped with duct tape, a strip of tape covering his mouth.

Oh, shit!

Jack looked back at the injured hunter. The man's hands were occupied, so he wasn't actually holding his rifle. But the weapon was within easy reach, ready to be snatched up at a moment's notice.

He'd blow me away before I got even halfway there.

Jack bit his lip as he surveyed the scene, searching for an idea. There was no way he was going to abandon Artem. But ...

What the hell can I do—

Before he could finish the thought, a rock sailed from the trees, directly over the hunter's head. It landed with a soft *thud* in the dirt beside him.

The man undoubtedly knew better than to fall for it: it had to be an old trick and Jack had even seen it himself a few hours earlier. But the man was looking before he could stop himself ... and as he did, Kayce burst from the brush. She was wielding a branch as thick as her arm, and the second she was within reach she planted her feet, set her teeth, and swung like Paul Bunyan with his axe.

The man heard her coming. He turned and had just enough time to throw a hand up before the club crashed into his injured arm with such force it snapped in half.

The man howled and dropped like a rock. But as Kayce raised her broken club his good arm shot out, hit Kayce's legs, and swept the girl off her feet.

Kayce screamed—

"Aaaaiiigh!"

—and fell flat on her back. She hit the ground hard, but recovered quickly enough to try scrabbling away. But this time the man was ready. And mad as a hornet. Before the girl had moved even a couple of inches, a powerful hand grabbed her leg and pulled her back. The man scrambled forward on his hands and knees, hooked Kayce by the belt, and flipped her onto her back. Before Kayce could react, he swung a beefy fist through the air and struck the side of her jaw—

There was a sickening *crunch* as her teeth cracked together.

—and snapped her head back.

She instantly went limp as a rag doll and lay still.

There was a blood-curdling yell—

"*Ahhhhhhhh ...*"

—so loud and unexpected Jack didn't even realize he was the one yelling. With no thought for himself, he was suddenly on his feet and charging the camouflaged commando like a runaway truck.

The man had just enough time to look up—his face white with shock and surprise—before Jack barreled into him. The collision forced the air from the hunter's lungs in a loud *whoosh!* But the man had training. And experience. He rolled beneath Jack's weight, rammed his boots into Jack's belly, kicked up with his legs, and sent Jack flying head-over-heels into the brush.

Jack landed on his back, smacking his spine against a rock that sent bolts of searing, screaming, scorching agony through every cell in his body. His nerves crackled like he'd been electrocuted. He hurt so bad he knew he'd broken a couple of ribs, but he didn't waste time checking. He rolled to his knees, turned, and lunged—

Still lying on his back, the commando ripped a pistol from his belt, aimed it at Jack, and pulled the trigger.

Jack cringed, expecting a bullet—

EEEEEEEEEE!

A wall of noise hit him like the kick of a mule. So loud and harsh and shrill he could feel it drilling through his body, straight through his bones and out the other side.

Stinging the fillings in his teeth like they were being drilled without Novocain.

Freezing his blood and shattering his ears.

Tortured beyond description, he doubled over, clamped his hands over his ears, and curled into a ball. His stomach churned—on the brink of heaving—his muddled brain spinning, unable to think.

There was a scream of anguish—

"*Aaaaaiiigh!*"

—high-pitched and wracked with pain—but he was in such agony that once again he didn't realize he was the one screaming.

EEEEEEEEEE!

It seemed to go on forever.

And when the agonizing noise finally stopped, the unexpected silence seemed as foreign and alien as the prehistoric forest. It took several seconds for his brain to stop spinning. And for the world to stop whirling around him.

He took several deep breaths, trying to clear the fog from his brain and settle his stomach. And after a minute or so managed to crack an eye.

The commando had regained his feet, though he was clearly favoring his left leg, which appeared injured. The man was still pointing his pistol-like noisemaker at him, grinning wickedly.

The man's lips were moving, but it was several seconds before Jack's ears cleared enough to make out the words.

"—doesn't it? More effective and a damn sight more painful than a taser." The man chuckled. "Believe me, I *know.*"

The man chuckled again, then glanced at his weapon, flicked a switch, and once again pointed the barrel at Jack.

EEEEEEE—

Jack instantly clamped his hands back over his ears. He rolled onto his back, screwing his eyes shut and clenching his teeth as he writhed on the ground.

—EEE!

The noise stopped and Jack heard the man laugh.

"Gets your attention though, doesn't it? I'll tell ya, I once had my fingernails torn off during an ... interrogation. And that didn't hurt *half* as bad as the first time I got blasted with one of these suckers."

He lifted the weapon for a third time.

Jack's voice was nothing more than a traumatized croak. "Don't ..."

EEEE!

The jolt of noise lasted only a second this time—maybe two—but the pain was so unbearable it instantly had Jack writhing in the dirt like a fish out of water. His brain was whirling, his throat hot with bile, and he abruptly vomited, spewing half-digested fish and apple/pears and foul stomach acid into the dirt. He retched again, and again, and again. And when he was empty, he dry-heaved for nearly a minute, his throat burning like he'd swallowed gasoline.

By the time his stomach finally settled, he was convinced that another blast of the awful noise would kill him.

That it would literally kill him.

He opened his eyes, expecting another blast, but ...

The man had turned away and was standing over Kayce, who—mercifully—was still unconscious. As Jack watched, the man nudged her with his boot, looking for a reaction.

The man chuckled and ... Jack saw a gleam in his eyes. A gleam that told him the guy wasn't done with her. And that what he wanted to do would be far worse than the agony of his freakin' noisemaker.

Shifting his gaze ever so slightly, Jack glanced at Artem. The young boy was lying motionless in the dirt, his eyes closed, looking almost ... peaceful.

He's unconscious ... the damn noise actually knocked him out—

Another thought hit him and he strained for a better look.

Shit! If that noisemaker made him throw up like it did me—with his mouth taped shut—he might have suffocated!

He held his breath as he stared ... but then saw the boy's chest rise as he breathed in through his nose.

Oh, man, Jack thought, overwhelmed with relief. *He's still okay!*

Even so, he knew that being unable to cover his ears, the kid must have suffered unimaginable agony.

No wonder he passed out ...

Jack slowly shifted his eyes and peered toward the man's rifle, which was still leaning against the log.

If I could just get to it ...

He tried calculating his chances, but knew they weren't good.

I can barely move as it is. I'll lurch and stumble trying to get there. And all that jerk has to do is hit me with another blast of noise and I'll drop like a rock.

He nevertheless continued staring wistfully at the rifle, knowing it was his only hope of getting away and possibly saving his friends.

But ... even if I got my hands on it, I wouldn't know what to do with it. Don't know if it has to be cocked or loaded or whatever you have to do with a gun.

He also knew that many weapons had a "safety" device: a switch that kept it from shooting when it wasn't supposed to. And that had to be flicked off before the gun could be fired.

But I don't know if every gun has one ... or where the hell it might be ... or what to do if I found it.

He flicked his eyes again toward the camouflaged hunter. Believing that Jack was thoroughly incapacitated, the man had lost interest in him and was instead focused upon Kayce. He was now several steps from his rifle, but Jack knew it wasn't enough.

The hunter leered at the unconscious girl. He licked his lips, then unsnapped his cargo vest and pulled it from his shoulders. Without taking his eyes off Kayce, he draped the vest over a nearby branch.

And began fumbling with his belt.

What the—

It hit Jack like a nail through his brain. And before he knew what he was doing, he was on his hands and knees. Determined to stop the man or die trying.

The hunter heard him moving and looked over with a scowl. He'd returned the noisemaker to its holster, but knew he no longer needed it.

"Stay right where you are," the man rumbled. He leveled a gnarled finger at Jack, then patted the noisemaker on his belt. "Unless you want another shot 'a joy."

Jack ground his teeth together. He was filled with fury, his blood hot as boiling lava. He wanted to rush the man ... to knock him on his ass and pound his head against the rocks until his brains were nothing but gooey gray mush leaking from his ears.

To punish the man for even *thinking* of hurting his friends.

To make up for having his own life stolen and every hope of a normal life dashed to pieces.

For all the horror and confusion and chaos that had been building inside him to the point his own brain was ready to explode.

But ...

He tried to breathe, struggling to calm himself. Knowing that he had to act. Had to do *something*. But knowing that the slightest mistake would get him killed.

And probably Kayce and Artem with me.

He forced himself not to look at the man's rifle, not wanting to give himself away. Because even though he didn't know a damn thing about guns, he knew that rifle was his only chance.

The man turned away. Leering down at Kayce, he unbuckled his belt and lowered his camouflaged pants.

But Jack was no longer watching. Just as the man turned, Jack heard a sound in the trees. A sound like the rumble of a airliner passing high overhead.

Where no airliner could ever be ...

He peered into the trees, searching for—

He felt a light tremor in the ground beneath his hands and knees.

And then another.

He slowly lowered himself to his belly. Flattening himself against the ground. Making himself harder to see.

The hunter was on his knees now, whispering to Kayce, though the girl was still unconscious and unable to hear. But even as Jack watched, he felt another tremor in the ground. And then heard a soft, barely perceptible grumble that he recognized as a growl.

The growl of a dinosaur ...

He shot a look at the hunter, who'd reached down to stroke Kayce's hair.

He's not listening! He has no idea something's coming!
Something big!

He looked at Kayce, then flicked his eyes for another glance at Artem, who was still lying motionless in the brush.

No way to help 'em, he thought miserably. *But—*

He took another look.

Kayce's not moving. And Artem's hidden by the brush. With any luck, whatever-the-hell's coming might not see 'em.

He turned to look—

There was a crackle as some bush or pile of leaves crunched softly in the trees. But the hunter was still too focused upon Kayce to notice. There was a crack—the sound of a dry twig snapping—and Jack saw the tops of the trees rustling, much closer than he expected.

It's right there! Right there!

Every fiber of Jack's being screamed at him to run.

To get as far away from the approaching dinosaur as he could.

To—

But not without my friends ... there's no way I'm leaving without my friends!

His heart was pumping so hard he could the blood pulsing through his toes and fingertips. Could feel it pounding against his temples. He tried to flatten himself even more, trying to melt into the dirt and leaves and old decaying brush.

There was a flash of gray in the trees, and—

Torvosaur! It's a torvosaurus!

The animal stepped past a tree, giving Jack a better look.

And it's the biggest freakin' monster I've ever seen!

The animal was creeping through the trees with the care of a hunting lion. There was a *crunch* as it stepped on a pile of dry leaves, and it froze.

And for several long seconds it didn't twitch, didn't blink, didn't move a muscle. Jack remained just as still, hardly daring to breathe.

And the hunter ...

The freakin' idiot has no idea the thing's even there! No idea at all!

A distant, faraway, rarely visited part of Jack's brain was screaming at him to warn the guy. To tell him to run for his life.

But ...

This might be the break I'm looking for! And it might be the only one I'm gonna get!

He knew it was risky.

Knew that a dinosaur storming through the brush could mash Kayce and Artem and even himself as easily as not.

But ... I won't get another chance like this.

A fly buzzed past his eyes. Even landed on his ear. But he didn't notice, every fiber of his being laser-focused on the dinosaur. Standing as still as it was, it blended perfectly with the trees. Was actually difficult to see. And Jack almost began to wonder if it was really there at all. If he hadn't simply imagined—

Without warning the torvosaur bellowed. Roaring with the power of a terrible, screaming jet engine, shaking the forest and sending flocks of startled birds squawking from the trees into the air.

Jack cringed and turned his head, almost as incapacitated by the thunderous bellow as from a shot from the hunter's noisemaker. But he looked back just in time to see the hunter reeling away in such shock and surprise that he stumbled and fell flat on his ass. The man gawked in horror, then fumbled for his belt—for his guns—but with his pants down they weren't where he expected and—unable to tear his eyes from the dinosaur—it took several seconds—

The dinosaur bellowed again—even louder than before—then charged from the trees. Pounding through the brush with the power of a freight train.

The hunter screamed—

"*Aaaaaiiigh!*"

—still fumbling for a weapon. The torvosaur's feet hammered the earth with such power they bounced Jack into the air with every step. The animal lowered its head and roared as it rushed the flailing hunter. The man screamed again—

"Aaaaaiiigh!"

—then suddenly had a gun in his hand, was pulling the trigger.

Nothing!

The man flailed at the weapon and Jack could hear him huffing in terror.

"Ah-ah-ah—"

The guy slapped at the gun, pointed it at the charging dinosaur—

EEEEEEEEEE!

Jack could actually *see* the awful sound waves as they slammed into the dinosaur. The animal stopped like it had run into a brick wall, stopping so fast it stumbled. Nearly fell. Bellowing in rage as much as agony.

EEEEEEEEEE!

The hunter kept the noisemaker pointed at the animal. Kept his finger mashed against the trigger.

EEEEEEEEE!

The dinosaur roared ... it took a step toward the dreaded noise, then had to turn away. Took a step back.

Roared in agony.

EEEEEEEEE!

The hunter kept the weapon aimed at the dinosaur. He wiped a hand across his face and then—careful to keep his weapon blasting—struggled to his feet.

EE—

The noise stopped.

Jack looked up in surprise ... and then in confusion as the hunter laughed.

"What's the matter?" the man called to the dinosaur. "Not so tough anymore, are you?"

The torvosaur roared, though not quite so ferociously this time. It shook its head.

And then took a step forward.

The hunter laughed—

Actually *laughed*!

—then calmly lifted his weapon, waited an agonizing moment, and pulled the trigger.

EEEEEEEEE!

The dinosaur tried to lunge—tried to force its way through the wall of horrendous, impenetrable noise—but once again had to turn away.

Took a step back.

And then another.

Blinking its eyes and shaking its head, torn between its powerful, instinct-driven need to attack ... and the terrible, blistering, incapacitating noise. Suffering misery so excruciating it was impossible to endure.

EE—

The noise stopped, and the hunter laughed again.

Laughing at the dinosaur.

"What's the matter, Big Guy? Can't handle a little noise?"

He aimed the gun, hit the trigger for a quick, split-second blast—

EE—

—did it again—

EE—

—and again—

EE—

—each time jolting the mighty animal with another bone-jarring blast of sound.

He's playing with it! Jack realized. *He's torturing it!*

Jack was already mad enough to rip the guy's face off. So infuriated he was no longer thinking of himself. Wanting to tear the guy to pieces. His face was flushed and his blood boiling. He wanted to rip the gun from the guy's hand—

The torvosaur bellowed, then rushed forward.

Full of confidence now, the hunter merely laughed. He waited an extra second—just to toy with the animal—then pulled the trigger.

EEEEEEEEEE!

The torvosaur stopped instantly. And roared. And once again backed away, roaring, shaking its head and snapping its teeth at the air. Clawing at the waves of debilitating noise with its puny arms.

EEEE—EE—E—ee—

The awful noise wavered—

—ee—ee—e—

—and decreased in volume.

The hunter looked at the weapon. Slapped it once, and then again, even as the sound skipped a beat.

—ee-e—ee—

The torvosaur turned and lowered its head. Then took a step forward, snapping tentatively at the air. The hunter shook the noisemaker, then pointed it at the dinosaur.

—ee—e—ee—e—e—

It's losing power! Jack thought in horror. *The battery's dying!*

With the noise wavering, the torvosaur was able to advance another step. And then another. Regaining its confidence and determination to attack.

The hunter shook the weapon desperately.

Frantically.

—ee—e—uh—uh—

The torvosaur lowered its head almost to the ground and bellowed, then rushed forward with incredible speed. The hunter screamed—

"Aaaaaiiigh!"

—and threw the noisemaker at the charging dinosaur, then turned and ran for his rifle. But the dinosaur was too close and moving too fast. The man had only taken a couple of steps before the torvosaur reached him. The great head snapped down, but the terrible jaws didn't open. To Jack's surprise, the animal swept its head sideways, striking the fleeing man in the side and hurling him through the air.

The guy howled, landing on his face several feet away. He yelped in pain, then—spiderlike—tried to scuttle away on all fours. But the torvosaur was already there, thumping a heavy foot onto the man's butt, mashing his hips and legs into the ground.

The hunter screamed—

"*Ayyyyyy!*"

—and the dinosaur dropped its nose.

Sniffed the screaming, writhing man.

Growled.

And then sniffed again.

There was a moan ... but it didn't come from the terrified hunter.

Jack blinked in confusion.

What the—

There was another moan, and Kayce lifted a hand to her face.

Kayce!

The dinosaur stopped in mid-growl. It turned its head and spotted the twitching, half-conscious girl. It blinked, then lifted its foot from the suffering man and stepped toward Kayce.

No, no, no! Jack thought in horror. *Nooooo!*

He pushed himself to his hands and knees, ready to jump to his feet and distract the animal away from his friend.

There was a crack—

Bam!

—and Jack jerked in surprise, then looked to see the hunter aiming a pistol—a real pistol this time—at the dinosaur. The man pulled the trigger again—

Bam!

—and again—

Bam!

—and again—

Bam! Babam-bam!

The dinosaur turned at the first shot and roared, even as the man continued shooting. But if the torvosaur was even remotely injured, it didn't show. In a quick, blinding motion the animal dropped its head and snapped its jaws shut around the man's chest. There was a sickening crunch of bones, the crack of teeth slamming together, a sloppy wet burble of ruined organs being pulped to jelly.

There was a single gurgling scream—

"*Aiiii—ug—gug—*"

—that ended as abruptly as it began. The dinosaur lifted its head—limp arms and legs dangling from both sides of its jaws—then whipped its head back and forth. The lifeless limbs flapped in the air, and a shredded arm came loose and flew into the brush in a spray of greasy blood.

The dinosaur threw its head back, sucking the man deeper into its mouth. The yellow teeth ground together, pulverizing bone and muscle and ruined organs to mush as blood and gore dribbled from the corners of its jaws.

The dinosaur chewed noisily, tossing its head back to let the hot blood run down its throat. And then—still chewing—the animal thumped back into the trees and disappeared.

Jack was breathing fast and hard—was almost hyperventilating—stunned by the violence and savagery of the attack. The strike had been so shocking—and so ... grisly—that now it was over, he wasn't certain it had actually happened.

But then he spotted what was left of the hunter's arm hanging from a nearby bush, jagged shards of bone protruding from the torn muscle.

Holy humpin' Hallie from Hell, he thought, his mouth suddenly dry as sand. *I can't believe that just happened!*

But even as he struggled for breath, a two-foot dinosaur crept from the brush on two legs. It advanced upon the bloody arm warily, sniffed at the warm meat, then craned its neck and latched onto a finger—

Jack could see some sort of watch attached to the wrist.

—and dragged the arm from its perch. After a moment the scavenger was joined by a second animal, and the two began squabbling over the prize.

Jack watched in disgust—

A soft moan snapped him back to the moment, and he turned to see Kayce roll onto her side.

Oh, shoot!

He struggled to his feet—

Man, I feel like I was hit by a frickin' truck!

—stumbled through the brush, and knelt beside his friend.

"Hey, take it easy," he advised. He placed a hand on the girl's shoulder and gently eased her onto her back. "Are you okay?"

"Not ... sure." She reached up and rubbed the side of her jaw, which was already bruising where the hunter struck her. "Wha-what happened?"

"Long story," Jack replied quietly. "But everything's okay. You're safe now."

She had to struggle to swallow before she could continue. "Wha—wha—what about Artem?"

Artem!

Holy buckets, Jack thought. *I completely forgot—*

He struggled back to his feet and staggered toward the unmoving boy. He took hold of the tape covering the kid's mouth, hesitated, and then with a quick tug ripped it free.

Artem arched his back and screamed.

"*Ahhhhh—*"

Jack quickly patted the boy.

"Hey, shhhh! It's just me ... Jack. You're okay, bud! Just relax. There you go, just take it easy, now ..."

The boy's eyes flew open—wide with fright—flicking from side to side, searching—

"Hey, everything's okay, bud. See? It's just me ..."

Kayce crawled over, supporting herself on her elbows.

"Hey, kiddo," she said. She reached out and smoothed the boy's hair. "It's just us. ... Are you okay?"

The boy blinked several times, still trying to regain his senses, then said, "I dreamed about pizza."

"Pizza?"

"With pineapple and pepperoni."

"Onions?"

Artem blanched. "Don't make me gag!"

"That's the ticket," Kayce whispered hoarsely. "He's gonna be okay."

Artem was recovering quickly, and while Kayce continued to soothe him, Jack tore off the tape binding his hands and feet.

"So, what's going on?" the boy asked. He reached up and rubbed his upper lip where the tape had torn off a layer of skin. "What happened to—"

"Everything's gone," Kayce said. "We're all fine. Everything's gonna be okay."

But even as she spoke, Jack heard animals begin to roar and bellow in every corner of the forest. The hair rose on his arms and neck.

Kayce and Artem both felt it too. A disturbing hum filled the air and Jack's teeth began to ache.

"Oh, hell," Artem whispered. He looked up at Kayce. "Someone's coming."

Jack ground his teeth, trying to relieve the ache.

"Who do you think it's gonna be?" he asked, fighting the smart. "More kids, or ... more hunters?"

"No way to know until we go for a look," Kayce replied, wrinkling her face in pain.

The hum quickly intensified and Kayce's hair began dancing from the electric charge building in the air.

"Well, damn," she said, scrunching her nose and shoulders as she braced herself for the coming *boom*. "Here we go again."

About the Author

Christopher Jaffrey is an accomplished musician who plays both acoustic and jazz guitar. He loves hiking and camping with his dogs, hunting for arrowheads, scouring the desert for fossils, and dreaming of dinosaurs. Jaffrey is the author of ***Dinosaur Strike***—the explosive sequel to ***Dinosaur Run***—and ***Flight of Horror***. He lives in central Utah.

Printed in Dunstable, United Kingdom